To Mr<u>s</u>

14 ^th̲ May

D1588576

From { J. Drumpson
{ C. aird.

AN INDEPENDENT YOUNG MAN

An Independent
Young Man

by

GUY
McCRONE

CONSTABLE & COMPANY LTD

LONDON

PUBLISHED BY
Constable and Company Ltd.
10–12 Orange Street, W.C.2

First published 1961

© 1961 *by Guy McCrone*

PRINTED IN THE REPUBLIC OF IRELAND
BY ALEX. THOM AND CO. LTD.

THE EDZELL/CRABBE FAMILY

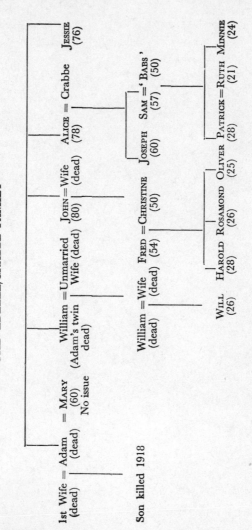

1

HAD the rock above him moved? Was it loose? Brittle? Will Edzell clung against the precipice considering what next he had better do. The rains and the frost of last winter must have loosened . . .

Was the rock still moving? What were those groaning sounds? These sounds of wrenching? He twisted his head, the better to look upwards. Above him the silver rock-lichen was slowly parting, tearing asunder like a rag to reveal a black, widening crack. The wrenching sounds were getting louder. Splinters and earth were beginning to fall. He pressed himself closer, trying to save himself. His hands were wet with sweat. Now he could see that a large piece of rock was coming. Would it take him with it as it came? Or was it possible it might fall past him? He could only cling and wait.

For a sickening eternity of seconds the sounds went on. Splinters came increasingly. Then the rock broke free. And for a time he was a mere clutching animal, pelted at and torn, in a shuddering, giddy world.

But now he became aware that it was past. Now he could hear the fallen boulder as it danced and rolled heavily down there at the bottom of the cliff below him.

He could not believe he was not down there too. Yet here he was. Still clinging. Battered and panting, but still clinging.

And what, in Heaven's name, must he do now? Keep his head for one thing. This was no moment to allow himself the luxury of terror.

But what had happened? What had the rock and splinters done to him? His head, it seemed, was bruised. That was all. The wet, clutching hands had got a cut or two. He could see some blood on them. But his leg? Had the main boulder grazed it? In his desperation merely to keep alive, he had not had time to feel. He changed his position and looked down. The trouser leg had been torn open and the leg itself was gashed—almost to his boot. Cautiously he tried to move it. With relief, he found that he could. Though the gash looked shocking, it could not be deep. The leg, then, was still of some use.

And now what was above him? Only ten or twelve feet to the top. If the rock had held he would have been up there long ago. No. The going should still be possible. The new made cavity in the cliff might even help.

Will moved up slowly, disregarding pain. Shaken, yet strangely alert; using all his climber's skill. And in ten minutes more he was crawling over the wiry sea turf that cushioned the hill top. For a time he lay, thankful merely to have reached it. He had set his powers against the precipice and, after all, he had won.

But as high excitement ebbed he began to be invaded by an increasing faintness. His leg? He must force himself to sit up and look at it. No. It didn't seem good. What next? How stop this bleeding? How get down from this place?

The precipice was a well known climbers' challenge. But there were, of course, gentler tracks on this little island mountain. Determination had got him up. But could it get him down again, even by an easier way?

For a time he continued to sit, trapped and impotent, staring before him. Then the world began to swing round him. His green platform, the blue above him and the clouds. The grassy stretches by the shore. The white lodge down there beneath him. The farm where he had left his rucksack. The sands of the crescent beaches. The early autumn sunshine on the calm, far-stretching waters. The luminous, grey ghosts of other island crags rising sharply from the Western Sea. All these became unsteady, spinning before his vision.

Then, in another moment, consciousness had left him.

2

The mistress of Stronn Island lowered her field glasses, ran to the front door of Stronn Lodge, and shouted "Murdo!" Having done so, Mrs Adam Edzell once again raised her glasses the better to follow what was happening on the summit of the Hog's Snout. For a little time she stood watching

intently, her capable, sunburnt hands holding the
glasses firmly, her stocky, sixty-year-old figure
planted, solid and motionless. Then as the Murdo to
whom she had appealed did not seem to have heard
her, she turned, smoothing back her greying hair, a
mechanical gesture betokening determined action,
and ran towards her kitchen garden where she found
him lifting the potatoes.

"Murdo, I'm sorry to take you from your work.
But there's a climber in trouble on the Hog's Snout.
I want you to come up there with me at once. I
think he must have hurt himself. I'll run upstairs
for my box."

As she came down again, the giant islander who
was her factotum stood waiting, grumbling into his
red-blond, viking's beard.

"Here," she said, disregarding his mood, "carry
this for me, will you?" She gave him the tin box
which contained, as every Stronn Islander knew, a
stock of medicaments and bandages. "It must be the
young man lodging at the farm who came off the
steamer this morning," she went on. "I've been
watching him with the glasses. The rock at the top
gave way. It was a very near thing. But he had great
courage. And he's a fine climber. That's what saved
him."

Mary Edzell had found herself a stick and put on
a battered cloth hat while she was talking. "The
path should be easy in this dry weather." She looked
up at Stronn Island's one fierce little mountain.
"Are you ready?"

"The young man should have taken his great
courage and his fine climbing up another hill on

another island and left me to lift my potatoes," Murdo said ungraciously.

"Never you mind what he should have been doing. We've got to get up there now, as fast as ever we can."

3

In Mrs Edzell's comfortable sitting room at Stronn Lodge there was a large photograph in a silver frame. It was the picture of a very young soldier who had been killed in Flanders in early 1918.

Her husband had never said much about this only child of his first marriage, And she had never pressed him to tell her. But often, especially since Adam's death, she had found herself picking up the photograph and looking at it, moved, it may be, by a regret to which her brusque downrightness refused to give a name.

Now, here on the top of the Hog's Snout, having done what she could for the injured leg, and, as the great creature she had brought up with her stood holding the slim young man in his arms ready to carry him down the hillside, Mary was astonished to find that this unknown climber had the face of the boy in the photograph; grown leaner and more mature.

CHAPTER 2

1

John Edzell hated—or so it pleased him to tell himself—the idea of anything so sentimental, so ridiculous, as today's birthday party. What did a hard old nut like himself want with that kind of nonsense?

"But John, dear, you're the head of the family! We all look up to you and want to pay you honour on your eightieth birthday," his sister Alice had insisted. Pay him honour, humbug! Alice had only been looking for self importance as usual; looking for something to arrange; or have the credit of arranging.

It was getting towards one o'clock on the last Saturday of September. A resplendent autumn day. John Edzell was at the top of his front steps, his heavy gold watch open in one hand, awaiting the arrival of his two sisters. Time they were here or they would be late for lunch. He stood looking about him, a large old man, still solid, his heavy features contracted to a scowl by the bright sunshine.

The idea of this party arranged in his honour by his sister did not irk him half so much as he liked to think it did. Old John's self importance had never been averse to homage, neither from his relatives nor from any other quarter.

The head of the Edzell family occupied an old villa called Lochview in the prosperous and quickly expanding Glasgow suburb—now turned borough—of Bearsden. It was a great, echoing house much too large for one old man and the middle aged couple who looked after him, built to a design that was ugly even for the late nineties: and made still more so by coloured panes of glass, beaten copper fitments, machine carved wood and glittering varnish. But yet, especially on such a day as this, the house was redeemed, given dignity indeed, by its setting. For it stood in apparent isolation, screened by the high old trees and shrubbery that cut it off from the sight of the ever extending acres of bungalows and small suburban houses in which it was actually engulfed; its only open outlook being where the green expanse of front lawn ran down to a pleasant little loch, floating a waterlily or two and fringed with a tangle of high reeds.

When young John Edzell had come here with his wife and little son, Lochview had been in the country. But its rural setting was now mere illusion; his son was now dignified by middle age; and his son's mother had been a memory for more than twenty years.

There was a sound of wheels on the gravel of the drive, then the large, old-fashioned car he had sent to bring his sisters came into sight from behind the screening shrubbery and ran to a standstill down there before him at the foot of the steps. Without bothering to change his expression to one of welcome—why should he, when it was only his sisters Alice and Jessie?—John Edzell snapped his gold watch shut, put it into a waistcoat pocket and stood waiting for the ladies to come up to him.

2

"Johnnie, my dear! There you are! A very happy birthday to you." Alice came up towards her brother with a youthfulness of step that was, perhaps, remarkable for her years. Then, having reached him, she added archly: "And I'm going to give you a kiss, you old bear, whether you like it or not!"

To all of which her brother responded with a grunt; though it was a grunt that sounded—or so, at least, his sister's optimism decided—a more responsive, a rather warmer grunt, than was usual.

Alice Crabbe was a frivolous woman of seventy-eight, possessed of much self conscious charm. A charm which tended, at times, to fill most of those who were near to her with black exasperation; an exasperation that was in no way diminished when those who were *not* near to her declared her to be the most fascinating old lady they had ever known. But at all events the bounding vitality which had carried her through what had, after all, been a life of quite sharp ups and downs, following a flighty, headstrong marriage at seventeen, had not yet deserted her. With her snowy hair and frail prettiness that suggested, quite wrongly, gentle resignation in lavender scented rooms, Alice still carried her years like banners rather than burdens.

She turned back now to call to her sister who

was helping the driver to collect parcels from the inside of the car. "Jessie dear! What are you doing? Why don't you come up and wish your big brother many happy returns? McNeil can bring up these things."

"She's coming. She's coming." The old man spoke impatiently. This was Alice all over. Concerning herself to make a graceful, unencumbered arrival, without bothering to help. "What are all these parcels anyway?" he demanded.

"Ah! What do you think? Birthday presents for you of course! I suggested that my family and, of course, Jessie should send their presents to me. Then I could bring them out here all together. That's why I asked you to send the car for us. Lovely idea, isn't it?"

He took an instant of time to wonder that still, after so many years, his sister Alice should be foolish enough to try to be arch with himself, but he made no comment. Then he turned to greet his younger sister Jessie who now, burdened and flushed, was ascending the steps followed by the still more burdened driver.

"How are you, Jessie?" he asked brusquely.

Jessie Edzell was a thin, good natured spinster some two years younger than Alice, with a tongue that was liable to run on unsupported by any substructure of thought.

"John! Eighty today! Just think! What does it feel like? Yes, McNeil. Put these things on the floor. Yes, anywhere. We can arrange them later. Eighty and looking like a boy! Many happy returns, John! Don't let that drop, McNeil! It's breakable! Just put it down there, please. Yes. Beside where I'm laying these things. And to think there's only three of us left now! Just three old Edzells left. How proud poor Willie and Adam would have been if they could only have been alive today!"

"Proud of what?"

"Well, John dear? But don't you see . . .?" Then as Jessie, now she came to think, could not quite see of what her dead brothers would have been proud, she took out a handkerchief with a hand that was once again free of parcels and wiped her eyes at the thought of them.

Alice was annoyed with Jessie. This day was of her arranging, and it must be brightly successful. This was no moment for her sister to be working up emotions about nothing.

"No sad memories today, Jessie dear!" she said, schooling herself with some difficulty to tones of indulgent patience, and patting her sister's arm.

Their brother stood detached, watching McNeil as he ran down the steps, took the wheel of the car and drove it away. Then he turned back. What were they going on about anyway? No. His sisters were just a couple of stupid old bodies. Why expect sense from one or the other of them?

But now the sight of Jessie reminded him of something. "This is the day you get your cheque," he said matter-of-factly. His younger sister received a fixed sum from him on the last Saturday of each month. "Here. You'd better take it while I remember." He withdrew an envelope from a pocket and gave it to her.

Alice flinched, stung, perhaps, by her brother's

lack of delicacy; or, it might be, by a pang of jealousy.

"Really, John! *Must* we think of business, even on your eightieth birthday?"

"Business is business, whatever day it is! Jessie expects this."

"Still, I should have thought that just today . . ."

"Well, you needn't bother thinking. There's Mrs McNeil putting in the lunch. Come and eat it, both of you."

3

The lofty, tasteless dining room with three places laid at the end of the large table did not suggest dignity or cosiness. Yet neither host nor guests took note of their surroundings. The room was as usual; as it had been for close on fifty years. The graceless furniture stood where it had first been placed. The only item of furniture that was missing, indeed, was the mistress of the house, herself. And she had been gone so long now that they did not feel her absence. An indifferent room. Containing three old, indifferent people, a stranger would have said.

Yet despite appearances, these old Edzells were not indifferent to each other. To say that there was love between them would be to say too much, perhaps. If love there was in their hearts, it was given rather to their children and their grandchildren; or by the spinster, Jessie, to such of the younger relatives as bothered to remember her existence. Still, the bonds that held them were oddly strong. Bonds of blood, of shared memories, of mutual understanding, of family interest. It had never occurred to them not to be attached, one to the other. Their very bickerings attached them.

For a time they spoke of the afternoon arrangements. The idea of providing tea for so many had flooded the inelastic mind of Mrs McNeil with horror. It must be catered from outside, she had firmly told Alice. And so boxes of ham sandwiches and commercial cake were even now waiting in the pantry to be duly refused by a younger, cocktail-minded generation of Edzells.

"So you've browbeaten everybody into coming, have you?"

Her brother's glum expression had not changed. But Alice, knowing him, caught a grace note of teasing in his voice.

"Johnnie, dear! Don't be naughty! Browbeaten! I wrote to everybody, of course. And I telephoned some of them as well, just to make them grasp how disappointed you would be if they didn't appear. But you can't quite call that browbeating, can you?"

"You're a great old body for making yourself important!" was her brother's gracious comment. He chewed steadily, looking past her out of the window.

Alice did not like being called old. And she genuinely believed that never in all her life had she accomplished anything except by her own great charm of manner. It must not desert her now.

"Well anyway, dear," she said soothingly, "I believe I can say that everybody in the family is coming.'

"And a member of it that neither of you expect!"
John and Alice turned to look at Jessie.

"I wanted it to be a surprise!" Jessie's thin face
was flushed with triumph.

"That neither of us expect, Jessie?" her elder
sister asked. "But who—?"

"She means the woman at Stronn Island that
Adam should never have married," John Edzell said.

At which Alice exclaimed: "Jessie, dear! You
don't mean to say you've asked Mrs Adam!"

But Jessie shook her head. "No. It's not Adam's
wife." And then, letting loose the floods: "I know
you don't count her. Although why you're determined not to like her—she's been very kind to me.
Really, very kind. You see, I am just back from a
fortnight up there, John. Perfect autumn weather.
Until just when I was coming home in the boat
early yesterday morning. Then all of a sudden the
sea—"

"Well, if it's not the Stronn Island woman, who
is it?" her brother roared.

Jessie looked red and offended. "I don't think you
should shout at me like that, John," she said resentfully. "Neither of you have given me a chance to
tell you who it is. He's a very nice young man. And
he wants to meet you all. That's why I asked him
to come today. Good manners and everything. A
young man we needn't feel the least ashamed of."

"Young man? Lord bless me, Jessie, why can't
you say who it is?"

"John, I've been trying to tell you! He's an
Edzell you don't know! He's our brother Willie's
grandson!"

Now, for once, Alice was startled into a lack of blandness. "Don't talk rubbish, Jessie! Willie was never married! How could he possibly have had a grandson?"

"In the same way as men who *are* married have grandsons, I suppose." Jessie spoke resentfully. This was how they had taken the great surprise she had planned. "You've only to see the young man to *know* he's an Edzell."

Alice, her Victorian sensibilities shrinking a little before her sister's indelicacy, looked at their brother.

John in turn was looking at Jessie "Where have you seen this young man? Is he in Glasgow?"

"Yes. He came back with me yesterday. Oh, don't imagine he's not a perfectly respectable young man, John! In fact I think he's delightful! He was staying at Stronn Island while I was there. Mary had brought him down from the top of the Hog's Snout and was nursing him. You know the Hog's Snout is the mountain they have out there And you see, he had been climbing—and—wasn't it extraordinary—she hadn't the slightest idea that . . "

But memory had withdrawn John Edzell's attention from the stream of Jessie's gabble. Alice could, if she liked, disentangle what she was talking about.

He sat silent now, his thoughts drawn back into another, younger world, remembering the handsome brother—the twin of his brother Adam—who had disappeared from among them. Remembering his parents' distress. His father's anger when it had come to his knowledge that the best and quickest of his sons had joined a company of actors. Remembering how, some years later, William had come to

town and how he had gone to the theatre with
another of the family—Adam was it?—and how
strange it had seemed to see William down there in
the bright lights of the stage. How their mother
had confessed to him that she had gone to see William at his lodgings and begged himself, John, to
say nothing to their father. And then the news that
William had died during a tour in America.

Here the old man's consciousness rose once more
to the surface to hear Jessie say: "Of course you
must all see him, Alice! Why shouldn't we get to
know him? He's an Edzell! And I don't see how
it's his fault that his grandparents didn't marry!"

4

And Alice was asking him: "Did *you* ever hear
that poor Willie had left a child behind him, John?
A son who could be the father of this young man?
It's quite understandable that nothing would be
said to us girls considering that he was . . ."

John looked at his elder sister, nodding "Well,
anyway we had an idea."

"Idea?"

"I remember a young woman coming asking for
the old man at the office."

"Our father, John?"

"Aye." John sat remembering for a moment, then
went on. "I can't have been married myself at that
time. It wasn't long after we heard Willie was dead.
My father wasn't there, so I saw her. Her story was

that she was carrying Willie's child."

"William's child?" Alice echoed the words, then sat thinking about them for a time. "And William was dead! Had she been engaged to him, John?"

"She said no."

"Then whatever kind of woman was she?"

The picture of an intense, thin-faced young woman draped in the loose, "emancipated" clothing of the turn of the century was still plain in his mind. "Oh, a queer arty kind of body. She said she was a political secretary, whatever that could be."

"But Johnnie, dear, what else did she say?"

"Oh, she had plenty to say! Said she believed every woman had a right to a bairn whether she was married or not."

"Cranky, dear?" Alice asked.

"Aye. Cranky."

Here Jessie was intrigued enough to emerge from her annoyance for a moment to ask: "And so she chose William to . . . ?

"Well, that's what she said anyway." John Edzell answered matter of factly. "And then she said she had heard he was dead and thought we would like to know a bairn of his was coming. She gave her address in London."

"But did she *love* William, Johnnie?" Alice asked.

"She didn't say."

"Well, really!" Alice shook her head. "Oh yes, cranky, Johnnie. She must have been a lady anarchist. Oh, very cranky!"

"Aye, cranky."

"And did you tell anybody?" Jessie asked.

"I told my father."

"And what did father say?"

"He said she would be wanting money and I was to leave her alone."

"And was she?"

"No. She said money had nothing to do with it. Said she had what she needed. Said she just wanted to be kind by letting us know."

Old John spoke with contempt, but his elder sister was forced to smile. "Perhaps with a woman like that the child wasn't William's at all!"

But now Jessie was turning excitedly from one to the other. "Just wait, both of you. until you see him. This young man is as Edzell looking as he can look!"

CHAPTER 3

1

ALICE opened her eyes to look up at her elder son. "Joey, dear! I didn't know you had come! What time is it? Has nobody else arrived?"

Joseph Crabbe looked down upon his mother with anxious concern. "Mother, this is ridiculous! The end of September is far too late for you to risk sleeping out here. You'll be in bed with a chill next."

After lunch, old John had dismissed Alice from his presence saying he wanted to talk to Jessie alone for a minute before he took his afternoon rest; thus forcing Alice's inquisitive reluctance into the garden, where, in a long chair, the warmth of the sunshine had sent her to sleep.

"Joey! Don't look so cross, dear! And answer my question." Alice reached for her son's hand and gave his fingers a petulant, coquettish shake.

"It's half past three and nobody else seems to be here yet. Where's Aunt Jessie?"

"She must be in the house." Alice's face clouded for an instant remembering John's dismissal of herself.

"The old man is inside too, I suppose?"

"The old man, as you call him, is only two years older than I am, Joey. Are you forgetting your mother is too old?"

Joseph withdrew his fingers and thrust both hands into his pockets. The emotion that dictated this quick nervous movement was not, perhaps, easily definable. But now he allowed himself a smile. "Well, mother, considering that I am on sixty . . ."

Alice shook her head wistfully and then laughed a little. "I wasn't quite nineteen when you were born. Ridiculous, wasn't it? But you and Sammy, whatever your ages, have always been just my own dear wee boys."

"Wee boys! We might be grandfathers! Sam will be, before long."

Alice did not answer this just at once. She cast a misty look across the shining surface of the loch down there in front of her, at a moorhen diving among the reeds, at the copper beech branches that hung down to darken the waters by the shore. Then she raised her eyes once more to her son's face. "Well, Joey. And why aren't you? You know quite well I've always wanted both of my sons to be happily married."

He did not bother to reply to her question. It was one with which she had tested him all through his adult days. A question he had never quite answered, even to himself.

But the family were forever making comment on Joseph's obsessive bachelor devotion to his mother; and how Alice played up to it. Nothing had ever been too good for her in the eyes of this, her elder son. Least of all the sacrifice of himself. "Joe? Oh, he would see all the rest of us minced if it would do mother any good!" his lighthearted younger brother Sam had always said. And once Sam's son,

Patrick, had been heard to remark that Uncle Joe was just an ass. A good, devoted ass, but still an ass.

Patrick's twenty-eight years did not know everything. For his elders were aware that since his boyhood, almost, Joseph Crabbe had been the support of his widowed mother; that his forces had been stretched by self sacrifice; that he had given her too much of himself.

At sixty he was a spare, keen little man with a head of thick grey hair, a red face, a foolish censoriousness of the rising generation, and a still more foolish fixation upon the flighty old woman who had taken the place of wife and child for him.

Now, he merely turned his head to see whose wheels were coming to a standstill up there behind them.

2

It was his brother arriving with wife and children in their family car.

"That's Sam," Joseph said.

"Go and bring them over here, Joey. Then we needn't disturb your Uncle John's afternoon rest just yet. Your Aunt Jessie can't have been with him all this time!"

Joseph, armed with a frosty, purposeful smile, went back across the lawn to where his nephew, young Patrick Crabbe had brought their car to a standstill. He opened both front and back doors and said: "Hello."

"Hello, Uncle Joe!"

Joseph looked beyond the large bulk of his sister-in-law at his niece, Minnie, who sat between her mother and her brother Patrick's wife.

"Wait a minute, Minnie. We had better get your mother manœuvred out first before you start talking. Hello, Ruth. Hello, Babs. Now steady!"

These last two greetings were addressed, the first to his nephew's wife, the second to his sister-in-law Euphemia, a name by which she never went except to Alice, her mother-in-law. For reasons never explained she had always gone by the more convenient name of Babs.

Babs was pink and blonde like her daughter, Minnie. But her fifty years on the earth had given her more time for expansion. Now, though she must be more than twice Minnie's weight, she disdained Joseph's hand and slid down out of her seat with surprising agility.

"There! Look at that! And no more of your talk about manœuvring!" she panted, straightening her large hat, pulled down the ample folds of her flowered dress and the foundation that supported it, dragged at the large pink pearls at her neck in an attempt to give herself air, then laughed. "Sammy, did you hear that? Manœuvre! Tell that brother of yours I want less of his impertinence!"

"We can't stay young and thin for ever, you and I, Babs." Sam Crabbe descended from the front seat carefully, shaking his head the while, affable but a little sad. He could, he knew, advance the pointer of the bathroom weighing machine even further than his wife could.

"That's rubbish!" Joseph spoke quite matter-of-factly. "You're only fifty seven and I'm sixty, and look at me! I'm thin."

"That's what I keep telling them, Uncle Joe. Look at you. They're fat because they eat too much. How are you?" Minnie Crabbe sprang from the car, and in almost the same movement flung her arms impulsively round her uncle's neck and kissed him.

"How are you, child? How are you? Look here, don't knock me down!"

Though her uncle's voice was incapable of soft inflection, rightly Minnie read affection into it. She and he had always looked upon each other as good friends. Minnie saw him with eyes that were pert but warm; he, with those that were stern, masking, perhaps, an ache. She was the only young person towards whom Joseph Crabbe was wholly without jealousy.

He set the plump young woman at arms' length and turned to his nephew Patrick and his wife who had come from the other side of the car. As he had seen the young man at the office this morning he did not bother to give him any greeting but turned to the girl by his side.

"How are you, Ruth? Looking after yourself? Pat looking after you?" Ruth was expecting a child in some weeks time. It was a natural reaction in Joseph to nip the buds of his envy by fussing crossly over those who might occasion their sprouting. "Take Ruth down beside your grandmother, Pat." He spoke in his sharp, one toned voice. "And put out a long chair for her."

The young couple smiled at him patronisingly and gaily. "Ruth's feeling grand, Uncle Joe," the young father-to-be said.

"Never mind. Go and do what you're told." Joseph turned aside to Minnie. "There's no need to stand about here. Come down and see your grandmother."

The large presence of Minnie's parents hovering over the old lady were already silhouetted against the loch's gleaming waters. Now Ruth had joined them and her husband had begun to take garden chairs from where they were stacked against a tree trunk and was setting them round for everybody.

Minnie put her arm affectionately through her uncle's and dragged him impulsively across the lawn.

3

But presently, as they were settling themselves, a second car had come to a standstill in the drive behind them; of so very different a kind from the conveyance of uncertain age which had just brought Sam Crabbe and his family, that it caused young Patrick Crabbe to exclaim: "Now there's a tidy job!" For there was nothing uncertain about the age of this one. It was three weeks old and was immense. And Paddy, who spent much time studying all the motor journals he could find lying around the coffee rooms of Glasgow, gasped at the thought of what it must have cost his father's cousin, Frederick Edzell of Priestlaw House, West Stirlingshire, who was, even now, descending from his seat beside the driver. But here Paddy's thinking was wrong. Frederick Edzell had not paid for this very handsome car. It was bought, maintained and expertly driven at the expense of Adam and John Edzell Limited of which he happened to be the chairman. Paddy was overlooking the fact that important companies must, in these days, see to it that their chairmen do not drive around in any old shandrydan.

"That must be Freddy and his family." Alice spoke in a tone of easy intimacy, but even as she did so, she had struggled out of her long chair with surprising speed and was moving across the lawn to pay the honour she felt their importance—and her own—demanded.

"Freddy! How nice to see you again! After all this long time!"

"A long time Aunt Alice!" Dutifully sentimental, Frederick Edzell bent to kiss this old woman he had not bothered to visit for years.

"Just like old times, Freddy! You remember how, when you were wee boys, I used to bring out Joey and Sammy to play with you, and how . . ."

"You've met Christine, haven't you, Aunt Alice?"

Christine Edzell, a slim woman of fifty, stood smiling a little mechanically. "Of course we've met! How are you, Aunt Alice?" She spoke brightly, bending in her turn to bestow a crisp, elegant peck. Mother, as the three very personable young people, who were at this moment likewise descending, well knew, had rolled up her social sleeves and had started in to putting through a very difficult afternoon; an afternoon they had all rather dreaded.

"The last time I saw you, I think, you were all in your prams. But I know your names, Harold. That's you, dear? You're the oldest. And Rosamond! And Oliver! It's wonderful to have you all here!" Alice's charm was working at full pressure, as she extended a hand in turn to the two young men and the young woman who were doing their best to respond with smiles that were, perhaps, wan a little and a little bewildered.

"Where's father?" Frederick asked "I don't see him."

"We thought he should stay in the house, Freddy, until everybody was here. He's wonderful, you know, dear. But he's not the man he was. Well, after all, at eighty . . ."

"You can take charge of the others, Aunt Alice, and I'll go in and find him."

"Very well, Freddy. I'm sure he'll be delighted to have you alone for a minute. But don't be too long. There's Mrs McNeil just bringing tea."

A self important, rather managing old woman, this Aunt Alice of their father's, Frederick Edzell's family decided, as they followed her across the lawn to meet these relatives they hardly knew.

4

Had any one asked Frederick Edzell to define his feelings each time he entered this, the home of his boyhood, he would have found it difficult to do so. Its old, spacious ugliness housed too many memories.

Pleasant, young memories of his mother and her anxious care for him. Bitter-sweet memories of adolescent discontents and longings; some of these kept to himself; some of them shared with her. The knowledge that neither she nor he were at their best in the presence of his father. Later memories of young manhood when he was being what his father liked to call licked into shape. When his young imaginings, his foolishnesses, his hopes, were being stripped from him one by one. When the reins were being drawn tight and he, Frederick, was being turned into the "first class" citizen and the man of business he had now long since become. It had been a rigorous grooming. And if it had turned John Edzell's son into the man his father intended him to be, it had been done at the cost of some cooling in filial affection.

But Frederick was nothing if not dutiful in everything he did. He visited his father punctiliously in the old man's semi-retirement, giving him news of the family firm, the only news that really interested, and looking after his affairs.

And yet, when John Edzell did go, his son knew he would be glad to have done coming to this place of his childhood, glad to be left to select his memories, glad only to remember this house with his mother in it, this garden he had dreamed around during his growing up.

His father knew his step and called from the deep chair in which he was resting. "Hello, Fred. Is that you?"

"Hello, father. Many happy returns." Frederick found him in the little room which had always been known as the library. Perhaps because it was leather upholstered and darker than the other rooms. Not because it contained any books. "How are you?"

"All right, I suppose. Bring your wife and family with you?"

This reference to wife and family was typical of his father who saw everything in terms of possession; and a wife and family, surely, were things you possessed.

"Yes. Christine's here with the boys and Rosamond. They've gone down to the others. I said I would come in and get you."

"Sit down for a minute. They can wait."

Frederick sat down as he was told. Even now, at the age of fifty-four with his position in life long since assured, some public honour, a wife from a level higher than his own, two sons and a daughter upon whose education nothing had been spared and a country mansion overlooking Loch Lomond, he still felt unsure and vulnerable in the presence of this old man. Feelings too far down in Frederick Edzell's roots for him ever to be rid of.

"And what have you been doing this week?"

Frederick did his best. He told of a board meeting in London. Of an interview with a cabinet minister. Of his hopes of a contract worth many thousands of pounds. Of changes in the personnel of the company.

John Edzell gave the impression of merely sitting listening. His heavy face set in lines into which a stranger might have read glumness, but which his son knew to be mere lines of repose.

And it would have surprised the stranger had he been told what was going on behind that heavy mask, or what these occasional grunts of assent meant.

The old man was experiencing a keen satisfaction at the sight of this large, middle aged man who was his son; satisfaction at hearing that son's quite unselfconscious recital of his own importance. He had been building up to this all his life. Fred was a successful extension of himself; in every sense his own creation. He had brought him into the world; then paid for his being turned into a gentleman; and thereafter, forced him to forget his grand ways and labour for a time like a navvy, withdrawing from him every privilege possible. Fred's mother had worried and found courage to protest now and then. But what did women know? He had known Fred would stand it all right. And now here he was, the finished product, sitting there in front of him. Yes. Fred had gone further than himself. He had education, address, everything. He was taking a place such as he, his father, could never have taken. But it had all been his doing. It was himself, John Edzell, who had pointed the way his son must take at every crossroads.

Never once did it occur to him that the gentle, not very colourful woman who had been Fred's mother might also have had qualities to give their son.

5

But now, as Frederick finished speaking, his father remembered a cloud, small, yet a cloud, moving across the blue of his complacency. "Your Aunt Jessie's here." He moved his heavy body uneasily in his armchair. "Have you seen her?"

"Well, we did," his son said, wondering a little. "She was standing at the gate as we drove in. She waved to us. She looked as if she were waiting for somebody."

"I brought her in here after lunch today," John went on, following his own thinking. "She's been staying with my brother Adam's widow on Stronn Island. There was a young man up there. His name was Edzell."

"Edzell!"

"He's the grandson of my brother Willie that ran away when he was young."

"I never knew that my uncle William was married."

"He wasn't married. But your Aunt Jessie is quite sure the young man's a grandson. That's what I brought her in here for. To ask her questions. She's such a silly body, it's hard to make her talk sense. But I think I got something. His name is William Edzell, she says. He's the son of a dead schoolteacher, that claimed to be my brother Willie's son."

Frederick could not interpret the look of ruminating displeasure in John's face. So he merely hazarded: "Well that all sounds very strange to me, Father." And left the old man to go on.

"He had some kind of accident up there. And the Stronn Island woman was nursing him. I got out of your Aunt Jessie that the pair of them had got very friendly, very close."

"Well, I suppose that's all right. And good luck to

them. What about it?" Frederick was still unable to see the direction of his father's thought.

The old man's face darkened. "You're the chairman of Adam and John Edzell, are you not?"

His son expressed assent by a look of blank curiosity.

"And who's got the biggest block of shares in the company?"

"Oh, we've always known that my Uncle Adam's widow had. But you know as well as I do that she has never given us any trouble. I don't believe she knows anything about money."

"She knew enough to catch your Uncle Adam when he was sixty."

"But if she has never troubled us, why should this new friendship start her troubling us now?"

Old John Edzell looked at his son with an expression of contempt. "You've still got a lot to learn, Fred," he said glumly.

"Where is this William Edzell? What does he do?" Frederick's tone was still determinedly light.

"He's got a job at the University, it seems. Your Aunt Jessie has asked him here today, although she had no right to do anything of the kind. She would be out at the gate looking for him when you passed."

"Well at least, father, we'll all get a look at him."

"Aye." Old John got up slowly. "Give me your arm," he said. "We had better get outside." And then, as though contact with his son's arm had sent a measure of warmth back into his feelings: "By the way, Fred. There's something I wanted to remind you about."

His son turned to listen.

"It was on my seventy-fifth birthday that I finished signing over half of all I had to you." The old bulldog features had actually relaxed. "I'm eighty today. Now they can whistle for their death duties! For that bit of it anyway! And here's another thing I have to tell you. I don't need much to keep me going now. So I am dividing some of the other half into three. A third share each for your two boys and your girl. I may live past eighty-five. Then they'll have to whistle for their death duties on that half too."

"But, Father, are you looking after yourself? Are you really sure you want to do this?"

The old man looked glum. "When could I not look after myself? And when did I not know my own mind? You can tell the three of them to expect this. Here, give me my stick."

6

As he supported his father across the lawn, Frederick at once realised that his wife, Christine, was making heavy weather of it. He realised this from the tone of her voice. Not that her voice was unpleasant. It was a very pleasant voice indeed. It was clear, bell-like and thoroughly well bred. But he knew from its pitch, its precision, and the stream of platitudes that were so beautifully enunciated, that she was out of tune with those around her and had been forced into giving a performance.

It could be said of Frederick Edzell that he had

married well. He had married at twenty-five. When, at the age of twenty-four, he had told his father— fearful and stammering—that he was head over heels in love with an English girl who was the sister of a friend he had known at Cambridge, John Edzell had grunted and looked sour. But he had asked questions. All of which Frederick was able to answer to his satisfaction. A few enquiries made behind the boy's back increased that satisfaction. The girl's background was impeccable and much better than Fred's. Yes. The boy had better be married if she would have him. Marriage stopped a man thinking about the wrong things. In the end it saved time and kept the nose to the grindstone. Besides, connection with this girl would mean a step up. To his astonishment, and still more to his mother's, marriage had been made easy for Frederick.

Christine Edzell had the temperament of watercress; a temperament that was wholesome, fresh and with a nip to it. She had never encouraged her husband to dream. What was a man for if not to be up and doing? To accomplish? And what was his wife for but to stand behind him, supplying him with resolution, support, a sympathy that was bracing, a sensible number of healthy children and a housekeeper-receptionist of competence, distinction and elegance? All these things Christine had required of herself; and all of them she had supplied and was continuing to supply in full measure. Privileged as she was, and with such a temperament, there were few times in her easy life in which she found herself at a loss.

But this was one of them. She was almost wishing

she had not yielded to a strange eruption of sentiment on Fred's part, following from an absurdly sentimental letter from this old woman who was Fred's Aunt Alice, asking them all to come to this quite unnecessary birthday party along with Fred's rather difficult relatives.

The children had, of course, protested. Whatever for?—they had demanded sitting round the breakfast table at Priestlaw House. Did grandfather really want this fuss? Couldn't they just drop in and see him some time? Wouldn't he like that much better? And why meet all these relatives they had never really known: whom they only felt obliged to recognise and greet for a moment when by chance they met in public places? Whatever could one find to say to them? The word "common" hovered large above the breakfast table. But they would not have been Christine Edzell's children had they brought themselves to utter it.

"Isn't Mrs. Samuel Crabbe called Babs?" Harold had asked in comic earnest. "Mother, darling, we just couldn't say 'Yes, Cousin Babs, no, Cousin Babs'. Surely you must see that!"

"I'll take on a bet with you that *I* do," his younger brother Oliver said.

And at this their sister Rosamond had laughed.

"Whatever I see or don't see, Harold," Christine had said, "I hope I can be sure there will be no bad manners." But diplomacy had prompted her to laugh, too, a little, for, seeing rebellion softened by humour, she had pushed her advantage and made them promise to do what their father so unaccountably wanted.

And now, sitting beside Frederick's old Aunt Alice and working very hard herself, Christine was glad at least to note that her children were behaving beautifully. But, of course, she had known they would. Scraps of their conversation reached her now and then.

". . . Yes. The South of France. I was staying only a fortnight ago with a French friend who has a villa near San Tropez." Rosamond was doing her best with the said Cousin Babs.

Christine's eyes could not help resting on her daughter's aspect with satisfaction; the fair hair, pulled back and knotted low on her neck; the quick, blue eyes set in a fair skin that was carefully and smoothly sunburned; the tweed suit of elegant austerity.

"San where did you say? That's not on the Riviera is it?"

"Well—San Tropez is not very far from Cannes."

"Oh, Cannes! Oh, I liked Cannes!" The large, hot face of Rosamond's neighbour expanded with pleasure. "They took us along in special buses to see the night life at Monte Carlo. And laugh! I don't think I ever . . ."

And just as Christine's attention was again reclaimed by old Mrs Crabbe she thought she heard something about paper hats. But to whatever Rosamond was being obliged to listen, her mother saw with satisfaction that Mrs Samuel Crabbe was receiving the respectful attention that might have been given to a duchess.

"Hello. There's father coming with grandfather!" Harold's voice was redolent of forced joy. It made

Christine wonder a little, until she realised that her elder son was probably glad to break away from small talk that had become heavy. She had, perhaps, least confidence in Harold's good manners. His idea of what was funny and what wasn't got the better of him, here and there, despite everything her early training of him had striven to do to correct this. But now his mother was pleased to see that his snub, cheerful face was composed and that his tubby body stood hesitant and deferential, as he waited while his elders struggled from their chairs in order to greet his grandfather.

It would have been hard to tell whether the gruff old man had any pleasure in returning their greetings. It was, it seemed, such a full-time occupation merely sitting down, merely regaining breath. But he would not have been John Edzell had he not, now he had time to sit looking about him, fallen into his old habits of assessment. These grandchildren of his, that he didn't often see these days. What about them? That girl of Fred's. Yes. He supposed she could be called a beauty. She should make a good marriage. The division of money he had now decided to make should help that. And the boy, Harold, who was with Fred in the business. A bit sparky, but he had the Edzell brain, it seemed. *He* was all right. But the young one, Oliver there, sitting on the grass between Sam Crabbe's son and daughter-in-law? He must remember to ask Fred about him. Fred, now he came to think about it, had never told him much about Oliver. Was Fred shielding the boy? Wasn't he doing well?

John Edzell sat watching his younger grandson

with the direct, unwavering stare of the old. That boy was like Fred's mother when she was young. The paleness that went with light red hair. That look of —was it uncertainty? There was something in that boy's face that stirred memory. But a man had no right to be uncertain. He had had a lot of that kind of thing to knock out of Fred in his young days.

"There's Mrs McNeil, darling." Alice was looking at her grand-daughter. "Go and tell her we'll have tea down here and help her with it."

Any interruption, even the bringing of tea out of doors and deciding how it was to be placed, was better than none. It made a welcome break in a difficult afternoon.

7

But soon there was another and better interruption. Jessie Edzell had appeared in the drive escorting a young man.

"Hello. There's Aunt Jessie!" Babs exclaimed. "I meant to ask where she was. Who's that with her?" But as nobody replied to this at once, but merely turned to look, Babs was obliged to take a large bite out of her ham sandwich and a surreptitious sip of tea to help it down and wait with the others.

The couple came slowly. The young man was lame, it seemed, and was using a stick, while his companion, twittering with pride and excitement, held up progress still further by bending enthusiastically towards him and thus impeding his vision with the crushed roses in her hat.

Alice reminded herself that she was mistress of ceremony. She got up. "That's Jessie with the young man, John."

"What young man?" her brother asked crossly.

"You know as well as I do, dear. We were talking about him at lunch. Jessie told you she had asked him." Alice turned to the Frederick Edzells, who were now all polite curiosity. "Your grandfather is just being naughty. He gets like that sometimes." A fact of which the Frederick Edzells were not unaware.

"I never said I wanted him to come here."

"Johnnie, dear, you mustn't talk like that. He can quite well hear you!—Oh, Jessie, dear, there you are! And this is—?"

"I hope you're not talking about me, sir. I *was* invited to come, you know."

John Edzell looked at the outstretched hand, then up at the lean, handsome face that was bending over his chair. "Who are *you?*" he asked, with an old man's perverseness, knowing very well.

"William Edzell, sir. Your brother William's grandson, I believe."

Frederick, the only one who was able to read his father a little, watched with interest as he again raised his eyes in a slow examination of the young man's face, allowing them to rest there in a steady stare for a time, then at length turning them aside to look across the loch.

"Aye," he said presently. "You look like my brother Willie. You'd better stay for your tea."

CHAPTER 4

1

YOUNG Will Edzell had known there were Edzells in Glasgow; relatives of the grandfather he had never seen. On the strength of his name he had meant, going warily and feeling his way, to let them know of his existence; going warily, since his father, sensitive to his own strange beginnings, had never visited any of them and thus had been unable to tell him anything about them. But now Will had begun to know these relatives almost at once. A magazine article on climbing in Scotland with a photograph of the famous Hog's Snout precipice on Stronn Island had caught his passion for climbing. And the statement that the island belonged to a Mrs Edzell, a relative perhaps, had kindled his curiosity and fixed his decision to go there before he took up the junior lectureship to which he had been appointed at Glasgow University. Thus, near-disaster had introduced him to Adam Edzell's widow and to Adam's sister, who happened to be her guest.

And now here he was sitting in the garden of another of his grandfather's old brothers, being received by all of them with enthusiasm and with an interest he might not have been accorded at another time. He was delighted, flattered and a little above himself, quite unaware that his merely appearing had been a straw to be snatched at. That it had given these people something to talk about; had broken the stiffness of an ill-assorted party and slackened tensions. He had, in himself, provided a young and unknown relative to be questioned, to be explained, to be summed up. In all of which Will was more than ready to co-operate; was delighted with everyone and equally ready to believe that everyone was delighted with him.

"Oh, I say, thanks. That's very kind of you," Will said as Oliver who, seeing him limp, had fetched another garden chair and had set it out for him. "You know, that is a strange business altogether! I don't suppose that before today most of you knew I existed. Except, of course, Aunt Jessie. We met on Stronn Island, didn't we?"

Jessie Edzell's face flushed with pride that this attractive young man should claim her.

"Did *you* know I existed?" he turned to the fair girl in the tweed suit.

Rosamond smiled, shaking an elegant head. "No. What are you anyway? Some kind of cousin? You look as if you belonged."

"Looks a bit like Paddy," Babs said, giving up her tea cup to be refilled.

"No. I don't think we can disown him, can we?" Christine was charmingly crisp.

"He's got an Edzell nose if that's any good to him," Joseph Crabbe said.

"Look here," Harold began waggishly. "Has no one got a form for you to fill in? Like on aeroplanes to Paris. *Date de naissance* sort of thing. Mother's maiden name. Grandmother's maiden name. You know what I mean."

Alice sat up. Surely these words had been unfortunate. Although Freddy's son wouldn't, of course, know why.

But the newcomer was actually laughing. "That, of course, is the whole point about me. You see, my grandmother never had anything *but* a maiden name. She was what was known in her day as an 'emancipated woman'. I suppose my own father was —what shall I say?—the ultimate expression of her emancipation. At any rate, as my grandfather died before he was born, she called their son William Edzell, too. As a kind of memorial, I gather."

Alice turned stiffly away, addressing her brother. "Johnnie, dear, you mustn't allow yourself to feel cold. I don't think you should allow yourself to sit out very long."

"My grandmother spent her life trying out new ideas. She was a social worker, or something, in London," Will went on. "For her time, she was said to be very advanced."

"So it would seem." Joseph Crabbe's voice was tart.

Will Edzell laughed at this, too, with a laugh that gave the other young people permission to laugh with him.

Alice felt helpless.

"But anyway my father and mother were safely married, so you can take it that I'm all right." Here Will looked about him. Wondering, for a moment if, perhaps, he had gone too far for these old people.

2

But as the others had found it hard to find common ground for talk and this unknown relative's story was of interest, Will was induced to continue with it, answering their questions.

His father, the second William Edzell, had, Will said, been duly sent to school in London by the strangely independent woman who was his grandmother. Later he had gone to London University. The rest of his comparatively short life had been spent as a schoolmaster in the English Midlands. He had married Will's mother, a farmer's daughter from the Lake District, when he was thirty; lost his wife when he was forty and his son was nine; and died in his early fifties.

It was a simple enough history. But it is one thing to tell what has happened to ourselves and to those who have gone immediately before us, and another to tell—or indeed to be aware of—how these happenings have shaped us into the sort of people we are.

The second William Edzell had been raised with a chip on his shoulder. His mother, determinedly eccentric, had made no secret of his beginnings. And as, especially at the turn of the century, the circle which would accept such eccentricity was small, it was not long before the growing boy had begun to feel himself looked at askance by his playfellows; and not much longer before he had begun to blame the mother who occasioned this. A strange upbringing full of resentments and discordant influences.

The cheerful Cumberland girl he had met on a climbing holiday and to whom he had given his unhappy heart, had done much towards dispelling these influences during the ten years of happiness she had been able to give him. But her early going had once again darkened existence for him, and though he now had a nine-year-old son to be fond of, it had put the chip firmly back on his shoulder.

For the remaining years of his life, Will's father had been devoted to him with a brooding devotion that might have found a better outlet in re-marriage. But his son and his son's education were everything. And thus Will had spent his adolescence in a gaunt, masculine world of schoolrooms and lecture rooms, varied by strenuous holidays walking and climbing in the company of a father from whom he learned to judge the world around him, if not with all the older man's harshness, at least with an over-quickness and unconventionality that would have surprised those who now sat round him here in the garden of Lockview.

3

It is pleasant to be twenty-six, to consider oneself a good talker and to find oneself the centre of an interested circle. But presently Will became aware that eyes were turning from himself towards the old man who was the reason for this gathering.

John Edzell was getting tired and impatient. He had not heard above half of what this talkative young man was saying, and the autumn afternoon was getting on. His granddaughter, Rosamond, now saw that he was trying to get up from his chair.

"Do you want your stick, grandfather?" she asked, helping him to his feet.

"Aye. I'm going into the house."

"Here it is. I'll come with you."

Most of the others had likewise risen, making gestures of goodbye or promising to come in and see him before they went. Which all agreed must now be soon.

As the old man turned round to orientate himself in the direction of his own front door, he found himself face to face with the stranger who now stood smiling at him.

"Goodbye, sir. It was very kind of you to allow me to come this afternoon. Will you let me come back some time?" Will held out his hand engagingly.

John Edzell did not take the hand nor did he answer Will's question. The others were not surprised at this. "My sister Jessie tells me you've been at Stronn Island," he said gruffly.

"Yes, sir. I had an accident up there. I was rock climbing. As you see, I'm still going a bit lame. But I'll be all right."

The old man stood thinking for a time, saying nothing. Then he asked: "Who looked after you?"

"Mrs Adam Edzell of the Lodge. She was very kind to me. Aunt Jessie was there too. Didn't she tell you?"

John Edzell continued to stand, seeming to think about that. His eyes sought and found his sister, then returned to the young man. "So you call her Aunt Jessie, do you?"

"Yes, sir. Why?"

But old John merely grunted and turned to begin, Rosamond walking beside him, his journey towards the house.

"He's tired, poor darling." Christine's tones were cool and kind as, with the others, she stood watching the retreating back.

Alice took the liberty of patting her arm affectionately. "Freddy's father is not as young as he once was, dear. He and Jessie and I are just three poor old bodies now, you know."

Christine could only reply to this with a little laugh that she hoped was both indulgent and sympathetic.

"He didn't seem to like my being at Stronn Island." Will said with a look of anxious innocence that may or may not have been entirely guileless. "I hope I haven't said or done anything wrong?"

There was a moment of silence before Frederick answered. "No. Not wrong. But you're right if you think my father doesn't like Mrs Adam Edzell."

"Oh? Doesn't he?"

"No."

Will waited for more but it did not come. Frederick's "no" seemed final. Will was disappointed. Having already heard the story from the the side of the mistress of Stronn Island, he would now be amused to hear it from the other side.

Christine Edzell looked at her wrist. "There's the

car waiting," she said to her husband. "If you're saying goodbye to your father, you might catch him before he goes in, Frederick. Tell Rosamond. The rest of us won't bother him any more. And then, perhaps . . ." She looked about her.

"It's an old family row, if you really want to know," Babs was saying to Will in a stage whisper. "The old boy never forgave his brother for marrying again."

Will decided it was best not to hear her just for the moment, but promised himself to ask her when the Priestlaw Edzells had gone.

Frederick hurried after his father to bid him a more intimate goodbye and to assure him he would be back to see him soon, while Christine made signs to her family to prepare themselves to be gone.

For an instant, as she gave her hand to Will, she found herself wondering if she ought to ask this strange, and presumably lonely, young man to visit them at Priestlaw House; if it would be kind; if her own children would scold her for doing so; and if it would be awkward to give an invitation to him in front of those others who were never invited. She compromised.

"You're alone in rooms, are you?" she said. "Well perhaps, sometime, if you cared, you might like to come out to Priestlaw House and see us." For which speech, settled later in the car and with time to consider it, Christine Edzel despised herself utterly. She was not that kind of woman. The young man, she told herself, should have had a proper invitation or none at all.

4

Will was enjoying himself immensely. "I say," he said, "I hope I didn't really make anybody angry with what I said about Mrs Adam Edzell." He was counting upon Bab's indiscretion and he was not to be disappointed.

"I've told you already it was a bad family row. They'll never get over it."

"It was never a low quarrel, Euphemia." Alice spoke in that cool voice that was intended to impose control upon her daughter-in-law's tongue. "We mustn't let our new cousin think . . ."

"It was bad enough, mother," Sam interposed, coming, for once, to the support of his wife. "Uncle John never forgave Uncle Adam."

"I sometimes think it would have been better for all of us if he had," Joseph snapped. "Certainly for Fred and *his* family."

"Better for us all, Joe? Why?" Sam asked.

"You know perfectly well why. You know—we all know—that that woman on Stronn Island owns more than half of Adam and John Edzell Limited. That if she liked she could . . ."

"Could what, Joe? Take it over? Put everybody out? Don't be silly! She knows when she's lucky. She must be throwing money into the sea to get rid of it!"

"And what's more, Sam, you know very well that our own firm is very nearly a branch of Adam and John Edzell; that half of the work we do now is for them."

"Your uncles were always very good to you two boys," Alice said.

Joseph snorted. "Uncle Adam was trying to help me when I started business, mother. It has all come from that. And it was for your sake."

"Joey, dear! Why are you getting so cross? This all seems to have arisen out of nothing."

"If Sam would only take the trouble to realise . . ."

"No, now, Joey . . ." Alice patted Joseph's hand soothingly as though he were a little boy, and for the moment he said no more. But Will was naughtily reluctant to allow the subject to drop.

"All I know of Mrs Edzell of Stronn Island—Aunt Mary as I now call her, actually—is that she was wonderful to me. She took me in and nursed me for —oh, for about a month. She told me she had *been* a nurse."

"She nursed herself into Adam Edzell's fortune!" Sam Crabbe's laugh was toneless.

"Mary Edzell has always been very kind to me. And I don't see why . . ." Jessie began.

But nobody cared to hear what she saw or didn't see. They knew that Adam Edzell, in his lifetime, had been the main support of his spinster sister Jessie; that his widow on Stronn Island continued this support; and that Jessie sometimes went to stay with her.

Will Edzell had received much kindness on the island and his loyalties were with the bestower of that kindness. All these people here were mere jokes to him. He laughed. "I'm sorry if I've started up anything unpleasant with my questions. Coming from the island, it's natural, isn't it, that I should want to know about Mrs Adam Edzell."

"It's a simple enough story." Joseph's matter of fact voice managed to convey that he did not approve of Will's probing. "Though I daresay Mrs Adam would give you a different version?"

"Will's answer was cautious. "Well, of course, she spoke about her husband, sir. Told me she had married him—when was it?—just before the war. They seem to have been very happy."

"That's always something." Joseph's tone was uncharitably curt.

Here Alice, feeling the lack of graciousness, interposed.

"Joey, dear, I think you ought to tell our cousin what happened. And just what we, and Uncle John, and Freddie and everybody felt about it."

"Uncle Adam went down to London to a meeting. He took a heart attack and was put into a nursing home. He was there for more than three months. On the day he came out he married the matron of the home. She was a woman who had come from the islands."

"She didn't waste much time, did she?" Paddy said.

"My poor brother, John, was very angry," Alice shook her head.

"But why poor, exactly? Why was he angry, granny? I could never quite see why," Minnie asked. "Did he feel Uncle Adam had been trapped into it!"

"Of course he had been trapped into it!" her father snapped.

Alice became reminiscent. "I remember poor John

would hardly look at her when Adam brought her back."

But now Will's mood had changed. What else they thought of Mary Edzell they could keep to themselves! To their surprise he stood up and said he must go. There were protests, offers of a lift back into town and invitations. He had left his motor bicycle by the front gate, he said. Yes, he would come to see them when his work was better arranged. No. He did not yet quite know when that would be.

They wondered a little at his sudden going and fell to discussing him after he was gone.

CHAPTER 5

1

FREDERICK EDZELL'S car had cleared Bearsden and was moving out towards the West before anyone bothered to speak. The family sat silent and relaxed, chewing the cud of its impressions. Parklands with trees and grass. The green velvet of a golf course, dotted here and there with playing figures.

"What's Babs' real name, anyway?" Harold's eyes were upon a man about to drive from a tee.

"Euphemia," Oliver said.

"How do you know?"

"Because I heard old Mrs Crabbe, Aunt Alice, calling her that. Why?"

"Oh, nothing." The player seemed to have driven well, though the car was moving too fast for Harold to see where the ball had gone.

Again there was silence as they ran on. Frederick was in his usual place beside the driver. His head and shoulders were divided from the others by the glass division. Now and then he could be seen exchanging a friendly word with the man beside him, though they could not hear what he said. For a moment, Christine caught herself wondering why, on the rare occasions when they were all together like this, Frederick almost always isolated himself from them. Was it chance? Convenience? Anyhow, why ponder over anything so trivial? Instead she asked:

"Do you think we ought to invite that young man who appeared?" Like many another of her kind, she found comfort, reassurance, in being a hostess.

"But I heard you invite him already, mother." Oliver looked out at a shabby van of white and gold halted by the green wayside and surrounded by city children who were licking coloured cones of ice cream.

"Not properly. I hate giving these half-hearted invitations."

"Then why not invite him properly?" Harold asked. "I quite liked him. Besides, any family worth anything ought to have one relative at least from the wrong side of the blanket."

"But he, himself, is not." Oliver withdrew his thoughts from the desecration of the countryside.

Harold touched his brother's arm soothingly. "I know, I know, Nol. But he's the best we can do."

"A bit red brick, wouldn't you say?" Rosamond said.

"Our sister is a snob," Harold announced.

"I didn't say I didn't like him." Rosamond's voice was indifferent.

The car had reached that point where, the road breaking through between plantations, Ben Lomond and the other mountains suddenly fill the distance with all the glory of Western Scotland. This was a daily sight for these people but, as for so many others, custom could never quite stale its wonder. Especially on mellow autumn evenings such as this.

They said no more now. Their thoughts were

driven inwards by the sight that lay before them; each pursuing a silent train of thinking.

Why, Rosamond wondered, had she bothered to say that? Harold had been right. It was snobbish. And absurd. But then she was a snob, she supposed. Snobbish and—despite her education—aimless.

Aimless. At least that young man could not be aimless. He must have learnt to earn a living for himself in his red brick university. As the car slid downhill in the direction of Loch Lomond, Rosamond ran an impatient hand over her sleek fair hair and looked gloomily at the moorlands about her.

Presently Christine came to the surface again. "All right," she said, "I'll write him a note. I suppose I'll find him at the University. I might ask him to lunch some Sunday. If he doesn't come, he doesn't come. And that will be that."

"But at least we'll have done our duty," Harold said with mock earnestness.

In some minutes more the car, having turned in at a gatehouse and having followed a long avenue overshadowed by high trees, had come to a standstill in front of Priestlaw House, an early Victorian mansion standing up among plantations and pleasant fields at some distance from Loch Lomond's island-dotted southern end. It had been placed high enough to allow the view from its front windows to sweep the mile, or thereby, of green country which lay between itself and the loch shore.

The family descended, then stood on the gravel of the drive for a time, aimlessly watching the car being driven away and looking about them. Relaxed and pleased, maybe, to find themselves done with the difficult afternoon. Reluctant, at all events, to go inside just at once.

"Look here," Frederick said, "just while I have you all together, I had better tell you what your grandfather intends to do with his money. He told me I could tell you at once."

"Not cut off his dear grandchildren with a shilling?" Harold's remark was facetious, but there was, perhaps, some apprehension in his look. "Well, Skipper, we all know he's quite capable of doing it, don't we?"

Frederick was called "the Skipper" by his children. No one could remember why.

"No, quite the reverse. You know he put half of everything he had into my name five years ago. Now he's arranging to divide equally most of what's left and give it to you three."

"Good Lord!" was Harold's cheerful comment.

"But what's he going to live on?" Oliver asked.

"He can get annuities at very good rates at his age. I expect he's doing that." Frederick turned to his daughter. "Well, Rose! You're not saying anything. It will be quite a good sum, you know."

Rosamond smiled at her father mistily. "I don't quite know what to say, Skipper. Give me time to think about it."

"She's wondering if there are any dukes going cheap." For this Harold earned the expected look of contempt from his sister. "I'll bet the old boy's doing this to diddle the Exchequer and not for our three dear sakes. He'll be hoping to live for five more years."

"Harold! How can you say anything so ungenerour about your grandfather!" Christine felt it her duty to exclaim angrily: "Frederick, do you hear that?"

For reply, Harold gaily put an arm round his mother's unresponsive shoulders. He noted his father made no comment.

Oliver smiled to his sister. "Mother's got her lead-them-not-into-temptation look," he said.

"Indeed, I hope you *will* take this seriously. All three of you." Christine looked at each of them in turn. She freed herself from her elder son's unwanted embrace and laid her hand upon her husband's arm. "Come along, Fred. It's time we were going in."

2

Frederick Edzell sat by himself on the steps leading from the terrace in front of Priestlaw House. He was smoking his after-dinner cigar in the darkness. The autumn night was warm. Behind him, the terrace itself glowed with the light from the french windows that opened upon it. But there, where the steps went down to a formal shrubbery, he was pleased to feel that for the moment he could not be seen.

A large white moon had bled the scene of all colour, as it hung there, high in the sky. In places, strands of silver mist lay upon the dark fields. Here and there the moonlight caught the distant water, causing it to sparkle coldly. The far off hills stood cut out in black against the luminous, star-powdered night. Somewhere in the trees near the house an owl was complaining.

"Hello, Skipper."

"Hello, Nol."

Frederick had not wanted anyone to interrupt him. He had wanted to sit here and let reminiscence take hold of him. These people he had seen this afternoon. His father, the aunts, the Crabbe cousins, belonged to him and were seen by him in a way that they could not possibly be by his wife and children. They were part of his roots. Part of his looking back. He had long since grown away from them. But now, in an odd manner, he was feeling the pull of the blood. Allowing it to awaken memories of his boyhood; of times he would not, he supposed, call back, even if he could.

But if this pleasant mood of regret for times and people he did not really want any more was to be broken into by anyone, it was better it should be broken into by the boy who was now sitting down beside him on the step.

"How did you know I was here?" he asked.

"Smelt your cigar. Saw the ash glowing." Oliver sat silent for a time looking out over the silent world before him.

This mute companionship pleased Frederick. But presently he became aware that the young man had not given himself up to enjoying the mood of the evening. The shadow beside him had lit and discarded several cigarettes. He was not quite surprised, therefore, by the note of tension in his son's voice when at length he spoke.

"Skipper."

"Yes?"

"Do you think I'll ever do any good in Adam and John Edzell?"

"Do you want to do any good, Nol?"

Oliver did not at once answer this unexpected question. He sat considering.

"It rather depends on that, doesn't it?" His father was searching for what was in his mind.

"Yes." But presently Oliver qualified this. "Well —it's possible to want to, and still be no good."

"Have you anything else you do want to do? Is it that, perhaps?"

"I want to go to Paris and learn to paint. I suppose, with this money that's coming to me from grandfather—"

"Now I see where we are!"

"But Skipper, wouldn't it yield me enough of an income to live in Paris without my having to ask you for anything?"

"Yes. If it's the amount I think it must be, I should say certainly."

"I've thought about this for a long time. Now it has become a possibility. But I want you to think it's all right."

Frederick puffed his cigar for a time. Somewhere a farm dog was barking. The headlights of a far off car flashed in and out as it threaded its way along a distant country lane. Nol had always painted rather well, he supposed. He, his father, had thought his work extreme to the point of unintelligibility. But people who seemed to know something about that sort of thing said they thought it quite good. Had that merely been easy praise for a charming young dabbler? Frederick could not tell. "If you go to Paris we'll lose you. You'll turn into a different person." He said this to give himself time.

"I don't see why."

"Inevitably. To do any good, you'll have to belong to that world over there. It's not a world— being the kind of people we are—that I would much want you to belong to."

"But, Skipper, is our world so wonderful?"

"There could be worse."

"And better. What do any of us do here but conform?"

"What are any of us here fit for but to conform?" Oliver's father turned in the darkness to smile at him.

"There's not a real enthusiasm among us?"

Frederick laughed. "Perhaps, my dear boy, you haven't noticed that your father is the very busy and not quite unsuccessful chairman of a large and important company."

"But do you put any real enthusiasm into it?"

"Yes. I think I've learned to do that."

"Did you ever have anything of your own you wanted to do instead?"

"When I was seventeen I wanted to be an actor. I even got to the length of confiding in your grandmother about it."

Oliver turned to him with excitement. "Skipper! You didn't! You! And what happened?"

"Your grandfather caught me declaiming 'to be or not to be' in front of my bedroom looking glass. That put an end to that."

"What did he say?"

"Shouted at me not to make a fool of myself. Said that one member of the family—he meant William Edzell, the grandfather of that young man we saw today—had made a fool of himself by taking to the stage and that *his* son wasn't going to be the second. Your grandfather was quite right, of course."

"But didn't you resent it at the time?"

Oliver's father turned to him trying to see his face, then he turned back to look in front of him, taking several draws at his cigar.

"Yes, I resented it," he said at length. "Bitterly. I was very young and very silly, I suppose."

A french window had opened behind them. Its light shone past them into the darkness. Then Christine Edzell's voice could be heard asking: "Do I hear talking down there? Wherever are you? What are you doing?"

Oliver got up.

"We'll talk more about this, Nol," Frederick said. "It's a big step, you know."

"Oh, hello." Christine's voice was now above them. "I have just been discussing that new young man with Harold, Oliver. I want to ask him to come for lunch either next Sunday or the Sunday after. Will you be here? You're not catching cold, down there, are you, Fred?"

3

Left once more to smoke in peace, Frederick sat thinking of his younger son and what the boy had just proposed to him. He, his father, had just told him it would be taking a big step. Yet he felt impelled to let him take it. Now, looking restlessly about him into the black and silver of the night, Frederick asked himself why he should feel this impulsion. Had old memories been stirred today? Old regrets? Old rebellions? Would the letting of Nol go to Paris give him a vague sense of revenge? Revenge against what? Against his father? Against the discipline that had turned himself into a success in life? That had made it possible for him to support a fine family and live in this beautiful place? There in the darkness Frederick shook his head. No. That didn't make sense. And yet—

A breath of night air caught the smoke of his cigar, rustled the leaves in the shrubbery, then died again. The owl had stopped his complainings. For the moment everything was still.

Presently there was a louder rustling. Frederick stood up, trying to see what had caused it. But presently the outline of Rosamond's spaniel ran out into the moonlight. He sat down again and called to the dog.

"Hello, Skipper. What are you doing?"

"You, Rose? I thought Charlie was out on his own and up to no good."

"Can I sit down beside you, Skipper? Or are you deep in thought?"

"I'm deep in thought. But you can sit down beside me."

The girl's elegance was caught for an instant against the moon as she came towards him. "Charles and I have been thinking too," she said as she

5

settled down. "Haven't we, Charlie?" The dog's nose was in her lap. "Long, deep thoughts."

"Would it be too much for a parent to ask—?"

"Oh, I don't know . . . Enormous moon tonight, isn't it? Funny seeing all these people today. Funny to think they're relatives."

"Did you like them? You haven't seen much of them, have you?"

"They were quite sweet." Rosamond dismissed them with an indulgent chuckle.

"What did you think of the young man who appeared?"

"I don't know. He's one of the things Charles and I have been thinking about. I liked him. A bit pleased with himself, perhaps. Harold called me a snob because I said he was red brick. But I didn't mean that I *disliked* red brick. Red brick people. Red brick voices. Red brick behaviour. There's sometimes a vitality about people like that. A freshness. You feel they're serious. That they'll achieve something. All the young men one meets have been given such a spit and polish that there's not much left of them."

Her father laughed. "You mean the people *you* meet, Rose?" He was thinking now of all the cheques he had been required to sign for the spitting upon and polishing up of the girl beside him and of her brothers. "Anyway, you're going to have another look at your red brick cousin. Your mother is asking him here one Sunday soon."

Rosamond did not reply to this. She sat for a time playing with the ears of her spaniel. But presently she said: "It's the breath of mother's nostrils to be inviting and arranging, isn't it, Skipper?" This was said with no rancour.

But it left her father wondering what was coming. "She runs things very well," he said diplomatically.

"Skipper."

"Yes?"

"I'm thinking of going to London to take a really serious secretarial course."

"You've done one already."

"I mean a really professional one. And now that grandfather has decided to—"

"I knew it!"

"What do you mean, knew it, Skipper? No, really! I'm in earnest! Mother doesn't need me here in the least now that she's well again. And I'm restless. I want really to get my teeth into something."

"That sounds ferocious."

"You know perfectly well what I mean."

Frederick heaved a deep sigh. Was this what the prospect of a personal income was doing to his children? Would his highly matter of fact elder son, Harold, presently come down here too, sit beside him and tell him that all *his* young ambitions were being strangled?

"Whatever are you sighing about, Skipper?"

"My dear child, I don't know." Why couldn't Rosamond "get her teeth" into a husband? "There's no young man who happens to be of interest, I suppose. You're twenty-six, you know."

"I knew you would ask that." Her voice was displeased.

"I'm sorry. Don't bother to answer me then."

But she did. "No. Honestly, Skipper. There's
nobody at all."

Frederick considered this too. It was surprising.
He was not blind to his daughter's good looks. And
admirers had been plentiful. What was it? Rosamond was a good, warm-hearted little creature,
really. But perhaps with young men she had been
too quick in judgment, too mocking, too remote.
Or was it, quite simply, that her heart had not yet
been touched?

But now the thought of Harold, and his possible
descent upon him, once more occurred to Frederick.
He stood up. "Rosamond," he said, "it's getting
cold. We'll discuss your going to London very soon
again. I won't forget. But remember, my dear girl,
it's very natural for someone of your age to be
restless and unsettled. It's a phase that will pass."

For which evasive platitudes, Frederick presently
hated himself utterly.

4

Will accepted for two Sundays later. At first, on
receiving the invitation, he had wondered whether
he should bother to do so or not. By nature he was
genial. But he had little experience of the ways of
rich people, such as these Frederick Edzell cousins,
and stood, perhaps—though he would never have
admitted this—a little in awe of them. Thus he
tended to find his compensation in judging such
people with a certain measure of disdain, setting his
own very real, if somewhat narrow culture, against

their prosperity, taking refuge in his scholarship.

In the rooms he had found for himself in Hillhead near the University, Will had sat, biting the end of his pen, looking at the masculine litter of books, of clothing, of team photographs, of photographs of his parents, and such other things as a willing and kindly landlady was wondering if she might dare arrange for him, and considering what he should reply to Mrs Edzell. Finally he had argued himself into going. The two young men had not been uncivil. The girl was certainly worth looking at again. And it might for once be amusing enough to play at ladies and gentlemen with Frederick and Christine Edzell.

It was a clear autumn Sunday. In nearby plantations and on the distant islands of Loch Lomond October nights of frost had changed the woods to flame and gold. The Loch itself lay blue, mirroring mountains that had already received their first sprinkling of snow.

Will arrived early, having given himself more time than he needed in order to find Priestlaw House. As he brought his motor bicycle to a standstill his hostess came out of the trees bordering the drive to welcome him.

"Oh, there you are, Mr Edzell!" she called as he dismounted.

"My name is Will, Mrs Edzell."

"Then mine had better be Cousin Christine, hadn't it? How are you?"

With a smile that more than matched her own very bright one, Will took her hand. "All right, thanks, Cousin Christine. Where shall I put this?"

He felt himself looking at his old bicycle with a smile of apology, made self conscious, perhaps, by the sight of a sleek sports car that was standing in the drive near the front entrance. For which emotion he at once despised himself.

"Oh, stand it anywhere. Yes. There. Behind Harold's car, if you like."

She waited until he had done this and come back to her, striking dust from his clothes.

"Now," she went on, "do come inside and have a wash, then we'll have some sherry. The boys should be about somewhere. Frederick wanted to go to church, so Rosamond nobly said she would go with him. I'm so glad you got down early."

As he washed his hands, combed his hair and hoped that Mrs Edzell would not notice an oil stain on the trousers of his best suit, Will found himself wondering for a moment why she had said she was glad he had arrived early.

"I ought to go more to church in Scotland," she was saying now as she took up the sherry decanter. "But then I was brought up in the Church of England. I can never get used to church up here. You must belong to the Church of England, too, I expect."

"My mother used to take me there when I was a small boy. I'm not Church of anything now, Cousin Christine."

"Oh, aren't you? I'm afraid I've made that glass very full." Her tone was impersonal as she gave it to him.

The topics of religion and mothers, he saw, were dismissed. Mrs Edzell had been making conversation.

5

Presently the others joined them. Frederick and Rosamond came back from church. Then Harold and Oliver appeared with two young men whom Christine had not expected and did not want. As a hostess, she was afraid Will might feel odd man out among these noisy, intimate friends of her sons.

"I brought these men here," Harold explained to the room in general when the new arrivals had been provided with sherry, "to get an afternoon's tennis. It may be the last one this autumn. So they had better not be filled up with too much lunch."

"I hope you will be able to lend Will what he needs." Christine said this as much to bring Harold back to good manners as to make sure that Will would not feel excluded; adding: "You play tennis, of course?"

"Yes. I play a great deal. Only . . ." Will's smile was rueful.

"Only what?" Harold was all polite concern now.

"Well, I think I told you the other day, I damaged a leg on the Hog's Snout on Stronn Island. It won't be ready for tennis again until next year. I'll score if you like."

"No. That's boring. My sister Rosamond can look after you. They say she's quite a nice girl."

Will obliged Harold by laughing a little. Rosamond raised her eyebrows as though to say: "My brother is a clown," but she did not speak.

Yet after a noisy, high spirited lunch in which most of the talk was about events and people about whom Will knew nothing, it was Rosamond who took Will in hand. She found him on the terrace sitting with her parents, the others having already gone to change.

"Would you like to walk about and look at things? Or won't your leg allow that?"

As he stood up to accept her invitation, will felt vividly aware of Rosamond's beauty. Her fine features, her expensive simplicity of dress, her elegance. She was the kind of young woman a man must try to keep himself from gaping at. There had been few of her sort in the world he came from.

She was puzzled by the withdrawn half smile that masked these thoughts as he stood, seemingly hesitating.

"Are you sure you want to come? You needn't if you don't want to. What about a stick?"

"Of course I want to come." His face was alive again. "Stick? Can I find a stick somewhere?"

But she had gone in to fetch one and was back at once.

Will found himself descending the steps from the terrace possessed by a sense of unreality. An unreality tinged with an irritation for which he could not quite account. The fine old house behind him with its lavish good taste. A way of life that was miles away from his own intellectual, inkstained, youth hostel existence. The flaming glory of the Scottish autumn spread out here in front of him; served up with the coffee they had just drunk on the terrace. Money could buy too much, it seemed; make the rough places altogether too plain. He wanted to stick pins into himself to make sure he was alive this afternoon. To stick pins too, into this blonde piece of perfection here on the steps beside him, to draw from her just one drop of real, red blood.

"Hello! Rosamond taking you for a walk?"

Four white clad figures had burst from the house, had hurried down past himself and his companion and now, carrying their equipment, were striding towards an unseen tennis court.

From the background of his own striving days, Will looked after them with something very near to resentment.

6

On her side, Rosamond felt at a loss. More, indeed, than she was aware of had Will been in her thoughts since that first meeting the other day in her grandfather's garden. Much of him had remained with her. His open, quick response. His lean handsomeness. His odd, bass voice with overtones of the English North Country in it. There was a hardwearing quality about him to which she could not feel indifferent, a quality, as she had told her father, not possessed by the young men to whom she was accustomed.

But there was another side to him, it seemed. All through lunch he had appeared at ease. The somewhat boisterous talk of her brothers and their friends, often to the exclusion of himself, had left him smiling and apparently unembarrassed. Yet now that she had him to herself, she sensed an odd— was it defensiveness?

No. Not altogether an easy young man. But since she liked him and wanted to know more about him, Rosamond decided to go on being straightforwardly friendly.

"Don't let me take you any further than you feel like walking," she hazarded as they halted at the foot of the steps.

"I may have hurt my leg. But even now I daresay I could still walk you off your feet."

She looked at him quickly. What an oddly boastful thing for him to say! But as his expression was entirely good humoured, she laughed. "Be careful!" she said. "In case you don't happen to recognise it yet, that's Ben Lomond over there."

He nodded.

"Well. This summer I walked from Inversnaid to Aberfoyle—if you have any idea of where these places are—taking in the top of Ben Lomond on the way."

He looked amused and apologetic. "No. I couldn't walk as far as that this afternoon."

"We had better go and see if there is anything left in the garden." She led him through a little pinewood which had been planted as a north-east protection to the old walled garden, a door to which they presently came upon at a sudden twist of the path. It was like most gardens of its kind, extensive and gracious, with high-growing herbaceous beds bordering paths that cut it into squares. The middle of each square contained vegetables and fruit trees. Against one wall there were glass houses.

"All this is as old as the house, I suppose?" Will asked.

"Yes. It was made when the house was built. There are old flues in the walls to keep the fruit trees that were trained against them from the frost. You can still see where they lit the fires. Coal must have been cheap in those days."

"It was. Women and young children helped to bring it up. To heat walls for fruit trees."

She turned to him uncertainly.

"It's perfectly true, what I'm telling you."

She was at a loss how to take this, wondering at the force of his words. "Yes. I've read about it. Poor things! But that's all past now, isn't it?"

"Yes, it's all past," he said. "It had to pass."

"It doesn't bear thinking about does it?" She was trying to interpret the earnestness of his expression.

"No."

They walked towards the glass houses looking at this and that; saying little more.

The vinery felt humid and warm. They stood in the green shade of the vines looking at the tumbling bunches of purple and yellow grapes with their delicate bloom upon them, as they hung ripe or ripening overhead. The air was redolent of hot-house earth and the aroma of the fruit.

"I'm not allowed to touch these," she said, "or I would cut a bunch for you. But Maclean would probably leave if I did."

"Who's Maclean?"

"Our head gardener. This place is really more his than ours."

"But surely he allows you to eat them?"

"Of course. But we have to take what Maclean brings to the house."

"That seems to me ridiculous. You pay him, don't you?"

She laughed. "I see you don't know Scotch gardeners!"

As he did not reply to this she opened another door saying: "These are Maclean's chrysanthemums. Absurd, aren't they?"

The single, artificial blooms stood in rows. Some of their petals so compact that they formed great balls of white or copper, some fell loose to give the appearance of beautiful, upturned mops.

For a time he hung about looking at them in an odd, dazed way until, indeed, she began to wonder what was wrong. But at length he answered: "Yes. Quite absurd."

She chanced to be standing near him. But at once she moved away quickly, alarmed, a little, by the sudden change of his tone. Was he angry? Was he going to try to make love to her? She had met with other young men whose throats had suddenly gone dry. From a safer distance her eyes sought his face. His tense expression told her nothing. But now he seemed to be trying to take hold of himself as he asked her: "Do you like living in this place?"

She was surprised at this. "Where? Here? Priest-law?"

"Yes."

"Why ever do you ask me that?"

"Interest."

"That's very kind of you." Her own voice was cold now.

"I'm sorry. I apologise for being interested."

At this she laughed. "Yes. I suppose I like living here. I've never known any other home. I'm part of the furniture."

"And that pleases you?"

She did not answer this, but he was determined now—he did not know why—to insert the pin to see if the red blood would come.

"Wouldn't you like to be doing something useful with yourself?"

Her colour rose. "What right have you to think I'm not being useful?"

"Then you are?"

"I'm leading the life my parents want me to lead. For the moment at least."

"And what is that? Meeting people? Visiting round the houses of people like yourself? London? Large hotels abroad?"

"You forgot to say hunting. I hunt in Ayrshire."

"I wondered about hunting."

"Well? And what's wrong with all that?"

"Didn't you ever think of having a profession? Or were you too bad at school?"

"I was quite good at school. And I happen to be a trained secretary, if that's of any interest to you. And I studied languages in Switzerland after I left school."

For a moment he stood, a smile masking what he thought. The question "So you were sent to a fashionable finishing school in Switzerland, were you?" reached the tip of his tongue. But instead he asked: "Then why don't you use your training?"

"I *have* used it. I got a quite entertaining secretarial job in Edinburgh. I came home last spring because mother happened to be ill. I daresay I could get another job tomorrow if I wanted it."

"And you don't want it?"

"Not for the moment." What she meant to do was no business of his. Then, while she opened another door which took them outside once more she added: "But that's quite enough about me. We'll go and see how they're getting on at tennis."

The four young men, used to each other's play, were engaged in a hard fought set. For a time Will stood envying them and regretting his own disability. Rosamond's brothers were playing against the other two. Presently, as they changed sides, the guests came over to exchange a greeting before they took up their new places.

"And which of these young men are you going to marry?" Will asked as they turned to go back to the house.

She stopped, looked up at him and said: "I would call that question vulgar."

"But then I am vulgar."

She stood still for a moment considering him, not displeased to find that she in her turn had made him angry.

"No," she said at length, "you're sensitive about something. That's all. I don't think you're as vulgar as you want yourself to be thought. No. I should call you arrogant." She turned away from him. "There should be some tea before long," she said, again walking ahead.

The terrace in front of the house was empty. As they halted at the bottom of the steps leading up to it they came level with each other. Their eyes met angrily. Then, suddenly each of them, feeling foolish, broke into a laugh that was embarrassed but friendly enough.

"Look here," he spoke low, conscious now of playing on the bass notes of his voice. "I'm afraid I'm very bad at making the right sort of conversation when kind young women show me round gardens. Will you forgive me?"

"Forgive you for what?"

"Well, anyway, thanks. I've enjoyed it."

"Oh, have you?"

"Yes." And then, rather surprisingly to himself Will found himself saying: "I'll try to behave better next time. Do you think there will ever be a next time?"

"My mother likes inviting people," she said. "Shall we go up?"

CHAPTER 6

1

Mrs Adam Edzell rose to her feet to show that she had finished. "Katie is a very stupid girl, Sandy. And you can go straight home and tell her that the doctor and I both say so. Do you want to be a widower before you've been married a year? A child coming and an almost certain appendix is not very nice is it?" She looked severely at the young fisherman standing there before her twisting his cap in his thick fingers; his dark eyes shifting anxiously back and forth between her face and the fire in the Stronn Lodge sitting room as its light caught and threw into relief the ribbing of his jersey, the boyish, swarthy face and the mop of black hair. "It's a hospital in Glasgow Katie should be in."

"Katie has just always been at Stronn, Mrs. Edzell. She never was going to Glasgow. But her Auntie Morag once took her for a sail to Oban."

These last irrelevant words, softly spoken in a language that was not his mother tongue, touched Mary strangely. She had to wait for a moment before she spoke again, and when she did so, she was using his own Gaelic speech, the speech of her own childhood. "Katie must go where she can be properly looked after, Sandy. Whether she wants to or not."

"She's frightened at the hospital, Mrs Edzell."

"Sandy, I was a nurse in hospitals before I came here. I had twenty years of it. Surely she can believe me when I say she will be all right."

He merely stood miserably continuing to twist his cap.

"Well? I've told you what the doctor said after he examined her this afternoon. He was very anxious when I saw him off at the jetty. Is there nothing to be done with Katie, Sandy?"

The young man looked bashfully down at the toes of his heavy rubber boots. "You wouldn't be going to Glasgow yourself, would you, Mrs Edzell? I don't think she would be saying no if you were going."

Mary's eyes filled. There was no presumption here. These words had been wrung from Sandy's simple desperation. This was her Island calling to her, herself a woman of the Islands, in a moment of trouble. She felt warmed and flattered as she turned away from him saying: "Sit down again Sandy and we'll see what we can do." She went to her desk and picked up the telephone. "The weather seems settled. Katie and I could catch the aeroplane tomorrow. I'll just make sure there are places for us."

2

Mary Edzell waved a brisk goodbye to Katie's mother and sisters, and, indeed, to most of the other women of Stronn Island who had come down to the jetty to see Katie Macdonald going off in the white motor launch belonging to the lodge.

"Go inside and keep warm, Katie," she said to the tearful girl as the launch backed out slowly into its own churning foam. "I've got brandy. I'll give you some in a minute."

"I'll not be wanting brandy, Mrs Edzell."

"You're doing what you're told today, Katie." She took a flask from her bag and turned to Katie's husband who was coming with them to the island airfield, the first stage of their journey, and who had just sprung on board at the last moment after helping to push off. "Here, Sandy, take this in to her. And don't drink any yourself. Katie may need it all before I get her to Glasgow."

Murdo, Mary's factotum, had backed in a wide circle of milky green until the bow was pointing seaward. Now he had come out of reverse, and the boat hung for a moment, swaying back and forth on the sparkling water. Then, as he put the motors once again into action the white launch sprang forward, building up wings of spray on either side of her as she gained speed; skimming the morning sea like a great white bird.

This launch was Mary Edzell's toy; her greatest self-indulgence. It was seaworthy and powerful. In reasonable weather it made her independent of the weekly steamer. She could go to the mainland or to another island whenever the fancy took her. "I can't use a motor car, so why shouldn't I have a motor boat?" she said to her friend the doctor when she showed it to him for the first time. "Now we can send for you whenever we need you." The doctor merely smiled. It was not for him to say that the islanders were few indeed who could buy for themselves such an absurdly expensive plaything.

Mary stood looking back at Stronn. The line of yellow sand. The white lodge with the smoke blowing from a chimney. The Hog's Snout with its sharp drop of precipice to one side. Could she, she wondered, detect at this distance where the piece of rock had broken away this autumn and all but carried young Will Edzell with it. She raised a hand to shade her eyes from the light, seeking to make it out. But presently she gave up trying and merely stood, watching the island withdraw by degrees; watching it become a luminous misty outline.

Her mind was still busy with the rescue. The getting of Will downhill. The nursing of him. The visits of the doctor. Later, the arrival of old Jessie for her autumn visit, all amiability and flutter. Stronn Lodge had been busy and cheerful, especially when Will was able to be up again and hobbling around.

Now the launch, coming out from the lee of the island began to pitch and fling back spray as her speed met the swell of a more open sea. Mary looked back into the cabin to see that Katie was all right. Sandy was sitting with his arms close about his wife. Mary smiled to herself and turned, reassured, to watch a flight of solan geese cross the blue above her. She stood up now exposing herself to the wind and the spray, exhilarated by the morning, by the tensions of this journey, and too, by the thought that in Glasgow she would be able to see Will Edzell again and, since she had grown attached to her patient, make sure that he was well.

Now, indeed, it occurred to her to wonder if, last night, she had been quite honest with herself. Had it been the thought of seeing this young man again that had caused her to jump at the chance of taking Katie to Glasgow? She looked back at the couple in the cabin. No. Not that. Another young fisherman on another island further north had once, long ago, held another young woman in his arms. But the winter seas had taken him and the girl had gone to learn to be a nurse in London. Still, that was a memory so distant now that Mary might have read it in a book.

Her thoughts turned again to the young man who was her guest this autumn. His looks had, of course, engaged her interest at once. Having no children of her own, it had, perhaps, been natural for her to wonder often about the son Adam Edzell lost so many years before, about the young soldier in the photograph. Then, early last month, it was as though she had found this son of Adam's lying wounded on the top of the Hog's Snout. A moment of sharp excitement. But one, of course, occasioned by a mere family likeness; by a very explicable chance, since her husband and Will's grandfather were twins.

But if Adam's boy was in temperament at all like Adam, he must have been, in every way but looks, different from Will. Her husband, when she came to know him at sixty, was a placid, openly generous, dogmatic sort of man. Will, on the other hand, was quick, endearingly ready to thank her for what she was doing for him and ready too, to give her the warm affection of a relative. And yet, as she got to know him, she guessed that there might be a brittle side to him; a side that could be tactless and defensive.

Meeting a wave that was larger than the others, the launch threw back a burst of spray that struck Mary's face and ran down her fisherman's oilskins. She took off her sou'wester and shook it, pushed back her wet grey hair, then pulled a man's red handkerchief from her pocket and began drying herself.

"Go back into the cabin, Mrs Edzell. We'll be getting some more of these," Murdo shouted from the wheel.

As she turned to look at the viking who was her servant, she saw, with no great pleasure, that he was laughing at her. "I'll do nothing of the kind, Murdo Macdonald! I like being out here. Sandy and Katie are better left to themselves."

Murdo turned to look at the inmates of the cabin, then turned back smiling indulgently to his mistress, saying no more.

Mary retied her sou'wester, steadied herself and looked round at the horizon as it rose and fell about her, at the blue, familiar shapes of far off islands, at the sparkling track of sunlight on the waves.

Will, she knew, had met her husband's family by this time. All of them, rather surprisingly, as he had told her in a letter. Now she thought of her own very brief attempt to make friends. She had met with little success. They saw her, it seemed, as a woman who had trapped their brother into marriage when he was recovering from illness and was sentimentally weak. Her Highland pride forbade her to justify herself, to try to convince them that a woman of forty-two might love a man of sixty well enough to want to care for him and seek to prolong his uncertain days. Adam's money had nothing to do with it, except in so far as it gave them power to retreat to the quietness and peace he needed.

Now, looking out across the sea, Mary asked herself why she had not been more bitter. Because, she supposed, she was determined, for his sake, not to be. After all, she never really knew the Glasgow Edzells. They meant nothing to her. And, while he was alive, she saw it as a duty not to bring useless resentments into the life of her invalid husband. She kept telling herself that Adam's last years must be his best.

And they had been. Or so at least he told her. At all events, the twelve years they spent together were the best of her own life, leaving an aftermath of loneliness which she sought to fill as best she could by helping and caring for the people of Stronn. So little was her interest in the Glasgow Edzells, that she would scarcely have known the make up of their families were it not for her continuing to support and befriend Adam's sister Jessie, as a special charge he had laid upon herself.

But now, since she saw that not even Sandy's reassuring embraces could prevent Katie from a serious threat of seasickness, and since his eyes were imploring her to come, Mary turned, put on the look of cheerfulness which was automatic to her former profession and went in to deal with her charge in the cabin.

3

"I shouldn't speak to grandfather about Nol this morning, Skipper. He's in a bad mood."

"He's got to be told, Harold." Frederick was assembling papers and putting them into his dispatch case.

"Rosamond and I will get the brunt of his annoyance. You'll be safely in the train."

"You both can take it." Frederick raised his eyes and looked at his elder son's smiling, a little apologetic perhaps, yet ruefully determined. "I promised Oliver I would tell your grandfather at once."

"That's all very well. I don't see any reason to be so conscientious. Besides it's none of grandfather's business."

"That's as may be, Harold. Nol will go on his own money, remember."

"Why did the old boy need to come into the office today? We *are* going to have a pleasant lunch party!"

This conversation was taking place in Frederick's room in the office of Adam and John Edzell Limited while father and son waited for old John Edzell to make himself ready to go out with them. Normally they would all have gone to their club. But since Frederick was leaving on an early afternoon train for London, and since, moreover, Rosamond had telephoned to say she happened to be in town and had better meet them, have lunch with her grandfather and thank him for what he was doing, it had been decided that all four should lunch in the restaurant of the station hotel.

Harold stood watching his father as he continued to select the papers he needed, wondering what was in his mind. "Anyway, do you think it's a good thing to let Nol go to Paris and turn himself into one of these painter fellows?"

"He wants to go, Harold. He would hold it against me if I tried to stop him. And I don't want Nol, nor any of you, to hold things against me."

The young man wondered why the Skipper was taking all this so heavily. This urge that troubled his brother was quite beyond himself. "And what will you do if he doesn't make a go of it?"

Frederick shrugged. "Let him come back, I suppose."

Which left his son still further puzzled. It surprised Harold that his father, so orthodox in most things, should suddenly turn round like this to support Oliver's passion for art. There must be more sides—or something—to the Skipper's character than he had suspected. Still, Nol's leaving the firm might be no bad thing for himself. It would leave the coast clear for his own importance. But it would be a miracle if his grandfather—

"Well, I'm ready." Old John Edzell stood looming large in the doorway.

And, of course, the miracle did not happen. It was, indeed, as Harold had foreseen a memorable lunch party. Although, certainly, his grandfather did not get round to threatening to cut Oliver off, yet he did not take the matter lightly. Indeed, he went so far as to shout at them in a way that was acutely embarrassing, especially with Rosamond there too.

And yet, Harold was, in many respects on his grand-father's side. But when the old boy thumped the table and protested how Priestlaw, their position, their background, were all of his making; that the Skipper, Rosamond, himself, all of them, would not have been anywhere at all if he, John Edzell, had not put them there. Well, surely that was just plain rubbish. There had been old Adam Edzell, too, who was no fool. And the Skipper had worked damn hard all his life, and wasn't quite mentally deficient either.

And now, his grandfather went on, Nol was being allowed to turn himself into a dabbler, a nobody. Where would Harold's father have been if he hadn't been disciplined and held firm at Oliver's age? And so on and forth.

And to add good measure and, Harold supposed, to give his grandfather opportunity to tune his anger to a still higher pitch, there had been a sudden, irrelevant outburst about inviting that young man Will Edzell out to Priestlaw. Another nobody! The son of a bastard! A young man who had no right to use the Edzell name. A stranger who pushed himself inpertinently among them the other afternoon. Un-reasonable hysterics, of course. The old man didn't mean half of it. But very uncomfortable in a public place.

But the astonishing thing was how stubbornly his father had stood up to these explosions. He had never seen him make such a firm stand before. Usually he was all submissiveness and pliability when the old boy took to lecturing him. Yet it had come to train time and the Skipper was gone without conceding anything. Indeed, he had actually got up and left them saying: "I am sorry I have excited you like this, father. Harold, you had better get him into a taxi and send him home," leaving himself and Rosamond with a quite impossible, raging old man on their hands.

And then, just as a taxi was being whistled up, here they were, face to face with Will Edzell and a weatherbeaten, elderly woman.

4

The sombre Glasgow morning had, so far, been a cheerful one for Mary. Rain and a threat of fog did nothing to mar her pleasure in again finding herself out and about in a world of bright, handsome shops and streaming, noisy traffic. It was everything that Stronn Island was not. But though she would not now have changed the one world for the other, it did, in its way, bring back her working days in London; in the same way, indeed, as had the hospital in which she had some days ago succeeded in placing Katie Macdonald.

And for Mary, there were still better reasons for cheerfulness. Now Katie could be said to be through the worst; and, speaking back to Sandy in the Stronn Lodge sitting-room where, by her instruction, he was told to expect a call each evening, she was able to tell him that his wife was out of danger. Following upon this she had telephoned to Will to announce her presence and to ask if he were free to lunch with her today. He replied with a joy that was flattering that in fact he was not free, but that he would cut everything and come.

They had met in the street just outside the restaurant, had exchanged greeting and had turned to go through the glass door that was being held open for them, when they came face to face with a large old man accompanied by a young man and woman, both of whom seemed to be doing their best to shepherd him towards a taxi waiting at the kerb.

"Hello! Good morning!" To Mary's surprise Will had caught the young man's arm.

"Hello? Oh, Will Edzell? How are you? Look, I'm just getting grandfather into a taxi. There it is waiting for us." Unceremonious and bothered, the young man darted across the pavement to open the door.

But Will was going on: "Aunt Mary, this is Rosamond Edzell of Priestlaw House. You haven't seen her before, have you? And her grandfather, you must know him."

The bloodshot old eyes now turned on Will, allowing themselves no glint of friendliness. Mary, now realising they were the eyes of her husband's brother, would had she been able, have left it at that, and continued into the restaurant, smiling vaguely perhaps, but saying nothing more. But the size of the large old man was making it awkward to pass. "And why should she know me?" he was asking.

The pitch of Will's voice became sharp with anger as he answered: "Because she's your brother's wife, Mrs Adam Edzell of Stronn Island."

Still blocking her way, John Edzell stood for a time looking down at Mary. At length he spoke. "So you're the woman that managed to get hold of my brother Adam's money, are you?" He turned and shuffled towards the taxi.

Mary did not answer him. Now, as he had moved, she was able to pass inside, followed by Will. "You shouldn't have stopped these people," she said.

"Aunt Mary, I'm sorry. I was determined to make that old beast recognise you."

Mary took some kind of control of herself and forced a smile. "You're just a great big bairn, Will!" She gave herself a moment, then went on: "I've been about in the town all morning. We will get our hands washed and have a drink and forget all about this."

But now as she stood with a glass of sherry in her hand, forcing herself into small talk, telling of Katie, of how she herself was staying with Jessie Edzell in the private hotel that was Jessie's home, Mary felt herself still quivering from the impact of John Edzell's words! Felt the sting more than she could have thought possible. She had long since known how Adam's family regarded her. But public rudeness like this was something—

"Oh, I'm so glad I've found you! They said they thought you would be in the cocktail bar. I told Harold I must come back and apologise!"

Mary turned. It was the girl who had been with John Edzell, his granddaughter.

"Mrs Edzell, I'm so sorry about grandfather just now. He was very angry about something quite different. So angry that he was almost hysterical.

Please! I'm sure he didn't know what he said to you. Anyway, do believe me, Harold and I have nothing to do with it. You *will* forgive this, won't you? Whatever he said was just an outburst. Something that had nothing to do with you whatever. But you won't—"

"I won't what, Miss Edzell?" Mary stood smiling, with every appearance of amused dignity, as Rosamond went on apologising a little wildly.

"Well, grandfather is an old man. And perhaps you can understand how old people behave sometimes."

"Yes, Miss Edzell, I understand old people very well. It was kind of you to think I might be hurt. But, you see, I didn't really hear what your grandfather said, so it doesn't matter, does it? Now run away and don't worry any more!" Mary held out her hand.

Rosamond took it, bestowed a troubled smile on Will and hurried off.

Having watched her out of sight, Mary turned back to Will. "Better go into lunch," she said.

"That was friendly of her." Mary now looked about her at the expensive traffic of the restaurant.

"I suppose so."

"Do you like her? What kind of young woman is she?"

But before he could answer, they were being required to choose what they should eat. Will, who was still almost dumb with anger, accepted with indifference what she proposed for him. He was not, it seemed, able to take control of his feelings as she had long since learned to do. And now that the waiters had left them, he sat morosely crumbling bread and saying nothing. She turned to smile encouragingly. "Well?"

"If that old man had been a young man, I would have knocked him down," he said glumly.

Mary laughed a little and laid a hand upon the hand that continued to crumble bread. "Then I'm glad he wasn't a young man. Don't worry about me, Will. So far as these people are concerned, I happen to be in a very strong position, you know. That old man can't hurt me."

But John Edzell *had* hurt her. Mary could not help reflecting over what had happened. She was, indeed, still very angry. Old injustices had been re-awakened within her, old insults to herself and to the memory of her husband. She had sought to go her own way, ignoring these, but now, at this moment, she was not sure that she wanted to continue doing so.

It was nice of this young man to be so angry on her account. To resent so hotly that she should be hurt. She was already aware of being very fond of Will, and this very gloom in which he had enwrapped himself was doing nothing to decrease her fondness. Now it crossed her mind that she might, in some way, use him as an instrument against these others. She was not a woman of affairs, but her advisers had once given her to understand that having Adam's major holding of shares in the family firm, she could take control of it if she cared to do so. She had merely laughed at the idea. What business knowledge had she? No. A mere, nebulous idea born of this moment's stinging resentment. Still——. Suppose she adopted Will as her son and began making her holding in Adam and John Edzell over to him? Suppose she demanded a seat on the board for him, increasing his financial influence over the others by degrees like the menace of an incoming tide?

And yet—and here Mary's commonsense, her sense of reality began to intervene—could it possibly be conferring a good upon Will to use him as the instrument of her resentment, even though she were giving him a fortune? She could not think so. And, indeed, it was quite probable that Will, with his equalitarian ideas and his quick independence, would not accept what she might propose.

If she decided to help him, to turn him into a rich man, to change entirely the texture of his life, she must do so out of her affection and respect for him. Not out of her dislike for others.

But hadn't she better wait a while? What, after all, did she know about him? Something. A month of nursing him had told her that he had pluck and independence. That he had been raised in a hard, somewhat narrow school, where nothing but scholastic knowledge counted. Of his sense of affairs, of his wisdom or the lack of it, of his emotional stability, she knew little.

It was this last thought, perhaps, that prompted her to say: "You haven't told me anything about that girl who came back to speak to us, Will? You didn't say if you liked her?"

"Why should I like any of these people?"

"Why shouldn't you? They've been nice to you, haven't they? You've been to Priestlaw. She came back just now because she was ashamed and upset."

"Politeness. Expensive, finishing school manners."

"Don't talk rubbish! Good manners don't mean bad feelings! Quite the opposite!"

He did not reply to this.

His companion determined to probe further: "A handsome girl. Beautiful, really."

"I suppose she's all right."

Mary burst out laughing. "Tell me about Priest-law," she said. "What are the rest of the family like?"

He wondered why she had laughed just then, and he continued to wonder, even when, an hour later, he had thanked her for his lunch and left her.

CHAPTER 7

1

IT was early evening next day. A dank and dark November evening with a rain so fine that it was almost a fog. An evening to send the heart of an exile from any sunny land, who chanced to find himself in Glasgow, straight down into his boots. But little Minnie Crabbe was no exile. She was born to the Glasgow weather. It was, indeed, second nature for her to draw cheerfulness about her like a cloak.

She descended from the bus which had brought her out from town to the western part of the city and stood now, buttoning her waterproof and putting up her umbrella. The high mist-haloed street lamps of Great Western Road. The streaming lights of motor cars and buses. The bright windows of the shops. As the traffic ran continuously and fast, she moved to join a group of people who stood with their eyes upon a policeman, waiting for the wave of his hand. As presently she crossed with the others, Minnie was actually humming to herself.

Now she remembered a dress that had been on display in the window of a shop near the end of Belmont Street. She had spied it this morning, but the arrival of the bus going into town had allowed her only a glimpse. Still humming, she crossed Belmont Street, a street running north from Great Western Road, to see if the dress was still there. It was. And she liked it, though she doubted if it would fit her plumpness. But one could always ask.

"No, Miss Crabbe. It's a very small fitting. For a teenager, dear, really. It's nice, though, isn't it? If we get in other sizes of it we'll let you know. Is there nothing else I can show you? No? Well, come back soon, anyway. We've some nice things coming in. Awful night, isn't it? You'll be wearying to get home for your tea. Well, bye-bye, dear."

Minnie continued up Belmont Street. She hadn't really wanted the dress. Her asking had been mere self-entertainment. But contact with the shop-woman's warm good nature had raised her cheerfulness by a degree or two. She was singing under her breath as she reached the end of this long grey street of respectable terraces, crossed the high stone bridge that spans the deep gulf of the Kelvin River, an abyss of blackness on a night like this, and turned into Doune Terrace, where her parents had their house.

But it was not all self-generated cheerfulness that caused Minnie's mood tonight. She had some family gossip that would interest those at home.

2

Doune Terrace is a pleasant row of late Victorian houses; its one disadvantage being that, built as it is on the wrong side of Belmont Bridge, it cannot claim to be in Glasgow's West End. If a letter be addressed to Doune Terrace, authority pitilessly demands Glasgow, North West, on the envelope.

This stigma apart, it faces south, looks into the trees and bushes which clothe the banks sharply descending to the river far below, and commands, across the chasm, a reassuring view of the University spire in the not too great distance, a reminder that the terrace, if not actually in the best part of the city, is almost within a stone's throw of it.

The house belonged to Minnie's mother who had, six months before her marriage, a bachelor uncle obliging enough to die and leave her a legacy of some few hundred pounds.

"We may as well have a nice house with it," Babs had said to the gay young man upon whom she proposed to bestow her hand. "We can furnish it as we go along." And as the price of houses in the slump years of the late 'twenties stood low, a house in Doune Terrace had been within their reach.

Thus the young couple had settled in and furnished "as they went along" with machine-made furniture, which was claimed to be the very latest on the day they bought it, but which somehow acquired a look of outmoded vulgarity on the day after. But, like clothes, chairs and tables express their users, and so this house, into the front door of which their daughter was even now inserting her latchkey, had about it an air of careless hospitality that was tasteless but warm; a hospitality that did not insist upon P's and Q's.

Some thirty years back, Mr and Mrs Samuel Crabbe had met each other at the rehearsals of an amateur performance of *The Merry Widow*. Having, both of them, but lately joined a club for the performance of light opera, they had been relegated to the chorus. But as Sam possessed, in these days, something of a voice, high spirits and good looks, he had almost at once received an offer to understudy Prince Danilo.

"Do you think I could ever manage it?" he had asked the pretty blonde chorister to whom he happened to have proposed marriage and who was still in two minds whether to accept him or not.

"Don't tell me you don't want a chance like that, Sam Crabbe!" she had answered, blushing archly.

And actually it had fallen out that in the middle of the Club's yearly run of a week at the Theatre Royal, the leading man having sprained an ankle in his exuberance, Sam had been called upon to take over his part; a part which he had filled, in the eyes of one young woman in the chorus at all events, quite magnificently. And if his splendid dash and swagger had been redolent more, perhaps, of the Plaza Dance Hall at Eglinton Toll than Maxim's in Paris; if his broken English had, perhaps, carried with it overtones of Sauchiehall Street rather than Middle Europe, yet they had sufficed to sweep up Babs on a wave of admiration that had finally decided her to direct the bowings, scrapings and elegant embraces, temporarily bestowed upon the Widow, towards her own enraptured self; and upon, she hoped, a more permanent basis.

3

Minnie was not altogether pleased to find her grandmother in the drawing-room of Doune Terrace. Mainly because—since it was already nearing six o'clock—she had expected to find the cocktail tray there. And surely, if ever there was an evening when a good fire and a cocktail were called for, this dank evening was it.

But her grandmother's visit meant, as Minnie well knew, a tiresome bringing out of little used silver tea things which her mother could never remember to ask the daily woman to polish, a long drawing out of the rite of tea drinking and bread-and-butter eating; and, above all, the moral pressure of the old lady's presence—a moral pressure of which only those born in the reign of Queen Victoria know the secret—which forbade the bringing out of bottles in her presence.

Things were at a low ebb as Minnie came in. Her grandmother was being tiresomely gentle and charming. Her mother was seeking a bleak solace in picking at the marzipan icing on a cake which had not been cut, while her father had abandoned himself to an open show of low spirits. He would have to kiss his mother, he knew, when she went, which made it quite impossible for him to slip downstairs to the dining-room cupboard and have a consoling swig before he had got rid of her.

Minnie felt she must do her best. "Hello, granny!" she bent to kiss the old woman, smiling encouragement meanwhile to her parents.

"Hello, darling. How cold your cheek is. Is it raining outside?"

"Yes, it's filthy. Father must call a taxi for you when you go." Minnie took a comb from her bag and, going to the looking glass over the mantelpiece, began to tidy her damp hair.

"Nonsense. I don't approve of wasting money."

The idea of getting his mother into a taxi brightened Sam Crabbe considerably.

But for the moment he was given no opportunity to press the matter, as the old lady was asking: "Did you have a busy day at the office, darling? How clever young girls are nowadays!"

Minnie was secretary to a businessman.

Ignoring the question, she spun round on her heel. "Who do you think I went into town with this morning?" she demanded, her hands still on her hair. "Somebody connected with our family. You would never guess who."

"It would be that young Will Edzell. We'll have to invite him here sometime, I suppose," Babs said, sliding another crumb of marzipan into her mouth and making a pretence of coughing behind her hand when she found the eyes of her mother-in-law upon her.

"No, it wasn't. It was Mrs Adam Edzell of Stronn Island. She's staying at Aunt Jessie's hotel."

"Her hotel, Minnie? And with all that money!" Babs exclaimed.

Jessie Edzell's home consisted of a room in a cheap private hotel in the West End. It was on the very top floor of what had once been a large and high Victorian house, and was reached by a narrow service stair. Here she lived among her few posses-sions, cheered—when she could not be bothered to make the long journey downstairs to complain about the lounge fire or the flickerings of the tele-vision with others of her kind—by the single bar of a small electric heater. It was not a life of luxury. But withal, Jessie, being still very active and fit for the stairs, did well enough.

"Mrs Adam will be economising." Sam winked without smiling at Minnie.

"Aunt Jessie was with her. She said she was glad to see me because I could tell Mrs Adam how to get to her lawyer's."

"Dear me! Could the woman not afford a taxi?" Babs exclaimed.

"Economising," her husband repeated once more. "What's she like, Min?"

"Sixtyish. Stout. Grey hair. Tweeds. Red face."

"Has Mrs Edzel been here for some time, darling?" Alice's voice was prim.

"A day or two. She brought some girl from Stronn down to a hospital."

"Then I think it's very unfriendly of your Aunt Jessie not to have told me Adam's wife was with her. The older Jessie gets the more secretive she becomes. I met Jessie out shopping yesterday and she didn't say a word about it."

"She would think you wouldn't be interested, mother."

"That's not the point, Sammy. Saying nothing can be a form of telling lies. The minister was preaching to the children about that very thing last Sunday."

"You would get a fright if we all took to telling you everything *we* had in *our* minds, mother." Her son gave a dry laugh.

Alice drew herself up. "I would be very sorry to think that, dear."

"What else about Mrs Adam, Min?" Babs interposed. Sam had a way of half-teasing, half-fighting
with his mother that only made things uncomfortable.

"I didn't speak to them much. The bus was full.
They were sitting and I had to stand. But Aunt
Jessie said she might look in here tonight. She said
she was coming across to that old Mrs Something
along the terrace. She'll tell you about Mrs Adam if
she comes."

"I wonder what Mrs Adam was seeing her lawyer
about?" Babs said idly.

"You could always telephone and ask her," was
her husband's comment. "Who are her lawyers anyway?"

But at this moment they could hear the doorbell
ringing.

"That could be Aunt Jessie," Minnie said. "I'll go
and see."

4

"Aunt Jessie, what are you doing out on a night
like this?" Sam asked by way of greeting.

"I've as much right to be out on a night like this
as your mother has," Jessie said, disappointed at finding her sister here too. "I promised to spend the
afternoon along the terrace with poor Mrs
Macalister, so I thought I would just drop in. You
know, that poor Mrs Macalister with chronic asthma
that I sometimes come to see up here. The one

whose husband drove his car and himself off
Gourock Pier. Or was it Greenock Pier? No. I
believe it was Wemyss Bay. Anyway, it was a terrible
thing. Some people say he meant to do it. He was a
gloomy kind of man, but poor Mrs Macalister was
very fond of him. You see, there was just the two of
them; no children. And so when he . . ."

"Jessie, dear," Alice interposed gently but with
firmness, determined to stop the flow. "I feel I
should tell you how disappointed I am that you
didn't say Mrs Adam was at your hotel, when I met
you shopping yesterday. I don't think it's nice to be
so secretive."

Her sister went red with annoyance. "I didn't
keep it a secret, Alice. I knew you didn't like her,
so I just didn't mention it."

"Don't you let mother bully you, Aunt Jessie,"
Sam said heartily. "But what's she doing in a
twopenny-ha'penny hotel like that, anyway? A
woman who has money to burn?"

"It's a very nice hotel, Sam," Jessie answered
primly. "And there are some very nice people in it."

"Of course there are, Aunt Jessie. Sam is just
being bad." Babs spoke kindly. "You wouldn't like a
bit of this cake, would you? The icing seems to have
got broken a bit, but it should be very good. It was
dear enough."

Jessie declined the offer. Poor Mrs Macalister's
tea, she protested, had been lavish.

"Did Mrs Adam find the lawyer's office all right?"
Minnie asked, seeking like her mother to smooth
things down.

"So she's been to her lawyer's, has she?" Sam

remarked with a grin. "She'll be leaving you all her money, Aunt Jessie."

"Adam's wife has always been very kind to me, as all of you know very well, Sam. I was just telling Will Edzell everything she had done for me last night."

"Will Edzell? So he's been seeing her, too, Jessie dear?" Alice asked with curiosity, forgetting now to be cold with her sister.

"Will? Yes. You know she had him at Stronn. He came in to see Mary last night, I think he was worrying about John's rudeness to her yesterday at lunch. It sounded terrible. Will was very angry."

"John? John who?"

"Your Uncle John, Sam."

The others sat forward on the edge of their chairs. What was all this about? A meeting between old John Edzell, of all people, and this woman whom it was regarded as a family duty to dislike.

"You don't mean to tell me that Mrs Adam had lunch with Uncle John, Aunt Jessie?"

"Oh, perhaps I shouldn't be talking about this, Sam. I daresay it's confidential in a way. Or at least —well people say things when they are angry or excited that they don't really expect to have repeated."

Sam saw his mother making to speak, but for once he managed to stop her by a commanding shake of his head. This was a story all of them wanted to hear. At all costs old Jessie's garrulousness must be given every encouragement. He smiled blandly. "Well, well, Aune Jessie; Wonders will never cease! You come here and tell us that Uncle John sat down and had his lunch yesterday with Uncle Adam's widow!"

"No, no, Sam. It wasn't like that at all! Mary had gone up to her room after dinner and Will had run in just to see how she was. It was while we were waiting for her to come down he told me. You see, Mary hadn't mentioned it. But at dinner I thought she was a little bit—well, you know, worrying about something. But, of course, after hearing from Will just what—but perhaps, really, I shouldn't—especially when Mary hadn't told me herself."

"So the young man had been at lunch with Mrs Adam and Uncle John, too?" Sam contined to prod.

"No, Sam! She didn't *have* lunch with your Uncle John! She and Will were going in just as John was coming out of the restaurant with the girl and one of the boys from Priestlaw. Will stopped them, meaning to be polite, I suppose, and John said something very insulting to Mary about being the woman who had stolen Adam's money or . . . I don't know. Anyway, it was awful, and Will was very angry. The girl came back later and tried to apologise. But, of course, John had said what he had said. Oh, I shouldn't be telling you all this! Mary didn't make much of it when she did come down. She said we had better forget it. All the same, I could see that Will and she were—" and here Jessie stopped for breath.

"Were what, Aunt Jessie?"

"Well, very upset, Sam. Who wouldn't be?" She looked about her a little guiltily and stood up. "Dear me! Is that the time? I must—"

"Sammy is sending us home in a taxi, Jessie dear.

I can drop you on my way."

"I thought you didn't want a taxi, mother," Sam said ungraciously.

But Alice now wanted her sister to herself. She looked at her son with a smile that was sweet and at the same time corrective. "But, Sammy, dear! Now that I could be giving your Aunt Jessie a lift! So if you mean to be so kind as to send two poor old ladies home on this wet night, I think perhaps— don't you?"

Sam Crabbe felt oddly apprehensive over this news of old John's rudeness. It would take some thinking out. He would have liked to keep his aunt longer and hear more. But presently Minnie returned from telephoning the taxi rank to say that one would be at the door immediately and the old sisters got up, collecting their possessions as they did so.

"Is this a new photograph you've had taken, Euphemia, dear?" Alice asked, picking up a handsome silver frame from a side table, as she made her way towards the door.

"You've seen that often before, mother." Sam's voice was a little sharp. "It's the photo Gladys Cooper signed for me herself at a charity bazaar a long time ago."

"Gladys who, dear?" Where are my spectacles?" Alice fumbled in her bag and put them on.

"Gladys Cooper, mother," Sam said. "The actress."

"Yes, dear. I can see now. Yes. It's a wonderfully beautiful face, isn't it? I thought it was you, Euphemia, dear, for a moment. But I see now it's not really like you." And Alice took her way downstairs, leaving Babs, who knew her mother-in-law had never approved of her interest in the theatre, wondering if the old lady were consciously trying to be unpleasant.

Sam gave the taxi man some money and remarked it was a nasty wet evening, wasn't it? He gave his mother and aunt the parting kisses that were expected of him and told them to take great care of themselves.

But presently, as the front door was banged and the night was once more excluded, Sam turned to his daughter, rubbing his hands in anticipation. Mrs Adam? Will Edzell? Lawyers? Well, what about them? Better get out the bottles and forget all about that.

CHAPTER 8

1

WILL EDZELL returned to his rooms in Hillhead,
bringing with him a sense of emptiness and a feeling
of depression. Unlike Minnie Crabbe, his more
tautly strung nerves were unable to extract much
cheerfulness from damp Glasgow nights. What was
he doing here in this ugly, rain-soaked northern
city? he asked himself drearily. What had his life,
his striving, his examination passing added up to? A
job in a big, dirty town; and these class papers waiting to be corrected, later tonight, there in a pile on
that end of his sitting room table which was not
covered with the cloth laid ready for his supper.
On other such evenings he might possibly have
found some sense of welcome in the crackling fire,
the drawn, plush curtains and the savoury smell that
was coming from his landlady's kitchen. These
things, after all, belonged to a way of living with
which, as student and graduate, he had become very
familiar.

As was his custom Will had let himself in with
a latchkey, then immediately come into his sitting
room still wearing his sodden overcoat. Now, seeing
the water dripping down upon the worn hearthrug,

he began to struggle out of it at the same time as he walked back into the dim hallway to hang it up.

"Your coat will be wet, Mr Edzell. Give it to me and I'll put it up on the kitchen pulleys." His landlady appeared and stretched out a hand to take it.

"Thank you." He gave it to her.

Her lodger was in one of his moods, the good woman told herself, as she shook the overcoat, let down the drying rod that hung from the roof of her kitchen, put the coat over this and hoisted it up again out of her way. She liked this young man with his handsome, lean face and his careless ways. But you never quite knew how you would find him. Sometimes, when he was so disposed, he would talk and joke with her with a respectful, confiding familiarity that was altogether engaging. At others, he would withdraw himself, seemingly indifferent, almost angry. At these times she felt sorry for him, telling herself sentimentally that it wasn't his fault. He had lost his mother early, he had told her. That would be the reason for these ups and downs. Presently, she hoped conventionally, he would be taken in hand by the right kind of young woman who would have the proper mellowing influence. Yes, surely these moods were the result of loneliness.

For tonight, at least, this innocent reading of her lodger's feelings was not, perhaps, quite wrong. Will felt empty and alone, having just parted from one of the few women for whom his life had given him the opportunity to have a warm affection.

He had just seen off Mary Edzell, together with her charge Katie Macdonald on the West Highland train connecting with the weekly steamer that would take them home. Since the weather appeared to have broken hopelessly, Mary had decided against returning by aeroplane and launch.

Now as he leant forward staring into the fire, his imagination was following the two women on their north bound progress, as the train threaded its lighted way high along desolate mountain sides and across remote moorlands, on what, in the autumn, had been for him a regal journey of gold and purple. But tonight all that would be changed. In their railway carriage they would see nothing. They might, perhaps, feel a labouring or a speeding up as the engine climbed or descended. That would be all. This, perhaps the most romantically beautiful railway journey in the world, would be shrouded in rain and darkness.

It is not, indeed, uncommon for a young man to become attached to some woman much older than himself, who has worldly wisdom and sympathy to give to him. And in the month of his convalescence on the island, he had been ripe for just such an attachment.

And in their several meetings here in Glasgow since that first one in the restaurant, it had surprised him to find how much affection he had for Mary; how warm his feelings towards her were.

He had always liked her, of course. And not only for her kindness to himself. He had never before met a woman of her type. On her island she had been buoyantly matriarchal. Mixed with her good nature there was a Highland tartness. A sharpness of the tongue, especially towards the servants, that had in the first days shocked his town bred sensibilities, until he came to see that the servants gave back as good as they got, that on both sides it was a half humorous demonstration of affection. Mrs Adam Edzell had, in short, a tang to her which Will could understand and admire.

And old John Edzell's insult had, if anything, heightened his feeling for her. His anger on her account had forged a closer bond. Yet she had shown her feelings over this so much less than he had. Her self-control had amazed him. Almost at once she had taken the talk in hand, seeking to keep things calm. Asking questions about the girl who had come back to apologise. About his injured leg and how it was mending. About his work. And how he was lodged.

Will picked up the poker from the hearth and stabbed the already blazing fire, caught, suddenly, in a hot wave of contempt. Contempt that these cool, rich people at Priestlaw House—yes, and these chattering underbred Crabbes—should have rejected this altogether excellent and motherly woman, just because, it would seem, old John and his sister Alice had, in their greed and smugness, decided she was an interloping schemer.

"Don't poke the fire like that, Mr Edzell. I made it up before you came in. You're just wasting good coal."

"I'm sorry." He laid down the poker and went off to wash, while the woman laid his evening meal upon the table.

Mary had quizzed him narrowly about them all. Will wondered why, as he dried his hands on the

8

carefully mended towel that was kept for him in this polished but much worn and old fashioned bathroom.

Now as he sat down to his high tea, he went over that lunchtime conversation. No. Mary's close questionings seemed strange. She had taken these people she could not like, one by one, demanding as clear a picture of each as he could give her, especially the Priestlaw Edzells.

Will poured his tea, buttered toast for himself, took up his fork and knife and began to eat and drink mechanically. Yes. He had had something to say about the Priestlaw people. Frederick Edzell, he said, was a typical rich man of business and that was all you could say about him. His wife was empty and well bred. That young man, Harold, they had met for a moment just then was—well—just what he looked; a bumptious, moneyed puppy. His brother, was, perhaps, a less aggressive variation of the same.

Will stopped eating and turned to look reflectively at the fire he had needlessly stirred up. Why had he said all this? Why had he drawn these harsh caricatures? Had it been because he was determined to show himself on Mary's side? Because he felt he must tell her what she wanted to hear? Or had there been in the behaviour of the Priestlaw Edzells towards himself something that had stung and rankled? But then, had he not come back from that Sunday visit, feeling it had all been pleasant enough? Even though these people might not, as he had assured himself, been of his kind, and would never mean anything to him?

2

And Rosamond Edzell, what had he told Mary about her? How had he described her?

Will laid down his fork and knife.

"I'm sorry, Mr Edzell. I thought you would have finished by this time. Oh, you've eaten nothing. Are you all right?" The woman had put her head inside the door.

"Yes. Perfectly. I'm sorry. I'm inclined to forget all about time when I'm thinking about my work." Red with confusion, Will began gulping down the remainder of his meal.

But he had not been thinking about his work. He had been thinking about Rosamond Edzell and the distorted picture he had drawn of her to the mistress of Stronn Island. A young woman with a glossy magazine beauty. Conventional and rich. Her element, an artificial world of county balls and race meetings; not the world of struggle most people must come to terms with. A useless, privileged creature with nothing in her head. A mere decoration.

Will finished eating and got up. Why had he said all this? Had Mary's questioning thrown him on the defensive? Had she seen this? Was that why she had laughed? And what had that laugh meant? That she didn't believe that he disliked Rosamond Edzell so much as his description had implied? That he did not, indeed, dislike her at all? That he had been seeking to contradict his own feelings?

"Thank you, yes. I have had all I want to eat.

Perhaps you would clear away at once. I'll want the whole of the table. I've brought home these papers." And Will had escaped into his bedroom, unable, this evening, to stand the usual few minutes of friendly platitude and gossip.

He flicked on the light, with nothing to do but wait until he could hear the woman go back into the kitchen. He went over to the little dressing table, took up his brush and began distractedly to brush his hair. But his face in the mirror as he leant forward mechanically to do this, looked sulky, almost angry. Will put the brush back, found a packet of cigarettes among a litter of books and papers, lit one and sat down to smoke on the edge of his bed.

Rosamond Edzell. She was the last kind of young woman who could ever be of any use to him. And yet that Sunday afternoon in the autumn woods and garden of Priestlaw had stamped itself upon his mind. Her aspect. The turn of her head. The litheness of her body. Her candid words about his own arrogance had stung and troubled him. But they had remained. And now there was that other picture of her in the restaurant, flushed, excited and eager that Mary Edzell should not be hurt by what that coarse old man had said. To Mary he had put down Rosamond's coming back to them as finishing school good manners. And Mary had only laughed!

Sitting there in his shabby little back bedroom, Will pulled deeply at his cigarette, suffering the fierce inquisition of his own thoughts.

Had he fallen in love, like any featherheaded playboy, with a beautiful girl about whom he knew nothing? And merely because of her looks? Merely because his own blood was young, hot and healthy? Was it as ridiculously crude as that? Was he, with all his intellectual self esteem, his respect for education, his contempt for wealth and privilege, no better, when it came to it, than any one of these?

He did not know. But however he had fallen in love, Will was now astounded to find that it had happened. Whether he liked it or not.

3

He had sucked his cigarette to a grey ash in a succession of savage puffs. Presently it was burning his fingers. Will got up and threw it into the cold bedroom fireplace. For no reason, he pushed aside the white cotton screen of his window and looked out. A dim yard and some lights in the tenement that turned its back upon his own. He could see the outline of a young man, a junior lecturer like himself, perhaps, who was washing dishes in a sink. A girl was holding up a child to whom he was required, it seemed, to say good night. Through another window, Will could see a shapeless, elderly woman dragging a dress over her grey, untidy head. Through yet another he could see a student studying in the pool of light made by a reading lamp. It was still raining lightly. The tops of walls glistened in the wet. Will dropped the screens again and turned back into the room. He heard the clank of dishes and the sound of the kitchen door closing. He could go and throw himself into his chair by the fire in peace.

Rosamond Edzell. Now he understood the rest-lessness, the disquiet that had been haunting his days. Why he had been hating himself and this new town he had come to live in. Why he had felt a lack of grip upon his work. His upbringing, all the bias of his thoughts, had been fighting an underground battle with his instincts.

But now at least the battle was above ground and he knew where he stood. He did not want to be in love with Rosamond. His prejudice despised her class. His scholar's pride despised what it pleased him to think of as her sophisticated ignorance. His hot, chip-on-the-shoulder independence shrank from the idea of even appearing to pursue such a young woman.

Will clasped his hands together, bent forward in his low chair, and sat quite still gazing intently into the fire, as though from its now glowing redness, he could wrest the answers he was seeking.

Yes, he was in love with Rosamond Edzell. He could see her in the restaurant. He could see her moving about that autumn garden. Bright, alive and desirable. Desirable most of all, perhaps, when she had stood still and deliberately accused him of arrogance.

But what if he did begin to go after her? What if he were to get onto his old motor bicycle and begin mooning around Priestlaw? They would be pleased to see him, wouldn't they? The guns of indifference and privilege would soon be swung round and pointed in his direction. He would not stand a chance with her even if he wanted it. He had better take hold of these crazy feelings. This thing that had happened had nothing whatever to do with common sense.

The picture of the young dishwasher at the back window with his wife and child recurred to him. That was how young intellect lived these days. It had been with a girl like that that he had, he supposed, taken for granted he would make his life. A girl who would understand his point of view. Who would understand his work. Who could laugh at improvisation. Who could make do. Who would join with him to find his own kind of happiness. Who would, in short, be a creature of his own world.

This conflagration in his heart must not be allowed to wreck his work. He clasped his fingers until the blood was wrung from them. He had a will and he would use it. He would beat out this absurd fire. Beat it out and grind the embers beneath his heel. She had called him arrogant. Very well. Arrogant he would be. Arrogant with proper pride. He was not going to be a fool. Nobody would ever know about this. Least of all Mary. Or, at least nothing more than she might have guessed already.

But now the thought of Mary brought him some comfort, some slackening of the tension. He had asked if he might come to her at Christmas. But she had told him that he had better think about it. The seas could be heavy round Stronn Island in winter. He might find he could not land, or that once having landed the waves might hold him captive for too long.

As Will rose from his armchair, preparing to work, he felt himself tired and lost. He picked up a student's paper and looked at it without taking in its contents. No. If he had to swim to Mary Edzell he would go to her at Christmas. On Stronn Island perhaps he might regain some peace of mind.

He pulled up a chair, dragged the pile of papers towards him and set himself stubbornly to his task.

CHAPTER 9

1

THE news that Mrs Adam had appeared in the city and renewed her friendship with Will Edzell, together with the rumour that she had been to see her lawyer, acted upon the encrusted smugness of the Edzell-Crabbe family like penetrating oil. Why this should have been so, or rather, why it should have begun thus insidiously to penetrate, it would be difficult to determine. Each and all of them knew, and had known for long, that Mrs Adam Edzell held a deciding number of shares in the firm of Adam and John Edzell from which up to now, she had been content to draw a very pleasantly large income. They knew, too, from Will's own lips, that he had stayed with her at Stronn Island and that Mary had nursed him for some weeks after an accident. From this they could guess that he and she were likely to be good friends.

There was nothing, then, strange or particularly alarming in what had now happened. And yet the oil had gone on penetrating. And their smugness had begun to loosen. Indeed, the more they thought about it the looser it became, manifesting itself in odd little outbursts of tell-tale anxiety.

Young Paddy Crabbe gave vent to one of these

outbursts in the presence of his grandmother when. on the Saturday following her grand-daughter Minnie's meeting with Mary and Jessie in the bus, Alice had dutifully toiled up three flights of an *"art nouveau"* tiled staircase in the Hyndland district to visit her grandson and his wife and to bestow her blessings upon their month old baby.

"What a little darling she is!" Alice, having got back her breath, looked down conventionally upon the small piece of pink immaturity that was her first great-grandchild, then up at the two rather sheepishly proud young parents. "No! I don't see her like anybody yet. Well, yes, perhaps. A look of your grandfather Crabbe, Patrick dear. Oh, yes! Quite distinctly! He used to look just like that sometimes when he was being naughty and trying to flatter me into doing things I didn't want to do. How adorable she is!"

"Looks to me just like any other plain, red-faced kid," Paddy said gauchely, unable to find a sensible answer to his grandmother's foolishness.

"He doesn't mean a word he's saying, does he, Ruth dear? He thinks there has never been such a wonderful baby, ever before," Alice said, turning to the young mother who was now looking none too pleased with her blustering husband. "And you're calling her Elizabeth Alice?"

"Yes. We thought of Elizabeth Alice after my mother and you. Her grandmother and her great-grandmother," Ruth said.

"That's a pretty name." Alice followed the young people to their small sitting room into which she was now invited, pleased that the name Euphemia had been passed over. "Very pretty, indeed," she repeated, sitting down, taking a cup of tea from her grandson's hand and giving it a little, engaging stir. "Only, darlings, no Bessies or Bettys or Lizzies or any of those horrible contractions please. In fact, I feel you would be much safer to put my name first. Alice Elizabeth. Yes. I think so."

"Ruth wants her own mother's name first," Paddy said, forbearing to pick up his own teacup for an instant and standing over his grandmother rather determinedly.

"Oh, do you really think so, dear? I'm not sure, you know. No. I think . . ."

It was here that Paddy burst out about the all pervading family worry, seizing upon it to divert the old woman's insistence. "And what do you think about Mrs Adam Edzell coming to Glasgow, granny?"

"But why shouldn't she come to Glasgow, Patrick, dear?" Alice was as concerned as everybody else, but it was her duty, she felt, to appear serene.

Paddy, knowing his grandmother, ignored her playacting. "You know she and Will Edzell are as thick as thieves. What about that?"

"Well, I don't know *how* friendly they are, Patrick. But it's always nice to think of people being friendly, isn't it? And especially nice for Will Edzell, who is a stranger up here and must be feeling a little lonely."

But Paddy was too much in earnest to listen to this nonsense. "You know that Uncle John met Mrs Adam somewhere in town the other day," he said, cutting his grandmother short, "And that he gave her a piece of his mind."

"Well, we don't really know much about that, Patrick, dear. That was the story your Aunt Jessie said she had got from Will Edzell. But your poor Aunt Jessie inclines to exaggerate sometimes, doesn't she?"

"Father heard her story at the same time as you did. He said that Uncle John must have been abominably rude. And we both agree that Uncle John would have done much better to have been nothing of the kind!"

His grandmother thought about this for a little, wondering what was in Paddy's mind. "Well, dear, you know I have always hated rudeness," she said presently, "but perhaps we should make allowances. Perhaps your poor Uncle John was worrying about something."

Rightly, her grandson took this to mean that his grandmother wanted to hear more. "So far, that woman hasn't given the family any trouble, granny —apart from getting Uncle Adam's holding in Edzell's, of course—but now Uncle John may have put it in her head to do something vindictive."

"Vindictive! Patrick, dear! But what—?" Here Alice stopped, then added quietly: "Yes, dear, I'm afraid I see what you mean."

"Especially with that young man, Will Edzell, on her side." Paddy was pleased to see that now the old lady sat finishing her cup of tea in silence. It was clear that she had grasped the situation. "Granny," he went on, "I think it would be a good thing for you to go out and see Uncle John. To find out what he did say and see if anything can be done about it."

"I could do nothing, Patrick. It would only make him angry."

"I wish you would go anyway, granny. Uncle John may tell you about it himself. Then you might slip in a word of advice."

Alice finished her tea and smiled wistfully at Ruth who had taken her teacup from her hand to replenish it. "Thank you, darling," she said. "Yes. Just like last time. It was delicious." And then to Paddy: "Well, actually I *am* owing your Uncle John a visit, dear. I might take a run out and see him soon. And for all your dear sakes, I might—"

"Some more bread and butter?" Paddy held out the plate to his grandmother.

2

On the morning following, old John Edzell lay snuffling in bed. He was suffering from a bad head cold and his housekeeper, Mrs McNeil, to whose edicts he paid more attention than to those of anybody else, had decreed he must stay there.

"I'll bring you up a nice breakfast, Mr Edzell, and you'll have the Sunday papers and stay where you are," she had insisted.

"I just want a cup of tea and I'm coming downstairs to the fire," the stubborn child of eighty had felt obliged to say.

"If you do that, Mr Edzell, I'll ask McNeil to telephone the doctor." The threat of a fuss was, the good woman knew, her best weapon.

Now, after an excellent breakfast of ham, eggs and coffee, a growl at the international situation, a further growl of approval at the financial editor's black prognostications and a little morning nap followed by aspirin washed down by half a glass of not very watered whisky, the old man lay content against his pillows, hands folded on the quilt in front of him, news sheets strewn around him. This cold, he decided, as his senses tingled and drifted pleasantly, might not, after all, be the beginning of his last illness. No. It was nice to lie here listening to the distant churchbells and to feel mistily that he might live to hear these bells on still a few more Sundays.

But soon the benign mists were dispersed. There was a sound of car tyres on the gravel outside. Annoyance returned with a bound. What was McNeil doing with the car out? Or was it Fred? Or some of Fred's family? Had the McNeils telephoned the doctor to say he was ill? Old John was actually on the point of struggling up angrily to go to the window, when his flushed and concerned housekeeper reappeared in the doorway.

"Whose car is that?" he asked crossly.

"It's Mrs Crabbe, Mr Edzell. She came out in a taxi."

"What has she done that for? Send her away. Tell her I don't want to see her."

"I said you had a bad cold, Mr Edzell."

"Very well, then. Tell her she'll catch it." But now the old man's eyes had shifted beyond his housekeeper's homely figure. "What are *you* doing, Alice?

You've no right to come up here. Can you not see I'm ill?"

"Johnnie, dear!" Alice advanced into the room anxiously. "I had a feeling I had to come out to see you this morning. I said so to Joey at breakfast. It was funny, wasn't it?"

"What is it, Alice? What is it you want?" her brother asked angrily.

But Alice had not yet finished her performance. "So I told Joey I couldn't come to church, this is his morning for helping with the collection, and that I must have a taxi and come out to you."

"Very nice of you." John looked sombre.

"I've asked Mrs McNeil to make me coffee," Alice went on. "When I heard you had a cold I thought it would be friendly to sit beside you with my cup and have a wee talk. Just us two old bodies."

"You had no right to ask Mrs McNeil to do anything of the kind. She's not your servant."

Alice smiled at her brother winningly. "Do you really grudge your sister a cup of coffee, Johnnie dear?"

For which she merely received a glare of hatred from the bed.

"Johnnie, there's something I have on my mind a little bit," she went on, dropping her archness and looking wistfully serious.

"Is there?" The old man clasped his hands gloomily before him, aware now that his sister was getting down to the real purpose of this untimely visit. "I'll give you the cold," he said, as she drew a chair to a confidential nearness and sat down.

3

"It's something that has been worrying us all a little ever since we heard about it. And perhaps it's been worrying you and your family, too."

"I don't know what you're talking about." This was not quite true. He was half ready for what was coming. But he only reached out for a large handkerchief, blew his nose until his face was the colour of beetroot, then looked at his sister angrily.

"I don't need to tell you that Mrs Adam Edzell has been in Glasgow."

Yes. He had thought that was it. "No. You don't need to tell me. But where did you hear that I knew anything about her?"

"She's been living in Jessie's hotel."

"And she told Jessie she had met me?"

"Yes, Johnnie. I think so."

"Think?"

"Well if it wasn't Mrs Adam, it was Will Edzell who told Jessie."

The old man stared at the wallpaper for a time before he turned to say: "He was there when I met her. I daresay he would tell Jessie what I said to that woman."

Alice thought it best to seem not to know too much. "Said, Johnnie?"

"I told Adam's widow what I thought about her. And you know what that is."

"But, Johnnie, was that wise?"

He was looking away from her like a sulky child. No. It had not been wise. It was difficult for him to admit himself in the wrong, but he knew, of course, that as a matter of plain commonsense his behaviour had been deplorable. If only Fred had not made him lose his temper about that boy. But now he wanted to know what the others might be thinking about his outburst. "What do you mean, Alice?" he asked, turning bloodshot eyes upon her once more. "What business is it of yours whether I was wise or not wise?"

"I saw Sammy's son, Patrick, yesterday. Sammy and he are just a little afraid, dear, that you may have made Mrs Adam angry enough to want to do something vindictive."

"Vindictive?"

"She has poor Adam's share of Edzell's, hasn't she? I'm not just sure what she could do with it, Johnnie. I'm such an old muddlehead, but Sammy and Patrick, and Joey, too, when I spoke to him last night, said that she could—"

"I know all about it. You don't need to tell me."

"Very well then, dear."

But this was getting him nowhere. He sat forward in bed, glaring at his sister. "Alice, what have you come out here to say to me?"

"Well, Johnnie, not to tell you to do anything, of course. You know I would never dare to do that, but—"

"But what?"

"Would you be very angry if I made a suggestion?"

"For God's sake, Alice, tell me what you've got to say!"

She took the plunge. "Well—dear. Wouldn't it be

a good thing to let Mrs Adams know somehow—oh, you would know how to do it—that you didn't really mean what you said to her the other day? Just so that if she had any idea of—well, dear—so that she wouldn't think of doing anything unfortunate."

"Apologise? To that woman!" He was almost shouting.

But Alice hung on. "Oh, not in person, of course, dear. I don't know—a letter. Or perhaps Freddy could—"

"Before I did anything of the kind, I would see Adam's widow in—!" but here old John was suddenly convulsed with coughing, and so Alice could tell herself she had not heard the last word.

She stood up. "Johnnie, are you all right? Look. I'll get you a glass of water."

He waved her away. Spluttered, choked into his handkerchief, blew his nose and then, having at last regained a voice that was at least articulate, utterly amazed her by saying through purple lips. "No. I'll do nothing of the kind. But the next time Fred's here I'll see what he thinks. I wish I had never met that woman! Go and get your coffee from Mrs McNeil and tell her to bring me some whisky."

Alice felt well pleased with herself. So she had, after all, succeeded in puncturing her brother's skin. "Johnnie, dear," she said gently, "I do hate leaving you like this. Is there really nothing I can do?"

But he made her no reply. He was lying back staring at the wallpaper in front of him once more, communing angrily with himself. Whether he was angry with the thought of Mrs Adam, or with his own behaviour, or with herself, Alice did not know as she descended the varnished pitch pine staircase of Lochview, jaunty from the sense of having done her duty by the family.

She found Mrs McNeil in the hall waiting to tell her coffee was ready. "Mr Edzell thinks a little half inch of whisky might help his cough." She smiled winningly. "And, Mrs McNeil, I think it might be a comfort to him if you rang up Mr. Frederick at Priestlaw and said his father was ill in bed and would be glad to see him." Here she dropped her voice to a whisper that was confidential and kind as she added: "Don't tell Mr Edzell you've done it. Just let Mr Frederick come as a surprise."

CHAPTER 10

1

SOME curiosity over the visit of Adam Edzell's widow to the city and her friendship with the new-found relative, had likewise penetrated to Priestlaw House. But it had touched them little. It was only Harold, worldly, and alive to advantage and disadvantage, who could be disturbed by any sense of menace. The others could, in their different degrees, only feel ashamed that Frederick's father should have been so outrageously rude to her. This feeling was particularly strong in Rosamond. She had done her best to apologise, yet still she could not help herself from flinching at the thought of it.

Harold had not seen his grandfather since and he was curious to know what he might be thinking of it, now that his rage over Oliver's going to Paris had, presumably, had time to cool down. For the old man could, in the end, be shrewd and objective enough.

On this same Sunday, therefore, when the news that old John had a bad cold and demanded to be visited was telephoned to Priestlaw, Harold's motives were not quite unmixed when he agreed to fall in with a suggestion from his mother. "Your father is just back from a heavy week in London, Harold. I'm quite sure your grandfather would be quite as glad to see you. I expect he's only nursing an ordinary bad cold and that's making him feel neglected. Don't you think so, Frederick?"

And Harold's father, having had quite enough of Oliver and Paris during his last meeting with the old man, was only too pleased to avail himself of his elder son's offer to stand between himself and a renewal of the battle.

"Well—you know, the poor old boy *is* quite worried." Harold, just having returned from visiting his grandfather announced to the assembled family that night before dinner. "That fussy old woman, Aunt Crabbe, or whatever you call her, had been seeing him this morning. She says that her people are afraid Mrs Adam Edzell might do something vindictive."

"What? Arrive at Lochview with a bottle of prussic acid?" Oliver was unable to be interested. His mind was on the fact that it was decided he would fly to Paris within the next few days.

"That's all very funny." Harold looked sulky.

"No. I don't think we really need worry about that." Their mother smiled encouragingly at her tubby elder son. "If your grandfather was sorry he was rude, so much the better. But vindictiveness is a very big word, surely. What do you think, Frederick?"

"I don't suppose I shall lose much sleep over it." Frederick's thoughts were engaged by the curious fact that his elder son was much more in the old man's confidence than he, himself, had ever been.

"Anyway, what is there to worry about?" Rosamond asked.

"Only that the control of Edzell's could go out of our hands." Harold took some sherry.

"Whose hands? The Skipper's?"

"And our brother Harold's," Oliver said cheerfully,

Dinner was announced.

"Come along, children," Christine said briskly. "And stop talking nonsense. Put out some of these lights, Harold, will you? What about asking that young man to come and see us again? I daresay he is feeling lonely."

"Yes. And when he's here, Harold can ask him if Mrs Adam Edzell is giving all her money to him." Oliver turned to follow his mother and sister.

2

Although nothing further was said now or in the next few days, Will Edzell's prospects continued to disquiet Harold. His immediate family, it seemed, had no interest whatever in the matter. If he were to revive talk about it, he would only expose himself to their ridicule. No. There was nothing he could do, his vanity told him, without appearing foolish, inquisitive or just plain absurd.

But unexpectedly, on the morning that Oliver was leaving, Christine, without knowing it, came to his rescue. Having, at breakfast, asked her younger son all the questions mothers ask of grown-up boys who are about to leave home, and having received all the off-putting replies and silences with which such silly questions are likely to be met, Christine sighed, looked out at the November leaves falling and blowing, as a breeze shook the trees that flanked the terrace outside, then, for consolation, sought in her mind for some kind of social arrangement to make.

"Dear me," she began, without thinking of the motive for what she was saying, "I had meant to ask that young man, Will Edzell, this Sunday. Oliver's going away had quite put it out of my head. Today is Friday. I suppose it's too late now."

"Why Sunday? And why this Sunday?" Rosamond asked.

"Mother will be feeling a blank without her little boy." Harold encouraged the proposal in the language expected of him. He would be glad to see Will Edzell and perhaps get some clue to his relationship with Mrs Adam.

Rosamond's quicker sensibilities took note that her mother made no reply to this. Was it possible that she could be feeling this separation a little? Even though it would be nothing for her to take flight any day and see how Oliver was faring?

"As I'm taking Nol across the ferry to the Airport it would be easy for me to run into Glasgow with a message. And perhaps I might see Will Edzell and get a reply from him at once," she said.

"I wish we had asked if his rooms had a telephone number. We might find out, I daresay."

"Not worthwhile, mother. Better to write a note and leave it, if he's not there."

3

Having duly seen Oliver through the barrier at the Airport and having duly waved goodbye to him, Rosamond turned her car back toward the ferry and the western part of the city.

It had been a wet, drab enough Clydeside morning. But now, as she drew up, taking her place among the traffic waiting for the ferry to return from the other side and carry them across, a ray of watery sunshine broke through, sending down a shaft of white light that caused the cobblestones of the landing ramp and the muddy river beyond to glisten and sparkle cheerfully.

Presently a great cargo ship came down, towering high and large in the narrow waterway, a detached community, independent and remote, living its own life as it passed down to the open sea between shipyards, factories and green fields. A fat ship's cook, hanging over the railings up there far above them, bestowed a facetious salute upon the line of waiting vehicles beneath him. Standing by the door of her car, Rosamond smiled and raised a hand in reply.

She felt gay this morning. She had not so far troubled to wonder why. Merely because she was young? Because the sun had decided to shine? Because she was stirred this morning, by an odd curiosity, an odd sense of adventure?

Now the ferry had come in clanking its chains and releasing the flood of traffic it had brought over. Now Rosamond had moved down and had been borne across. Now they had reached the northern shore and she was driving through a riverside town towards the west of Glasgow.

But why this feeling of excitement? What was there exciting about coming into town to deliver an unimportant invitation to an obscure relative she scarcely knew? Wasn't it just to please her mother? A mere gesture of good nature?

And yet as she climbed the scrubbed stone staircase leading to Will Edzell's rooms, Rosamond became aware that these unaccountable feelings had in no way diminished, that her heart was beating more than the climbing warranted, that, perhaps, she was not altogether her own collected self.

Indeed, she was aware of warmth in her cheeks as she now stood on the doormat, listening to the distant class bell of the University clanging out for the eleven o'clock lectures, and waiting for someone to open.

A grey haired woman appeared. She was sorry, she said, but Mr Edzell was over at the University. Was that the eleven o'clock bell that was ringing? He sometimes came in at this time, but not often. Who, could she say called, please?

"His cousin. I have a message for him from my mother. Perhaps you would give it to him." Rosamond found herself looking about her uncertainly. "Or—perhaps I—Could I come in and write him a note?"

This proposal suited the curiosity of the good woman admirably. In the gloom of the stairway she had suspected that this young woman was more than usually handsome. Now, as Rosamond turned from looking for an instant from the window of Will's sitting room, and received paper and pencil from her hands, the landlady saw that this cousin of Mr Edzell's was more than handsome. That she was beautiful.

"Thank you. Shall I sit down here? I won't be a moment."

The woman regretted that she could find no reason to stay while Miss Edzell wrote her message. She would have liked to remain in the room merely taking her in, savouring her looks, her clothes, her perfection. Still, there was the solace of romantic speculation. What did her lodger think of this cousin? What did the cousin think of him? How did they stand, one to the other? Was this the girl who was to save Mr Edzell from his dark moods? And give him the life of mellowing happiness that she, his sentimental landlady, had planned for him?

But the outside door had opened and closed. And there was his step in the hallway. She had better tell him he had a visitor. No. Why should she spoil the pleasure for him? Why shouldn't he open the door and find this beautiful young lady waiting for him?

4

He had banged into the room and slammed down some books upon the table before Rosamond quite realised he had come in. She had not yet settled to writing her message. She was standing, looking at photographs on his mantelpiece.

They stood now, facing each other, equally at a

loss, equally taken aback. Quite automatically she held out a hand.

He took it, then let it drop, seeking, in confused self-consciousness, for something to say.

"I'm sorry to surprise you like this," she said hurriedly, surprised in her turn that he should look so embarrassed.

"Have you come up here to see how the poor live?"

She stood facing him, gathering her confidence about her. Why had he said that? she wondered. Was it merely an awkward joke? She looked him up and down, taking him in. The worn, belted raincoat, none too clean. The untidy hair. The lean, flushed face, with—was it lines of strain she had not remembered seeing there before? She was about to take him to task for what he had just said, then, wondering if she discerned a wounded look in his expression, decided to let it pass.

"Are those your parents?" she said, turning back to the mantelpiece.

"Yes. My father and mother." Her question, it seemed, had been reproof enough, for now he seemed anxious to take up her tone of friendly politeness. "Of course, the photograph of my father was taken very much later than my mother's. I was only nine when she died."

She took down his mother's picture, hanging over it for a moment, giving it a little, polite smile of approving homage, then put it back. She could think of nothing to say about it that would not sound conventional or forced. As she turned to meet his eye once more, she felt he understood this.

"Look here," he was saying as he stood undoing the buckle of his belt, "do sit down. Cigarette?" He pushed at his hair to tidy it, then threw aside his raincoat. "I had some sherry somewhere. Or I could probably get you a cup of coffee."

She sat down and took a cigarette from the packet he had fished from his pocket. "Please don't worry about anything else."

"Sure?"

"Of course," She bent forward and lit her cigarette at the lighter he held for her. Now that he had recovered himself, the force of Will's attraction for her was again making itself felt. The colour in her face had deepened as she looked up to thank him. "You must be wondering why I came up here," she went on.

He waited, standing over her, smiling.

"It was with a message from mother. I was on the point of writing a note when you came in. I happened to be seeing Oliver off to Paris. I told her I should run up and leave it. Oliver is going to Paris to learn to paint. I don't suppose you knew he had left Edzell's for painting, did you?"

"Seriously? Or as a rich young man's hobby?"

This time she answered sharply. "Why shouldn't he take it seriously? And how do you know how rich or poor Oliver is?"

"I don't suppose you'll let him starve in a garret like—whom shall I say?—Oh, according to pattern, anyway?"

"No. I don't suppose we shall. But why do you keep on asking me these rude questions? As—as if it was some kind of sin not to be—to be destitute?

You're not quite destitute yourself, are you?"

He took the reproof, turning away from her almost shamefacedly. "Will you forgive me?" he said, throwing himself into the chair on the other side of the hearthrug. "I say these things because I *am* rude, I daresay. A rude devil. That's all, I suppose."

"No," she said. "I don't suppose that *is* all. But I'll forgive you this time."

"Thank you."

His uneasy, apologetic smile received a serene smile in return.

"Mother would be glad if you can come down to see us again. She wondered if lunch on Sunday would be all right. That was the message I came to give you."

For reply, the strange, unpredictable young man had risen from his chair without saying a word and was now, as Rosamond turned to see what he was doing, standing, looking out of the window. Alarmed a little by this odd behaviour she rose to her own feet and stood, her eyes upon his back, waiting.

He turned round abruptly. "Would *you* be glad if I came?"

She could not understand the strange harshness of his voice and she found herself resenting it. But she saw no reason why she should not answer coolly: "I? Of course. Why not?"

"That's very polite of you."

"What else do you expect me to be?" Rosamond laughed uneasily and turned to throw the end of her cigarette into the fire. When she turned back again, Will was standing beside her on the hearthrug.

Again the wounded, defensive look that somehow touched her. But why this tension? She forced a bright smile. "Well? Shall we take it that you're coming?"

He turned away from her again dropping his voice as he answered: "All right. I'll come this time. Thank you."

"Good. And other times, too, surely?"

As he turned back to reply, she saw with amazement that his face was actually working. "I—I don't know. I—don't think so."

"Will! Why should . . ."

"I've said I'll come on Sunday. We'd better leave it at that." He had moved away abruptly and was now at the door turning the handle. He was asking her to go!

There was nothing now for Rosamond to do but say, once again, that they would be happy to see him and go quickly.

5

She was in no doubt of what had happened, as she started her car and began to thread her way out from among the high sandstone tenements of Hillhead. Will Edzell was in love with her, at what level she could not tell, but surely this smouldering rudeness, hovering so near to emotion, could add up to nothing else. Yet, though she attracted him, he did not want to be attracted. Why?

Dropping down the hill, Rosamond was halted by

the control lights at Botanic Gardens, then, receiving the green light, she joined the traffic rushing westward out of the city.

She was surprised and oddly shaken by what had happened. Other young men had lost their heads about her, pleasantly or unpleasantly. She seemed to be the kind of young woman who, all unsought, prompted declarations. But never before had a young man betrayed his feelings and at the same time betrayed that these feelings were unwelcome to him.

Automatically she turned at Anniesland, making for Bearsden and the open country.

Well, what of it? What did it matter what Will Edzell felt or didn't feel? What did this young man of no background, who by chance bore the Edzell name, have to do with herself? She need never see him again. Even on Sunday, she could go elsewhere if she did not want to meet him. But perhaps now he would not come. Perhaps now he would simply not appear, sending, or perhaps not even sending, an apology.

"He can do what he likes," Rosamond said aloud, then found herself wondering just what it was that had excited her into talking to herself. As she had reached the open country, she decided to turn into a farm road, stop the car, light a cigarette and think.

Now in her mind she ran over this morning's happenings. Oliver's going to Paris was nothing. Being rich and mobile, they were for ever seeing each other off at some railway station or airfield. But why, she wondered, had she been so ready, so anxious as it now seemed, to take a message to Will

Edzell's rooms? Curiosity, was it? Just to see how he lived? "How the poor lived" as he had put it? Again she saw Will's lean face as he had said this and heard again his short, ungracious laugh. Strange young man. Why should she be curious about him? Why should she have any particular interest in him whatever? Was it possible that she, in her turn, was attracted?

With a gesture of impatience, Rosamond lowered the car window and pitched her half smoked cigarette out upon the sodden grass by the roadside. Attracted? She could not tell. But now it came to her that Will Edzell, since that visit some weeks ago, had taken a strange possession of her mind. She had thought about him. Had remembered their talk in the garden at Priestlaw. Had wondered about his background. His odd, uncompromising manners. And she had kept seeing his face, moody, almost unfriendly at one moment, then suddenly lit up, when he had willed it, by that quick smile. What kind of person was he?

Rosamond looked about her. Cows were grazing in the wet field beside her. A flock of crows had settled in one more distant. In another, farmyard dung was being thrown out from a cart. She saw these things and did not see them.

Did she even *like* this young man, into whose rooms her curiosity had driven her this morning? She could not answer this. But she knew now that the thought of him touched her feelings strangely. That their meeting this morning had disturbed her.

Was she in love with him? She did not know. But she had better not be. Since obviously Will, whatever the feelings he had been unable to conceal, had also shown that he wanted to be left alone. Yet why should he? She was not deformed. Ugly. Suppose then that she *did* decide that she wanted him? At first it might annoy her parents, particularly her mother. But wouldn't it be an excellent thing for Will? And the Skipper was an imaginative, helpful person. And this money now coming from her grandfather, together with what Will earned, should surely make life quite possible for them? And allow Will time to work. For what? A professorship, she supposed. Well, then. There was no possible disgrace in being married to a professor, was there?

But suddenly Rosamond saw where the train of thinking had brought her and laughed a little uncomfortably. She had actually been making joint plans for herself and a man she hardly knew. A man she was not even certain she liked. This had, indeed, been a curious morning!

She pushed the starter of her car and backed it out into the main road, continuing towards home.

CHAPTER 11

1

WILL was to remember the two days which elapsed from the moment the door had closed behind Rosamond until he set out for Sunday lunch at Priestlaw, as a time of racking tension, of self-examination, of uncertainty, of blowing hot and cold. At one moment he would blame himself for having consented to go. At the next he would tell himself that there was nothing else he could have done without seeming childish and unreasonable. That he might easily have told a polite lie, excusing himself, did not, in his overwrought state, occur to him.

Raised among men, knowing little of women, yet strongly male, his emotional defences were of the weakest. And, if anything had remained of them, Rosamond's surprise visit had brought them down to the ground. The thought of her was now a trouble and an obsession.

And he was ashamed of himself. Bewildered and ashamed. Bewildered that his heart and his senses should thus become invaded; and ashamed that this intellect of his, upon which he had prided himself, this very serviceable instrument which he had, up to now, spent so much of his time disciplining and training, had little or no say in the matter, that it should have fallen back, surprised, before other forces within him.

On the Saturday, after a night of little sleep, Will went out into the country and spent most of the day in a long, exhausting walk. A walk in which he did not much note where he was going, so deep was he in debate with himself, so busy examing this absurd, inexplicable trap into which his emotions had led him. For it *was* absurd, as he kept telling himself. What did he know of Rosamond? Of her mind? Of her sympathies? Even making all allowances for her background, for the frame inside which she lived, a frame for which, incidentally, he had little understanding and less sympathy, what kind of young woman was she? Was her character soft or hard? Deep or shallow? He could not tell.

And about tomorrow? Was it going to make matters worse or better for him if he went? And so, on that unhappy Saturday, Will had plodded on, arguing with himself, seeking for decisions that were out of his reach. A young man, like any other, hopelessly and unexpectedly in love for the first time.

But on Sunday morning it seemed that the matter of his going had somehow settled itself. Having slept better, out of sheer exhaustion, perhaps, Will found himself mechanically taking out the clothes he had worn at Priestlaw on his last visit. So he was going today, was he? It was, almost, as though he were asking another young man the question. Now, as he dressed, he felt oddly detached, as though his senses had been made numb by the emotional storm of yesterday.

This unaccountable feeling of moving in a dream

remained with him all morning. It was, indeed, still with him as he rode down to Priestlaw through the wet, sinking beauty of the very late autumn; still with him as he parked his bicycle in front of the mansion house. And more strange still, with him as Rosamond met him at the front entrance and took his hand. Was this the young woman who had roused all the trouble within him? This young woman now so anxious and so concerned?

2

"Will, I've been looking for you. We've just had very frightening news about my brother Oliver. I wanted to catch you before you saw mother and the Skipper."

"News? What news?"

"Come outside again. Just for a moment and I'll tell you."

Will followed her from the entrance and, still slightly limping, fell into step with her as she began slowly to pace in front of the house. His wits were still misted by these last overwrought days, but Rosamond's presence, the force of her anxiety had now begun to clear them.

"Oliver was spending yesterday in London. He flew to Paris this morning. Less than an hour ago there was a call from the Airport to say that he was among the passengers on a plane that had overshot the runway at the Orly airfield in Paris and that there was a report of casualties. We listened to the news just now at one o'clock. But they didn't tell us any more." Here Rosamond stopped for a moment, then added, in a voice she had to control, "except that the plane had caught fire."

He turned to look at her face, saw her distress, then, as he waited to hear what else she had to tell him, he found himself laying a hand upon her arm.

She smiled wanly at this gesture of reassurance. "Harold has gone into Glasgow to get more news, if he can. I don't know if it was a good thing to do or not, but he said he couldn't sit at home and do nothing. He was going to the air office in town." Rosamond took another step or two, then turned. "That's all, really," she said. "The Skipper and mother know all this, of course. But I didn't feel like telling you in front of them. We'd better go in now."

"They probably won't want me," Will said. "Not with all this uncertainty. I had better go away again." He stood undecided for a moment. "Unless, of course, I can help. I've got my bike. I might be able to do some despatch riding or something."

In her turn Rosamond caught his arm. "No. Don't go away. We're expecting you. Look, there's the Skipper."

Frederick greeted Will from the doorway with the words: "Has Rosamond been telling you?" He was looking older.

"Are you sure you want to be bothered with me now, sir?"

"Come in, come in. We're glad you've come. You've got to have your lunch somewhere, haven't you?" Frederick's voice was hoarse but it was friendly.

3

It was midnight when Will got back to Hillhead. Although outside it was more damp than cold, his room seemed inhospitable and icy as he came into it, snapped on the light, threw down his overcoat and looked about him. There was a note on the table, left by his landlady before she went to bed. She had not lit the fire, she wrote, since he had not appeared by supper time, but he would notice she had put in an electric heater if he wanted to warm himself. There was a saucepan containing soup, waiting if he wanted it, on the gas stove in the kitchen. Will turned on the heater, sat down and lit a cigarette. Presently the happenings of this extraordinary day began to recede from him, began to fall into perspective a little, as he lay back considering them.

This morning he had driven to Priestlaw suspended, as it seemed, in his own exhausted feelings. So isolated, indeed, that even his meeting with Rosamond, who had been the cause of them, had been a meeting almost without sensation. But at once the unlooked for had happened. Instead of the polite, somewhat impersonal reception he had expected from them all, he had found himself in the middle of a family with all its guards down; a family given over to apprehension and distress. If he had harboured any thought that cool good manners betoken shallow affections, now he knew that he was wrong.

Will sat forward in his chair, stretching out his hands to warm them at the glowing bars of the heater.

He had gone down this morning to visit strangers. He had come back tonight having spent the day with friends. Even Christine, the least comprehensible to him, had seemed to be glad of his presence. Indeed now, as he sat thinking things over, it was Christine who had, perhaps, won his greatest admiration. In a sense she had been very much herself. Going in ahead of Rosamond and her father, he had found himself alone with her in the drawing room for a moment. "You've heard the news, Will? Help yourself to sherry. We're waiting to hear just what has happened." Her eyes were red, he saw, but now before himself, her control was complete. "And please, just while I've got you alone, do try to stiffen Frederick a little. He's blaming himself for having let Oliver go to Paris at all. Which, of course, is quite ridiculous. But then I daresay we're all— well—not at our most sensible this morning."

Just then there had been a ring of the telephone. "Take that, please, Will." Her voice had dropped to an apprehensive whisper. "It would be a help if you would take the telephone calls—until we know—just what has happened." It had been Harold to say that he had arrived at the air office, that they had heard there had been burnings but few deaths. No names were yet available. Harold would stay where he was until names came through.

Will sat back, puffed his cigarette to a finish and took out another.

By the time he had finished with Harold's message all three had been standing round him. Christine's face was fixed and colourless, but she had stood, her hand on her husband's sleeve, more anxious for his feelings, it seemed, than her own. "Well. It's lunch time, I suppose. We had better go through. I don't want to eat anything. But Will has got to be fed. And you two had better put something inside you."

And so she had gone on, tense and staccato, but firm with herself through all that dreadful afternoon. And Frederick had sat, as it seemed, merely waiting, bent forward, an unhappy man; while he, Will, together with Rosamond, had sat there with them, making a poor pretence at normality, looking at books, the Sunday papers, talking together sometimes, trying as best they could to fill in the unbearable hours. More than once Harold had telephoned again. Rather to keep in touch than to give fresh information. Calls that had merely served to tighten the rack.

And then towards five o'clock the news they had been waiting for came. Oliver was suffering from burning and shock, they could not say how seriously, but at least he was alive and had been taken along with others to hospital.

Now, as it came back to him, Will stood up, crushed his cigarette against the tiles of the fireplace, threw it upon the unlit coals and thrust his hands deep into his pockets. For it was here that Christine had lost control at last. Her feelings had escaped in a storm of wholesome weeping.

"Tell Harold to hang on for a moment, Will," Rosamond had said.

It was Frederick who made the decision. "Come along, Christine. You and I are leaving for Paris. Will, tell Harold we're going tonight. Tell him to

get train tickets and sleepers if he can. And plane
bookings for us from London in the morning."

4

Will looked about him. Why was he standing here
letting the events of the day excite him? He had
work to do tomorrow. Hadn't he better go to bed?
He bent to turn off the electric heater, picked up his
damp waterproof in order to hang it in the hallway,
then put out the light. As he began slowly to un-
dress, his state of mind this morning came back to
him. His dazed, preoccupation with Rosamond.

And now? The centre of today's happening had
not been Oliver Edzell's sister, but Oliver's father
and mother. Rosamond and he had merely stood by,
doing what they could.

Will kicked off his shoes and tore at his necktie to
undo it, half noting, irrelevantly, how a sudden rain
squall outside was shaking the frames of his loose,
old-fashioned bedroom window.

He and Rosamond had been mere good friends all
day. After Frederick's decision to go to Paris she had
gone off to help her mother to pack, while he had
gone with her father to his dressingroom. In due
course, Harold had appeared with travelling arrangements made, there had been a hurried unconversa-
tional meal, then Frederick Edzell and his wife had
driven off to a night train, leaving the three young
people to themselves. As the lights of the family car
had disappeared into the darkness, Will had turned

on the doorstep to say he had better think of getting back to Glasgow, too. But Harold had held him.

"No. Look here, you can't go away yet. Stay and have a drink or something." Even Harold had been human.

"No, Will. Of course you're going to stay. We can't do without you. Why not stay all night? Harold can give you what you need."

Will stood up to finish undressing, then, once in his pyjamas, he lit yet another cigarette and sat down on the edge of his bed.

Rosamond. Today he had come to know Rosamond, too. The creature that had bewitched his senses had put on flesh and blood. She had done well today, showing herself to be sensitive, quick to help and warm. Any other good-hearted young woman would have done as much in like circumstances, he told himself. Her performance had been praiseworthy but unremarkable. But then she wasn't any other good-hearted young woman. She was Rosamond.

"No, Will. You're going to stay. We can't do without you." What exactly did these words mean, he wondered.

He had stayed late, sitting with Rosamond and Harold by the fire in an intimacy that would have seemed impossible before he set out this morning. They had talked of what had happened and what was likely to happen. Then, at length, despite protest, he had stood up to take his leave.

A day of feelings to which Will could not yet put a name. And yet, tonight, although he could not have explained this either, he felt an easement, a

lightening of the spirits. "We can't do without you."
Was it that? The new-found sense of comradeship?
He did not know. But now perhaps he would be
able to sleep.

Why had he lit this cigarette? He hadn't wanted
it. He stood up, stubbed it out on the tin lid he
used as an ashtray on his dressingtable, took up his
towel and toothbrush and limped off barefoot to
the bathroom to finish up for the night.

5

Will woke up to a surprisingly normal working
Monday. Normal, in that, although he felt tired, he
was able to take pleasure in the thought that today
his work must come first. He looked to it as a
pleasant refuge from emotion. In the evening, he
told himself, he would telephone to Priestlaw to ask
if further news had come from Paris. That would be
time enough.

This mood of wilful detachment remained with
him all through the day until late in the afternoon,
when he found himself turning back from the
entrance to his lodging, having heard the sound of a
car coming to a standstill and the shutting of a door.

Now he was sorry, almost, to see that it was Rosamond. He would have been grateful to her, just for
today, to be left alone.

"Will! Hello!" she was calling after him. "I went
in to the office this afternoon. I knew Harold would
be doing everything to get news and I couldn't bear
to sit at home and wait for it. My parents have

arrived. The Skipper talked to Harold on the telephone from Paris. They had themselves driven straight from the airport to the hospital. Can I come up and tell you about it?"

"Of course! I can get you tea or a drink or something?" Now as he led the way upstairs, he found himself half pleased, half disturbed by her request. Why couldn't she merely have given him the news down there by the car, then gone? Or at least left to himself the politeness of asking her to come upstairs for a moment. He turned his latchkey in the door of the flat and called to his landlady. There was no reply. Then, having knocked at her kitchen door and having no reply to this either, he turned with a shrug to his guest standing behind. "No one there. I'm sorry it can't be tea. Unless you like to go and make yourself a cup."

She laughed at this. And he thought her laugh was a little brittle. "I don't suppose a strange young woman would be popular if Mrs—whatever her name is—found her prowling about her kitchen!"

"I've got some sherry." He held the door of his sitting-room for her, snapping on the light as he did so. "Tell me how your brother is?" He saw now, as they stood looking at each other in the light, that her face was flushed, that she looked strained and might be near to tears.

"He's going to live, Will. He has been burnt on one side and cut quite badly. And, of course, he's badly shocked. Poor old Nol!"

"Fond of him?"

"Of course! What a queer question to ask! He's my brother, isn't he?"

"I'll look out the sherry bottle. Sit down. You're looking tired."

"Am I? I'm sorry."

"Nothing to be sorry about." Presently he turned back to her with the bottle and two glasses.

She was not sitting down, but standing on the hearthrug with her hand on the mantelpiece, looking at the photographs she had already seen and now and then dropping her eyes to look into the fire. "Anyway, it was quite a day for all of us yesterday, wasn't it? How thankful I was that you were with us, Will. I don't know how I should have got through that dreadful afternoon without you."

"Very kind of you to put it that way."

"Don't you believe what I'm saying? Can't you answer me nicely, just for once?"

"Sit down and have this sherry. You don't look as if you had slept much last night."

"No. I don't think I slept at all."

"Then it was ridiculous for you to drive into Glasgow today, when you could quite as well have got all the news you wanted over the telephone!" He was bewildered by the tone of his own voice as he said this. Why did he sound hoarse and angry? He didn't mean to be.

But in a moment he was to be more bewildered, for now Rosamond, still standing in front of him, had burst into tears and, in yet a more bewildering moment, he was holding her in his arms!

"Will!" At length she had broken from him, and, turning away still weeping, was trying to take hold of herself by pouring out two glasses of sherry with a hand that was none too steady.

He had not yet refound his tongue and merely stood looking at her.

"Will," she had turned back to him, "I hope you really meant that?"

"Meant, Rosamond?"

"For I discovered yesterday that I had fallen desperately in love with you!"

He heard himself laughing at this with a high laugh that was not his own. "And do you think that *you* haven't been putting *me* through it?" For further argument he could only take her into his arms again.

And yet, when at last they had taken up their glasses, telling each other they must be sensible, Will, while he knew himself to be happy—if a state of high excitement can be called happiness—also found himself wondering if this strange girl, who so unaccountably had told him she loved him, had not come up here expressly to bring about what had just happened.

CHAPTER 12

1

ROSAMOND came home to find her brother Harold asleep before the library fire. Her arrival roused him just enough to cause him to open his eyes, say: "Hello, where have you been?" and shut them again.

"Having dinner in Glasgow with a young man."

This information did not interest Harold very much. Instead, he came awake enough to open his eyes once more and say: "I felt I had to look in on grandfather and tell him about Nol. The evening newspapers had got hold of the fact that Nol was in the Paris crash yesterday. 'Younger son of prominent Glasgow businessman—' that sort of stuff."

"How did grandfather take the news?" Occupied with her own thoughts, Rosamond was walking about the room.

"He was a bit low about it. I suppose, after all, he feels we all belong to him in a way. And, of course, he's blaming the Skipper. Saying that Nol should never have been allowed to go to Paris and all the rest of it. Our dear father is in for a devil of a time when he gets back. Lord! What a weekend this has been! I'm worn out!" While he was speaking Harold was becoming more and more wide awake.

Now he got up and crossed to where a tray of whisky was standing.

"Any more news of Nol?" his sister asked.

"Not a thing."

"Harold?"

"What?" Tumbler in hand, he turned to look at her for the first time this evening.

"Will Edzell and I have decided to marry each other."

"Good heavens!"

"You might at least say you were pleased."

Harold returned to his place by the fire and sat, for a time, watching the bubbles rise in his tumbler. "Well, it's your affair, isn't it? Or is it? No. Perhaps it's all our affairs."

"What does that mean?"

Instead of replying to this, her brother said: "I think you said once that he was red brick."

"He *is* red brick. That's one of his attractions."

Harold took a gulp of his drink and sat eyeing his sister, while he held it in his mouth, savouring it before he swallowed it down. Rosamond, now he had taken the trouble to look at her, seemed keyed up. There were bright spots in her cheeks and her eyes shone. He was not sure how to take all this. He would have to consider it. The repercussions of this marriage, if it took place, might be enormous.

"He was absolutely wonderful with mother and the Skipper yesterday afternoon while you were away, Harold. I don't know what we should have done without him!"

"Hello! Steady! Steady!" Harold got up. There

had been tones of pleading and—was it hysteria?—in his sister's voice. And now he saw that her eyes were full. It was time to smooth her down a bit. "Yes. Will Edzell's a good chap. Look here, I'm going to give you some whisky whether you want it or not. You're looking washed-out. Then you'd better go to bed. Your young man shouldn't let you stay out so late."

Rosamond meekly accepted the glass from his hand. "He drove me down just now, but he wouldn't come in."

"Drove?" It was on the tip of Harold's tongue to ask her if she had come down riding pillion on the back of Will's motor-bicycle, but he controlled the impulse.

"He insisted on driving me down in my own car. He's gone back in it. I've allowed him to keep it up there for the night."

"Allowed?"

She looked up to find a quizzical smile on her brother's face. "Oh, there's nothing to laugh at, Harold!" Now she was very near to tears, indeed. "I didn't mean *allowed,* of course. *Told* if you like. Will had to get back to Glasgow somehow. He has an early lecture tomorrow. I'll take this upstairs with me." She turned to go.

"Rosie, come here." Harold crooked a finger as she turned back. "I'm sorry," he said; then went on: "We only kiss each other once every ten years or so, don't we? We might consider the ten years up to-night." He bent to kiss her. "That's just to say good luck to you."

11

2

Half an hour later Rosamond pulled back her curtains, threw open her windows, got into bed and put out the light. Now, lying in the comforting, familiar darkness of her own bedroom, she was conscious that her body was tired. Tired by the strains of the last two days. But her mind, it seemed, was on a knife edge, turning over the happenings of today and yesterday, alert and over-excited.

Outside, the wind had risen a little. She was aware of its low complaining as, here and there, it shook drops of water from the trees upon leaves that had already fallen upon the stone terrace beneath her window.

Will should be home by now. She was glad to think of him making the short journey safely and warmly in her car, instead of exposing himself to the discomforts of the night on that bicycle of his. But discomforts of that sort were, of course, soon going to stop for him now that he belonged to herself.

Will. As she lay there in the darkness Rosamond became aware that tears were running from her eyes. She could not tell if they were tears of happiness, of tenderness, or merely because she was unstrung. At all events they did not matter. There was no one here to see them. And her cousin, Will Edzell, was to be her husband.

She had spoken nothing more than the truth when, breaking from his arms up there in his lodging, she had said she had fallen desperately in love with him. His attraction was for her intense; as she now knew her own must be for him. They could not help, it seemed, setting each other alight. And yet for her, too, there was so much more than that. Her future husband, as she saw it, was to give her life direction. While she, on her side, would support him, building him up, removing every obstacle from him on his journey towards academic distinction. His grittiness of temper, his ability, even, to make her angry, his red brick ideas, were for her a part of him. But hereafter, she told herself, it would be her happy duty to control these things, to see to it that these difficult qualities did not stand in his way.

Now Rosamond could hear the lock of the french window beneath her as it was turned. She could hear a step, then Harold's cough. He was not yet gone to bed, it seemed, and was looking out to see what kind of a night it was. The window was closed again. She could hear what sounded in the distance like the barking of a fox.

But this evening, their first evening together, there had been nothing difficult about Will. He had been shy with her, a little unsure of himself, gentle and utterly lovable. She had said they must dine somewhere and told him she wanted it to be her party, seeking, perhaps, to save him expense. But in that, at least, he had been firm. She must come with him. They had eaten in a little city restaurant she did not know, a little place of no consequence. But Will in his old tweed jacket, with its leather reinforcements at elbow and sleeve, and his baggy flannel trousers, had just been as she wanted him to be. They had found a quiet corner, talked about each other, and she had been tremulously happy.

And Will, too, surely? Well, of course! Rosamond turned about in bed, listening to the sound of the trees and the raindrops falling? Was he not in love with her? And had he not said so? Had she not known that ever since she had run up last Friday to invite him here to Priestlaw? And hadn't she known it this afternoon as she ascended the stair and watched him put his key in the latch? Here Rosamond stopped short in her thinking and sat up excitedly in bed. Had she, Rosamond Edzell, actually gone upstairs with her cousin deliberately intending to make him propose marriage to her? Rosamond drew up her knees in the darkness, locked her hands about them and rocked back and forth as she thought about this. No, she decided presently, laughing noiselessly at the thought. Not deliberately. Instinctively, maybe. But not deliberately.

She unclasped her hands, lay back once more and re-arranged the covers about her. Besides, however it had come about, wasn't it a good thing? Weren't they both deeply in love and glad to have found each other? What did it matter about the wherefores and the hows?

The night wind sprang up still more freshly. The rain had stopped and now the moon was showing its rim above the black outline of a hill bordering on Loch Lomond.

But she was past being aware of such things. She had fallen asleep.

3

Some mornings later Rosamond appeared in Will's rooms; a liberty she had taken to permitting herself and which, had Will been in any normal frame of mind, would have made him testy, since, like most students, he was impatient of interruption when his thoughts should have been upon his work. But he was in no normal frame of mind. His senses were still surprised, delighted and bewildered.

Rosamond had forbidden him to talk about ways and means, about dates and arrangements. It was no use, she had said, to talk of these things until her parents came home and were told of the engagement, no news of which had been sent to Paris, where there must be, as all at home felt, quite enough to think about.

Will had been more than pleased to let things go. End of term work was pressing upon him and it had not been made lighter by the emotional upheavals of these last days. He was conscious that somewhere, just round the corner, practical difficulties and necessary decisions were waiting. But, telling himself that his job must come first whatever happened, he was, for the moment, content to linger in the brittle world of happiness in which he now found himself.

"Will, I've run up to tell you something. I see you're working. I won't stay a minute if you don't want me to."

"You'd better say good morning first." Will laid down his pen, stood up from the table, and took her into his arms. "That was just to show that I don't

ever want you up here at all," he said releasing her
presently and added, suddenly self-conscious; "Will
your ladyship please have the goodness to ignore the
hole in the elbow of this old jersey?"

A little to his surprise the beautiful girl beside
him became solemn. "I don't want to be anybody's
ladyship," she said taking his hand. "And if you take
your jersey off now, I'll patch the elbow for you."

"Never mind. I don't suppose I could find any
wool to do it with. What was it you came up to tell
me?"

"Will, the Skipper is home. He had to come home
for business reasons. Nol is still very ill, he says. He
wants me to leave for Paris tomorrow to be with
mother. I may be away for a week or two."

After Rosamond had taken up the hand she had
been holding and kissed the knuckles of it, Will was
amazed to find, as he took it back, that it was wet.
Her eyes, as they looked up at him, were brimming
over. He was still quite unused to this; unused to
find his own, striving, independent self, of importance to anyone. For a time he could not speak, he
could only stand, his lips trembling, looking down
upon her. But presently, feeling that something
must be said, he drew her once more to him and
spoke over her shoulder. "It's the first time I've met
this kind of thing, Rosamond." His voice was unsteady. "I mean—that anyone should care whether I
was left alone or not." And then in a moment: "Of
course you've got to go. We're going to be happy for
the rest of time, aren't we? Surely we can spare a
day or two of it. Have you told your father about
us?"

"Not yet, Will. He was dead beat and very full of Oliver, when he got in last night. I'm glad you feel I have to go. Because I felt that, too. I told him I would, last night. I couldn't say no. Can you come out to dinner tonight and we'll talk to him together? In fact, I'm not asking. I'm telling you to come. You'll have all the time in the world to finish your term work while I'm in Paris." Then in reply to a shrug and a somewhat strained smile from Will: "That's a good boy. And by the way, I think Harold should put a notice of our engagement into the *Glasgow Herald* quite soon. Don't you? He can do it for us. Why should you be worried? Your father's name was William, too, wasn't it?"

At another time this would have caused an explosion. The world of social conformity, of polite newspaper announcements, was a world that Will had been brought up to turn his back upon. But now he could say nothing. The tendernesses of these first days still tied his tongue.

But Rosamond could only see that his expression had become strained, that he looked exhausted. "My darling," she said, "you look worn out. On top of everything else you've been overworking. You had better stay the night at Priestlaw and we will deliver you back here again in time for your work tomorrow. I wouldn't insist on your coming at all, if I didn't have to go away in the morning."

"I'll be all right."

She put her arms about him as he stood now, limp before her. "Look, Will. I know how clever you are, and I also know how hard you have to work. But very soon you are going to have a wife who is quite determined to make things easy for you, to look after you and arrange your life. You belong to me now." She kissed him gaily, with a crispness that reminded him of her mother.

"I'll phone Harold to come here and get you on his way home tonight. No. You mustn't bother about anything. We have a supply of spare toothbrushes!"

Having returned from seeing Rosamond drive off, Will drew up his chair and sat down once more to his work. For a time he could not bring his mind to bear upon it. For the thoughts that interrupted were disquieting and unaccountable.

CHAPTER 13

1

IT was Joseph Crabbe's custom, on six working mornings of the week, to enjoy a solitary and unhurried breakfast with the *Glasgow Herald* propped up against the coffee pot. This had long since come to be the best half hour in the day of Alice's fussy, but much devoted, son. Then, when it was time for him to be gone, being a man who hated all things slovenly, he would stand up, fold the paper to look as far as possible as though it had not yet been unfolded, see that his spotted bow tie sat straight, that there was neither crush nor crumb on his well, but sensibly cut, pepper and salt jacket, go to say good morning to his mother, who breakfasted in bed, hand her over the newspaper, then take his way downstairs from the Hillhead flat, spruce, red-faced, and fully ready to resume the day's battle with a life that had never been particularly easy for him.

This morning Joseph went through his routine as usual, except for one very minor detail, a detail which, however, was significant enough. He did not refold the sheets of the *Glasgow Herald* into their proper order; he folded them carefully so that his mother might read the social and personal column first. "There, mother," he said. "There. Where my thumb it. Read that. That's something to interest

163

you. I see you have your spectacles on already."

Alice looked up at her son through them. "It's fish morning, Joey, dear," she said smiling meekly. "You know very well that your old blind mother has to wear her spectacles to see the bones."

"Well, that's grand then. I've got to go. You can amuse yourself by reading what's there."

"No, Joey, wait! You'll be sure to let me know if any more news comes through about that poor boy of Freddie's, won't you? His sister must be in Paris now."

"Yes, yes. Of course."

"And Joey—!"

But Joseph had escaped for the day, and now there was nothing left for Alice to do but lie back against her pillows, adjust her spectacles and read the astonishing announcement of the fact that young Will Edzell was to marry his cousin Rosamond.

Several times she laid down the newspaper, stared before herself in amazement, then took it up to re-read the words. How had this come about? And what was it going to mean? Really, it was too bad of Joey to run away, as he had done, without any comment on this extraordinary happening.

It was terrible for this self-elected oracle and centre of the family to feel so very much in the dark. Where could she go to get news? For a minute Alice almost determined to get up, take herself into the next street where, she knew, Will Edzell had his lodging, boldly climb to his door and ring the bell. But the young man would probably be across at the university; besides, she and Joey had shown him no hospitality, established no rights over his friendship. Jessie might know something. She saw him from time to time, Alice understood. Although Jessie, with her new habits of secrecy, had never quite said so. No. She, Alice, had better go to John. Indeed, she had been meaning to go, anyway, ever since there had been news of his younger grandson's accident in Paris. If the weather hadn't been so dreadfully wet, and if her going would not have brought down an anxious scolding from Joey on her head, she would certainly have done so already.

But now? Alice got out of bed with her mind made up. She could count upon her brother having remained at home in this weather. And the situation, surely, she felt, warranted the expense of a taxi all the way out to Bearsden and all the way back.

2

"What are you doing here on a morning like this?"

Alice stood smiling down upon her brother. She had found him sitting in an armchair in the large, draughty dining-room of Lochview by a fire that had newly been piled up, was just then sending up columns of steamy, grey smoke into the chimney, and was giving forth little or no heat. But it was here, she knew, that her brother was mostly to be found after breakfast, doggedly reading his newspaper and enjoying his morning moroseness. "I came out to see *you*, Johnnie. It *is* a frightful morning,

isn't it?" Alice turned to look out for a moment.
Rain was lashing the windows. Trees and evergreen
were bending and dancing in the storm. "Mrs
McNeil took my waterproof to dry just now. And it
was wet only with getting in and out of the taxi."

"You've no right to be wasting your money on
taxis." Her brother grabbed at the *Glasgow Herald*
that looked like falling from his knee.

"I thought you would be so worried and unhappy
about the news from Priestlaw." Here Alice turned
round a dining-room chair and sat as nearly over the
fire as she could put herself, pulling up her skirt as
far as her ideas of propriety would allow her, in the
hope that she might get some heat. "I felt I really
must come and see you. Have you any news of
Freddie's poor boy this morning?"

Old John did not bother to relax his glum expression. He disliked his sister sitting on a chair higher
than his own, looking down upon him in this uncomfortable fashion. But in the main he was glad
enough to see her. "Fred's coming out to see me
today. The boy's much the same. His mother's staying with him. The girl is over in Paris to keep her
company."

Alice sat looking down upon her brother. Knowing him, she saw that he had been upset by his
grandson's accident. And knowing him, she saw, too,
that from his manner of mentioning Freddie's
daughter, he had not yet seen the announcement in
the newspaper he now held in these knotted old
hands. She felt genuinely sorry for him and a little
alarmed at what he might say when she drew his
attention to it. But the taxi was there outside in the

rain ticking up waiting time. And had she not, after all, come out to know before all the others what old John thought of this engagement? She bent over, took the sheets from his hands and folded them at the appropriate place. "You don't seem to have seen that." She pointed a finger.

"What is it, Alice? What are you doing?"

She disregarded his querulousness. "Put on your spectacles, Johnnie. And tell me what you think of that?"

He put them on and sat up, bending his heavy old body forward, the better to read the lines of print she had shown him. She could not see his features thus, but she saw the colour rise on his brow and spread backward beneath the sparse grey hair on the top of his head. For a time he hung in this position but at length he sat back, his bulldog face alarmingly scarlet, and looked at his sister.

Alice turned away, nervously clutching her skirt still higher and gazing down into the grey, rolling smoke. "Well, John?" She forced herself to ask at last. After all, there *was* the taxi.

"Well, what, Alice?"

"What do you think of that?"

"Think? I think that young man's nothing but a rascal! He wants my grand-daughter's money! That's what he wants!"

"But has Rosamond got any money of her own, John?"

"I'm not telling you what the girl has got, Alice. It's none of your business. But there's one thing I *will* tell you. That she's not going to marry him if I can help it!"

"But what can you do, Johnnie? Nowadays young people are so—?"

"Oh? Do you think there's nothing I can do?" And with this, John Edzell retreated into his own anger, refusing to be drawn.

"You will be discussing it with Freddie when he comes to see you today, won't you, dear?" Alice said, making a courageous attempt to induce her brother to yield up still more fodder for family gossip.

"Mebbe I will, and mebbe I'll not."

Alice got up. This was really too bad. "Surely you can trust your own sister, Johnnie," she said, offended.

"Trust you to what? To tell everybody else?"

"Johnnie! How can you be so unkind! And when I bothered to come out on a morning like this! Well, dear, the taxi's waiting. I'll get my waterproof from Mrs McNeil."

But as the taxi splashed its way across the switch-back road back into Anniesland, then down Great Western Road, Alice found herself becoming cheerful. After all, she had got this quite important piece of news to give the family; that John Edzell was shocked by his granddaughter's engagement and would do everything to stop it.

But who was there to tell? And at this time of day? For she must tell someone. She directed the driver to the hotel where her sister Jessie lived.

Alice found Jessie in an iron hard basket chair in the lounge of her hotel before a much better fire than the one left behind at Lochview. Jessie was happily describing the astonishing beauty of certain chrysanthemums, at present to be seen in the

Botanic Gardens, to a lady from England, a new-comer to the hotel, telling her how easy it really was to get to the Botanic Gardens from here, once this dreadful rain was off, of course, and giving her careful instructions about how to go, which glass house to enter, which section of it to go to, and in which corner of that section the astonishing chrysanthemums were to be seen. The lady, who was a nice person, but deaf, sat smiling at Jessie. Since she saw the newcomer bend to give her talkative fellow guest a rain-sodden good morning kiss, the lady's good breeding concluded that they must be intimate friends and thus would prefer to be left alone. So, continuing to smile, she stood up, murmured something about "upstairs" and left them.

3

An hour later, Jessie Edzell turned back into the hotel after seeing her sister to the door. She felt troubled. Simple-hearted she might be, but that did not mean she was insensitive, nor yet disloyal. Being a reader of picture papers only, she had not seen the announcement with which Alice had succeeded in making their brother so angry.

Jessie took her place again by the fire in the deserted lounge, her hands folded primly in her lap. At first she had received Alice's news with innocent pleasure. What could be more delightful than that a clever boy like Will and a beautiful girl like Rosamond should become attached, one to the other? What could be more ideal? What could be more

romantic? But Alice had treated this talk with contempt. Couldn't Jessie see that, as John had said to
her this morning, the young man must be a rascal?
(Well, Johnnie had called him rascal. But it might
be more charitable, mightn't it, to call him—well—
an adventurer?) But, at all events, what right had
Will, a nobody, to trap the affections of a young lady
of position like Frederick Edzell's only daughter?
The thing was absurd. Was there any wonder that
Rosamond's grandfather had burst out that he would
do everything in his power to put an end to the
engagement.

At which Jessie had been really shocked. "Alice!
How do you know John is going to do any such
thing?"

"I know because he told me."

"But what can he do, Alice?"

At this Alice had looked knowing and said:
"What, indeed, Jessie!" Then added in a moment:
"Oh, he's a poor foolish boy, dear. Don't think I
don't feel very, very sorry for him."

Which Jessie, now sitting here thinking things
over, did not, for all her innocence, believe. Then
Alice had gone on about how the family all, in
greater or lesser degree, depended on Adam and
John Edzell Limited, and how this young man's
being the husband of Fred's daughter couldn't be
anything but a bad thing. Jessie could not see any
reason for that either. She only knew that she liked
Will. She clasped her hands tightly together, as now
she sat wondering if there was anything she could
do. The family, she knew, looked upon her as a
foolish old woman. Perhaps she was. She was used to

being considered so. But foolish or clever, Alice had not been able to persuade Jessie's old maid's partisan and romantic heart, that Will Edzell was not an honest young man, who happened quite simply to have fallen in love with his beautiful cousin and that the path of their true love must be made to run as smoothly as possible.

"Terrible morning it's been, Miss Edzell. It's clear now, though. There's a wee blink o' sun. Are ye not thinking of going out for a wee turn?" An untidy denizen of the hotel's lower regions had come up with a bucket of dross, had dropped on her knees before the fire, had smothered all its warmth and was now sweeping the hearth.

"Well, I don't know." Jessie stood up, masking with a smile, as was her habit, this rough disregard of her comfort. "Yes, I think perhaps I should." And as she did so it came to her that it might be kind to run up, though she had never been there before, to Will Edzell's rooms on the chance he might be in and offer him her congratulations. There was no reason why she, at least, should not show her goodwill.

No. Mr Edzell was not at home. At this Jessie had smilingly asked Will's landlady if she had seen this morning's announcement. It was gratifying that the woman shook her head, for it gave Jessie the satisfaction of a long drawn-out and enthusiastic telling.

"And you see," Jessie had concluded, "I'm an aunt of his so, of course, I'm greatly interested. Well, at any rate, he calls me aunt. I'm not an aunt really. You see, Will's grandfather was my oldest brother. No. It would be Will's father, whom I never saw—

12

he lived far away in England—who would be my real nephew, I suppose. Yes. That's right. So Will is only my grandnephew, if you see what I mean. Do you think I might come in and write him a little note?"

Will's landlady had not tried to follow Jessie's talk about relationships. She had merely stood a little dazed, summing up this excitable old lady and deciding that however irresponsibly her tongue might move, she had, presumably, a heart that remained in the right place.

"A note. Did you think I might come in and write one?" Jessie repeated, seeing that her request had not been taken in the first time.

That evening before dinner, Jessie was called from her attic room. She found Will waiting.

"I was passing, Aunt Jessie, and I came in to thank you for the congratulations you left this morning.

Jessie was puzzled by his aspect. Will looked anything but the radiant young lover. Standing there in his rain-splashed waterproof, he seemed dispirited and tired. Still, it was a nasty wet night and probably he had had an exhausting day. "Come in and take off your coat and tell me all about it. This is most exciting! And when did it all happen?"

The inmates of the hotel were gathered round the fire, laughing at each other's forced jokes and awaiting the call to dinner. A young business man, entertaining friends, had a bottle of commercially mixed cocktail. Those who were not his guests were pretending not to notice it.

Jessie and Will sat down away from them on the other side of the room.

He tried to answer her questions as she would

want to have them answered. Yes. Of course it was
exciting, wasn't it? No. They had no plans. Rosamond most unfortunately had had to leave for Paris
three days ago. No. Oliver was no worse, but his
state was still critical and, as Rosamond's father had
promised to send her to her mother, they had both
felt, Will and she, that it was only right she should
go. After all, it couldn't be for long, could it?

The gong sounded.

"Will, why don't you stay and have dinner with
me? It won't be very wonderful and I haven't got
anything to—" here Jessie looked across at the cocktail drinkers. "But if you—" here she halted, lacking
confidence to stress her invitation further. She was
surprised, a little, by his immediate acceptance.

"Thank you, Aunt Jessie. I would like to stay if
you would let me go immediately afterwards. I've
got a pile of work waiting for me."

With some food in him, Will seemed to revive,
Jessie was glad to see. That beguiling, bright smile
of his made its reappearance and he made dutiful
little jokes to amuse her. But it was, as even she
could guess, a brittle performance punctuated by
moments of withdrawing into himself. She continued
to be puzzled. Was it Rosamond's leaving him so
soon after promising to marry him? Was it his work?
Could he possibly know anything about her brother
John's threat? Jessie wished she had the courage to
ask him. The mere telling might help him. She
wished she were not so bad at this kind of thing.
She had never felt so spinsterish, so angular. It came
as a relief when, dinner finished, Will, repeating
that he had work to do, had risen to his feet, excused

himself and left her.

Jessie sat on at her table after the others had gone, oblivious of the hotel waitresses who were now shaking crumbs from the tablecloths, banging the table legs with carpet sweepers and noisily re-laying the tables for breakfast.

The more she thought of Will the more frustration she felt. At other times he had seemed to her so carefree, so fit for himself. But now he was different. She wished she were clever enough to tell just in what way. At this point, perhaps, the boy needed a family to support him, people who could stand behind him and give him advice. And Alice's account of her visit to John? No. It wasn't fair. What right had they to decide he was a rascal? She knew him much better than they did, and—

"Are ye feeling all right, Miss Edzell?"

"Oh? Yes. Thank you. Has everybody else gone?"

"Ye've dropped yer bag. And look at all these pennies!" The girl had bent down to pick up the bag and put back the coins that had fallen from it. "Ye must be goin' to do an awful lot of telephoning or something. There ye are now, dear. That's you." The poor old soul had tears in her eyes, she noticed, as Jessie stood up, thanked her and made to leave the room.

Telephone? At the door of the dining-room Jessie halted. The word had given her an idea. Would it be impossible to telephone Mary at Stronn Island? She could manage local calls in the hotel telephone box fairly well, but even with them, she got fussed and could never be quite sure whether you pressed button A or B. But what on earth did you do for a longer distance? And how, for instance, did you know the amount of money to put in?

"Was there something ye were wanting?"

"I was wondering—would it be very difficult to put a telephone call through to Stronn Island? It's in the sea, quite far away. I don't know how many sixpences—?"

"I could try for you. Have you got the number?"

"Yes. I think I have it on a letter upstairs. That would be very kind of you."

"We could ask the directory."

"No. I'll get the letter. And then I can be quite sure."

Breathless from the long ascent and descent to and from her high bedroom, Jessie stood outside the telephone box while the girl performed the necessary mysteries inside. Once, as they seemed to be taking so long, Jessie opened the glass door to ask if she did not think another shilling would be a good thing. "No, no, Miss Edzell. It's jist these Hielan' post offices." But at length the girl turned, pushed the door open and gave the receiver into Jessie's excited hand.

"Mary? This is Jessie. Jessie Edzell. You sound so far away!"

"It's all right, Jessie. I can hear you. Is that better? What's the excitement? Are you all right? Where are you?"

"I'm not excited, Mary. I'm just in Glasgow." Jessie heard Mary's laugh and wondered what she had to laugh about. But the laugh was reassuring and brought Mary closer. "Mary, did you see the newspaper today?"

"No. There was no boat. Why?"

At this it all came tumbling out. "Because there was an announcement that Will—you know who I mean—young Will Edzell is to be married to Fred Edzell's girl, Rosamond. And Will was here tonight to see me and seemed to me to be looking miserable. I don't know why. The girl has gone to Paris to her brother who has had an accident. It may be that. But I don't know—I don't think so. And Alice told me that John said he would do anything to stop the engagement. That Will was just a rascal. Isn't it dreadful? I feel that somebody must help! But I don't know what to do. It should be such a happy event, shouldn't it, Mary? I don't see why—and fancy thinking that Will was a rascal! Mary! Mary! Are you still there?"

"I'm here, Jessie. But you haven't let me talk much, have you?"

"I'm sorry. I'm so stupid. Mary, is there anything we can do?"

There was a moment's pause at the other end of the line, then the voice came back cheerfully firm. "Oh, yes. I think there's something we can do, Jessie. But I'll have to know far more about it first. So he wants to marry old John's grand-daughter, does he? I wondered about that the last time I saw him. There's the three minutes up. Thanks for telephoning me. You did the right thing. And don't distress yourself about it any more. You'll be hearing from me."

"But Mary, what can we possibly do?"

There was no reply. Mary had not wanted to incur for her the unnecessary expense of another three minutes.

CHAPTER 14

1

"THE plain fact is, Fred, I'm dreadfully worried. We know nothing but good of this young man, in so far as we know him at all. But that isn't very much. How could it be?"

"He behaved very well while we were waiting for news of Oliver, Christine."

"Yes. I know. But one afternoon isn't everything. And his background is so different from Rosamond's, isn't it? I *do* wish they had given themselves time to know each other better. Are you alone in your private office?"

"Of course. Or I wouldn't be speaking to you like this."

"You saw them together before Rosamond left to come here. He spent the night at Priestlaw, she tells me. Would you say they were very much in love?"

"Well—how can I tell? Yes. I should say they were."

"Have you seen your father yet? Is he in town to-day?"

"No. But he telephoned. The announcement was in today's *Herald*. I'm seeing him on my way home tonight. He disapproves."

"Poor Fred!" Christine's dry little laugh of commiseration came to her husband all the way from

Paris. "Oh, I wish I were at home to talk to you about this!"

"I wish you were, Christine. But you say Nol is perking up today? That's the main thing. You may all be home sooner than we think. There's our time up. Take care of yourself. And bless you."

Frederick had a careworn expression as his elder son came into the room. "That was your mother talking from Paris," he said.

"Rose arrive all right?"

"Yes. She was at the hospital seeing Oliver just now."

"How is he?"

"Better today."

"Good. What does mother think of the engagement?"

His father merely shrugged at this. "Look here, Harold," he said, and his voice sounded tired, "your grandfather wants to see me on the way home."

"And so you're obeying the crook of his finger as usual, I suppose? You truckle far too much to that old man, Skipper."

This, too, Frederick answered with a shrug.

"And I suppose, as we're in my car today, I've got to come with you?"

"If you would. Have you much more to do tonight?"

"Letters to sign. That's all. Are you expecting a rough passage with grandfather?"

Frederick looked about him expressionlessly. "You know he blames me for letting Oliver go to Paris. And he doesn't like Rosamond's engagement."

"In fact we're going to have quite a homely little

chat. Right. I'll be ready within half an hour. Will that do?"

2

Harold paced back and forth in the library of Lochview, watching his grandfather and his father as they sat facing each other by the fire. The old man's mind was occupied entirely, it seemed, with what he could only see as the rascality of Will Edzell and the foolish susceptibility of Rosamond. The accident to Oliver and his father's so-called iniquity in letting the boy go to Paris no longer appeared, now that the news was a little better, to occupy his grandfather's mind. Why did his father stand these insulting tirades from the old man? Why did he let him rant like this? What could his grandfather do if they, both of them, simply got up, turned, walked out of the house and left him shouting? His father was a gentle person, but, after all, he was not weak, either with himself or with others. When he must do so, as his son was well aware, Frederick could impose discipline very sharply.

It was not in Harold's make-up to understand how the relationships of the two older men, one to the other, went back into their roots; how his grandfather still felt at liberty to rage at the son he could still at times see as a soft and rather feckless youngster. And how his father, however sick of these tirades, still found a compensation for his weary feelings in assuring himself that it was, in the end, only the old man's unfortunate way of showing concern for his well-being and for the well-being of those who belonged to him.

"But after all, grandfather," Harold said, losing patience, "I don't see why you should lecture the Skipper like this. It's not his doing."

"Your father could stop it!"

"I don't see how. Rosamond and Will have taken things into their own hands."

"Have they? You mean *he's* taken it into his own hands. He's looking for a wife that can keep him. That's what he's looking for!"

"I don't think Will Edzell is that kind of young man at all, father," Frederick found himself saying. For himself, he was still unsure about the wisdom of his daughter's engagement. And his telephone talk with Christine this afternoon had done nothing to reassure him. But old John's unreasonable violence had driven Frederick, for the moment at least, into becoming Will's advocate. And he was prompted to say: "Perhaps it would be a good thing if we could ask the young man to come out here to see you? You might get a better impression of him."

To this the old man said nothing for a time. He merely sat looking gloomily, now at his son, now at his grandson. Yes. The young man, if he had impertinence enough, could come out here if he liked. It would give himself, John Edzell, great pleasure to tell him what he thought of him. "All right," he said at length, much to the surprise of the others. "You can send him here and I'll see him."

"I'll make a point of telling him tomorrow." Harold, albeit uncertainly, felt that his father had scored a diplomatic trick. "It's time we were getting home." He laid a hand on Frederick's shoulder, a gesture which was, in part, one of sympathy.

"No. I've got something else to say to you."

"What is it, grandfather?"

The old man's eyes turned back to fix themselves upon Frederick. "I've given you more than half of all I have already." He spoke slowly, then remained for so long regarding his son without speaking that Frederick felt obliged to say:

"I know, father. It was very good of you."

"Death duties," was the only comment.

Harold stood still now, feeling that something ominous was coming.

"And for the same reason, as you all know very well," the old man went on presently, "I had split most of the other half into three for your children. I suppose you were fool enough to let your son go to Paris on the strength of what was coming to him? Well, you can tell your daughter Rosamond that the papers are drawn up and waiting for my signature. And you can tell her at the same time that it depends on her whether I put pen to paper—and that goes for all three of them—or not."

"But, grandfather, surely—!"

It was typical that Harold should fly up at this, while Frederick, who had been used to threats and will-rattling all his life, should say nothing whatever. Now, and not for the first time, he merely sat looking at his father detachedly, asking himself if he could, anywhere, find within himself a single spark of a son's affection for this hard old man.

"Very well, Harold. *You* can speak to your sister. I don't care who tells her."

Frederick got up wearily. "Yes, time we were getting home" was all he said, looking towards Harold. He had been put through this kind of thing so often, yet it still made him sick at heart.

3

Until his engagement Will had felt that he belonged to no one but himself. But now this, it seemed, was abruptly to be brought to an end. He seemed to belong to everyone. Late last night, after he had got home from dinner with old Jessie, Mary Edzell had telephoned to him from Stronn Island, scolding him for not letting her know the important news sooner, and asking what his plans were.

"I've no plans, Aunt Mary. All I can do now is to sit here and wait."

"When do you expect Rosamond home?"

"I don't know. She may well be in Paris over Christmas. In fact, I don't see how they can get back before it, Oliver being as he is."

"Well, that's only ten days away. You had better think of coming out here to me after all!" Then, as there was no immediate reply to this from Will's end of the telephone: "Will! Will, are you still there? Well? What's to keep you? When can you be free?"

"Early next week, I expect."

"And what are you going to do? Sit with your hands folded waiting for letters from Paris? You can telephone that girl of yours from Stronn and her letters can follow you here. Jessie said you were looking ill. What's wrong with you, anyway?"

"Nothing. I'm all right."

"Just stubborn? Is that it? If I could I would come down to Glasgow and bring you myself! But I've got my people to look after here. Children's Christmas tree from the mainland; we don't grow them here. And things for the old people and all the rest of it. Will, I'm in earnest. I know it can be stormy at this time of the year, but all the same I must see you now."

There had been a warmth and urgency in Mary's voice, which had made him want to accept at once. But he had had a first letter from Rosamond which told him she would be telephoning. He would discuss going to Stronn with her and let Mary know.

And Sam Crabbe's thick voice had come to him, redolent of apology and jovial invitation. "Minnie was giving her mother and me a row just the other day for not having you over long before this, Will. We're quite ashamed of ourselves. But you know how the time slips along. Well, if you can't be definite about when, for the next day or two, just give us a tinkle and drop up for a quick one any time you feel like it."

Even Patrick had sent him a correct little note of congratulation, apologising for neglect and offering hospitality.

And above all, there was that first letter from Rosamond written on the Paris aeroplane. A letter which, since their love was still so new, plucked at his heartstrings. With joy certainly. But with bewilderment and anxiety, too. And too, an obsessive longing for this girl who had shaken his existence.

And now her brother Harold had telephoned before breakfast to ask if he might see him today, and when and where? No. Clearly, Will Edzell, whether he liked it or not, could no longer say he belonged entirely to himself.

4

Harold's reception of Will could almost be called determinedly friendly as he led him across the empty clubroom, offered him a cigarette and called for mid-morning coffee. He was not so blunt that he did not realise the question of Will's going to see old John would have to be approached obliquely. There had been time to remember his grandfather's insult to Mary Edzell at the door of the restaurant while in Will's company and, very rightly, Harold concluded that Will must have resented this for her sake. But the reasons why Will should go to pay his respects and try to put himself into the good graces of Rosamond's grandfather were so strong now, that they must weigh against any dislike Will might have taken to the old man. For—and quite overwhelmingly, as Harold saw it—there was this matter of money. Rosamond and Will just could not afford to do without this further distribution which Harold's grandfather might or might not make. Harold, who, as a man of business, knew his family's resources, was aware that it would be a very useful sum indeed. And what about losing his own share of it? And

Oliver's? No. If the penurious lecturer who had attached himself to his sister could not be brought to see reason and be prepared to do all he could to bring round the old boy, then really he was out of his senses. Still, tact, Harold felt, since he did not yet know his prospective brother-in-law well enough, had better be used until at least he saw how far Will was likely to be amenable.

"Coffee all right?" he asked affably. "Sure you won't have a drink?"

"Not at half-past eleven. I've got to go back and do some work."

Harold had confined himself, while they had awaited the coming of the tray, to family gossip. Rosamond's arrival. Christine's telephone call. What she had said about Oliver's condition. Details of the aeroplane crash. Regrets, for Will's sake, that Rosamond should have to leave home just now. Fears that she might not get back before Christmas. His guest was taking this with the right amount of friendly interest and concern. But now he could see that Will was wondering why he had been brought here.

"My father and I went out to see my grandfather yesterday evening," Harold said.

Will waited.

"The old boy has been worrying about my brother quite a lot."

As an answer seemed expected of him, Will said: "You would be able to reassure him."

"Yes. He's fond of us all in his way. Although you might not believe it."

"I daresay."

All this was not very promising but Harold felt he must get on. "We were talking about your engagement to Rosamond, Will."

"And?"

"Well, you know how slow old people are at getting used to new ideas."

"I'm not sure that I do. And do I take it from this that he doesn't like his grand-daughter being engaged to me?"

"Oh, it's just because he's old and not very—what shall I say?—flexible. I've often seen grandfather like that before."

"What has it got to do with *him*? Who has asked *him*?"

"No. If you'll take my advice, Will, I wouldn't take it like that. If it's only for Rosamond's sake. He'll come round all right, I expect."

"He can come round, or stay round the other way for all I care!"

Harold laid a hand on Will's knee. "My dear man! Surely this is unreasonable! The old man is Rosamond's grandfather. You can't want to make her unhappy by starting a family row first thing." As Will had no reply to this, Harold felt he could go on. "As a matter of fact, one of the reasons I asked you here this morning was to tell you that grandfather has asked you out to see him." Harold held up a hand to prevent Will's quick reply and continued forcefully: "Will, it's in your hands whether grandfather accepts your engagement to my sister or not."

"I've told you I don't give a damn what he does! I've lived independently all my life and I'm not starting to bow the knee to anybody now!"

"But, after all, what have you got against grand-father? Was it his rudeness to Mrs Adam Edzell the other day?"

"Wasn't that enough?"

"Will, let me assure you it was something quite different that had annoyed him."

"That may be." Will got up. "Is that all you have to say to me?" Then, as though recollecting that some politeness was due to Rosamond's brother: "I'm sorry, Harold. But Mrs Adam is my friend."

"Listen! Rosamond is going to be your wife! No, please, Will! Sit down again. I've something else you've got to know." Harold waited until Will had seated himself reluctantly. "When we saw grand-father last night, he told us that—oh, I suppose because of death duties—he's dividing up the remain-ing half of his estate between Oliver, Rosamond and myself. And, you see, if you—I mean everything seems to have gone through except the final sign-ing up. If Rosamond—well, it's really in *your* hands."

Now Will had stood up again and was looking down at him with eyes that were narrowed with anger. "Are you sitting there trying to say to me that I'm marrying your sister for her money? I've always hated money! We—we haven't even said the word to each other yet!"

"My dear good man! You'll have to, sooner or later! That's all very fine and large. You and Rose are not children! You can't live on air!"

"I can earn my living as I've always done! We'll both have to do with that!" Will held out his hand. "I'm going to get my hat and coat!"

13

"No. Don't run away. I'll come with you and help you to find them."

It was outside on the steps of the club that they finally parted. Again Will held out his hand. His temper, Harold guessed, had begun to cool a little.

"I'll be writing to Rosamond today," Will said. "And I'll tell her I've seen you."

"Right. Well, anyway, thanks for coming into town." Harold stood watching his receding back until—still with a slight limp—he disappeared into the crowd, then he turned to get his own overcoat. Better report this talk to the Skipper. He might be able to help.

"Free for lunch, Skipper? I've seen Will this morning. He came down to the club."

"Well?"

"He was quite unreasonable."

Frederick looked worriedly at his wristwatch. "I'm sorry about that. I can't lunch with you, but I've half an hour now. Tell them outside that we're not to be disturbed."

Harold came back, lit a cigarette and took a chair on the other side of his father's desk.

"And in what way was he unreasonable?" Frederick asked. Harold's usually cheerful, bluff features now expressed concern. His father found himself wondering if Harold had been abrupt and tactless as he so easily might be.

"Said he had no intention of going out to Bearsden to see grandfather."

"Oh, why?"

Harold shook his head. "Will seems attached to

Mrs Adam Edzell. He still resents what grandfather said to her."

Frederick turned to look at the view of roofs and chimney pots outside his window, then he turned back to say: "We were all ashamed about that, weren't we?"

"But at least Rosamond apologised." His father had, now and then, a way of seeing everyone's point of view, Herald reflected. A habit that was not always helpful. "Oh, we all know grandfather's an old monster—"

"Not quite, Harold. You can't say—"

"Well, as near as makes no difference, Skipper. But so far as our family is concerned we can't get past him. This division of what he still has being held up because he doesn't like the man his granddaughter is going to marry is frightful, of course. I mean, this using it as a lever to make Rosamond drop Will."

"I've had many a threat like that from your grandfather."

"Poor Skipper!"

Frederick smiled wearily and once more looked out of the window. "I've survived them," he said.

"But suppose he carried this one out? After all, I've a good idea what this division would mean. To say the least, it's a sum that would be very useful to any one of us."

"Haven't you got enough money already, Harold?"

At this Harold chose to grin broadly. "Has anyone ever enough money? No, honestly, Skipper. Just think. It would allow Rosamond and Will to marry without any worry. And what about Nol? What kind of health is he going to be left with?"

Frederick said gravely: "Yes. There's Nol."

Harold was pleased to note that he had touched his father upon a very vulnerable spot. "After all," he said in a moment, "I take it that Will is not quite a fool. It's not impossible to get round grandfather. *We're* not asking him to drop Rosamond or anything. All he's got to do is to go out and see the old boy and try to bring him round. If he can't, he can't. But I do think it's up to him to try. For Rosamond's, for his own, for all our sake's."

"I wish I had your mother at home to talk to," Frederick said, with what seemed to his son to be maddening irrelevance.

"Well, she's not," Harold said testily. "Skipper, look here. You do see my point, don't you. I know you keep seeing everyone else's as well, but—"

"I see your point, Harold." Again Frederick looked out of the window. "I wonder what Rosamond would think," he said abstractedly.

But now he had given Harold an idea. "Why shouldn't I write Rose and tell her everything, Skipper? Don't you think that's a good idea? She can be quite practical if she tries. And she has every reason to be now. She's bound to be thinking of ways and means. It's up to her to deal with this temperamental young man of hers. Don't you think it is?"

Frederick turned from the window to look across the table. He was recalling his thoughts, though his son could not be sure from where. "Yes," he said. "I think it would be a good idea to tell Rosamond."

CHAPTER 15

1

ROSAMOND put down the receiver, thanked the switchboard girl and left the telephone room. For no particular reason—to get a breath of fresh air, perhaps—she crossed the entrance of the large, impersonal French hotel, lively, even on a Sunday afternoon, with a come-and-go of visitors, braided porters, white-gloved pageboys and obsequious reception clerks. A doorman swung the revolving glass door for her.

She had noticed rain on her sitting-room window as she left it to go downstairs in order to make her telephone call to Will in Scotland. But now, coming outside she found the boulevard lit for a moment by a stray shaft of weak December sunshine. The bare branches of trees on either side of it were actually casting watery shadows. The air was surprisingly mild.

More than one passer-by turned his head to look at this girl so deep in thought, as she strode slowly away from the hotel, her hands thrust into the pocket of her tweed jacket. A beautiful, elegant creature, American surely, or perhaps Scandinavian, with that sleek, fair hair.

Will. She had been glad to speak to him, of course. And yet, in a way, she wished she had not. Distance had somehow changed the quality of his voice. The notes, bass yet boyish. The light, North Country flavour, that now could mean so absurdly much to her, had been, indeed, distinguishable, but not as they should be. Instead of bringing him nearer, their talk had somehow set him, emotionally, further away from her.

"But Will, tell me, darling, how are you really?"

"Grand."

"I don't believe it."

He had laughed at this. "Well, anyway, a bit end-of-termish. When we are married you'll get to know what that means."

"I shall feed you on things to keep your strength up."

"I won't take them. I hate coddling. Rosamond, listen. Mrs Adam Edzell wants me to go out to Stronn Island for Christmas. Is there really no chance of your getting home?"

"Darling! I can't see it. It's—it's cruel for both of us. But we decided to be sensible about that, didn't we? No, Will. I most definitely think you should go. I should feel so much happier if you had someone to look after you. You like Mrs Edzell, don't you? Besides, why should I have the family prejudice now? If *you* like her, so should *I*. Will, I want you to go. Do you hear me?"

"It's a day further away from you."

"Rubbish! I've got a pencil here. What's her telephone number?"

Rosamond stopped her pacing for a moment and looked about her, conscious of being in Paris alone without Will. When she came here with him, she reflected, they would go to an hotel she knew on the Left Bank that was cosy and old-fashioned, but not too old-fashioned, and had, of course, every necessary luxury, as well as the right atmosphere. It would be a wonderful Paris for them. Something quite different from this. For in the better districts on the Right Bank everything could look so very much alike. The well-built properties, the handsome shops—characterless, once you had got over their Frenchness—the trees, the kiosk on the corner. These stretching thoroughfares could be so repetitive. She turned to go on walking.

And just now on the telephone Will had told her of having met Harold. She could not quite make out what kind of meeting it had been, nor what exactly had been its purpose. Will had sounded strange about that. She had, of course, quite understood Will's reluctance to go and see her grandfather. The restaurant incident was only too clear in her mind. And yet his defensive refusal nagged at her somehow. She wished she knew more about it. It had been so difficult on the telephone. If only she were at home, she could, she felt, manage Will. He was a professor in the making, an intellectual. She could not expect him to grasp practicalities. In the life they were going to lead together the practicalities must fall to herself.

She looked about her. The sun had gone in and there were spots of rain again. She was surprised at how, in her abstraction, she had wandered so far. Rosamond turned about abruptly and made for shelter before the rain began in earnest.

2

"Here's a letter from Harold to me!" Rosamond turned back to her mother who had been waiting while she got their keys and asked for letters. It was late in the afternoon of the next day. They had been visiting Oliver. "This one's from Will." She put it into her coat pocket. She would read it in the solitude of her bedroom. "It's not often that Harold does me the honour."

"Nor his mother either," Christine said, preceding her daughter into the lift. "I wonder what it's about?"

To please her Rosamond tore it open as they travelled upwards.

"My dear Rosie,

"I've been having a spot of bother with that young man of yours. I've discussed the matter with the Skipper and we both decided that it would be a good thing to write to you, as the one best able to deal with him."

The lift had arrived at their floor and the boy had opened the doors.

"It's not too late to have tea, is it, mother? If you'll ring for it I'll come in a moment."

"What's Harold writing about?"

"I'll tell you at tea."

Christine had to wait some time before her daughter appeared. At once she saw that Rosamond was troubled. But, having some experience as a mother, she forbore from putting direct questions. "I was nearly coming to look for you," she said casually. "Nothing wrong?"

"*I'm* all right."

"Will all right?"

"He's all right too, I suppose."

"You suppose, Rosamond?"

Rosamond took her brother's letter from her pocket. "I think the best thing you can do is to read that for yourself, mother."

Presently Christine pulled off her spectacles, put down the letter and looked up at the girl who was now walking about this hotel sitting-room, so conventionally French, with its brocades, its loop-laced curtains, its gilt and its marble table tops. She was as worried now as her daughter. Engagements to marry, as Christine's own calm temperament had always told her, should, of course, be well thought out things. After all, you had to found the rest of your life upon them. And now—and not for the first time—she wondered if Rosamond had given much thought to foundations. The girl's heart had, it appeared, been taken by surprise by this unlikely cousin. Not that she didn't see Will's attractions, had not, especially that Sunday, liked him very much indeed. But his merely being the kind of person he was seemed to Christine to raise all kind of difficulties. She had spoken no more than the truth when she had told her husband on the telephone the other day that she was dreadfully worried. And now, already, the young man was making tiresome difficulties for all of them. What had she better say?"

"Well at any rate, you've got to agree with Harold that grandfather is an old monster!" the girl said swinging round in her walk and addressing her mother angrily.

"Rose! I haven't said anything yet! Give me time! No. I think it would be a very good thing if your grandfather made that division now. First of all for Oliver, of course. And certainly for you and Will. Oh, I daresay your father wouldn't see you both stuck but—"

"It's this using it as a means of—. What has he got against Will anyway? It's that that's so monstrous! Can't you see, mother?"

"My dearest child! Will you calm yourself!"

"I *love* Will, mother! I want to be his wife! I want to be everything to him! I never dreamt another human being could suddenly become so much to me! I want to help him, manage him, if you like, build him up! I never believed that anything so wonderful—" But here Rosamond's tirade was drowned in tears.

"Rose, darling! I've every kind of sympathy with you! I see it was horrid of the old man. Still, you know very well that I myself have not always had it easy with your grandfather. I've been hurt countless times by things he did to your father. And I've been hurt on my own account, often enough too! But you can't say that we—all of us—haven't done very well on the whole. Can you? This will work out all right. You'll see." Here Christine stopped, realising that she had merely been talking for the sake of saying anything to calm her daughter. It had astonished her that Rosamond should show so much feeling. She was amazed and troubled at the girl's outburst and what it had laid bare. Was it wise, was it reasonable that she should be throwing herself so completely at the feet of this unknown young man? She had talked of building him up. But would he, would any man, want to be taken thus in hand? Want to be ruled by a wilful girl, even if that girl adored him?

"Darling," she said presently, forcing a smile. "I wish you were a tiny girl again so that I could just pick you up and take you on my knee." She put on her spectacles and once again took up the letter. "Sit down and drink your tea and let me have another look at this." She wished Frederick had written to Rosamond instead of Harold. It was in her husband's nature to soften the edge of things, as it was in her son's to deal in hard outlines. And yet, they had, each of them, it seemed, agreed that it was Rosamond's business to make Will see reason. Christine could not disagree with that. And the girl, when she had swallowed her anger, would surely agree too.

At length she put down the letter. "You know, I think on re-reading this that perhaps they've been taking your grandfather's threat too seriously. Time and time again we've known his bark to be worse than his bite. I think you might write to that boy of yours and tell him so. We haven't talked much about Will together yet, have we? But if I can judge him at all, I should say he could be very clever with people if he tried. He's attractive. And if you'll allow me to say so, I think he could be politic and charming if it suited him. Remember how he was in your grandfather's garden in the autumn."

"All of which means, I suppose, that I should order Will to see grandfather whether he wants to or not."

"Well? What do *you* think? You talk of helping him. And I sincerely hope his ideas of being helped fit in with your ideas of helping. That's as may be. But anyway, as we know that Will is not rich, this money your grandfather talks of dividing couldn't fail to be a help to you both. And darling, what about Oliver? Surely it is not too much to ask of Will to try to make his peace with a foolish old man?" Christine's eyes followed Rosamond as she again got up moodily, went to the window, thrust back a net curtain and stood, watching the movement on the broad, rain-glittering street.

Presently she turned. "Do you think I should wait until I'm home again, or do you think it would be best to write to him about it?"

"Surely that's for you to say."

"By what they said at the hospital this afternoon we may well be here with Nol for some time yet."

"You make me feel dreadful, keeping you in Paris like this."

"Will understands all that, mother. No. I think I'd better write to him. And tell him to be a little more realistic."

3

It was early afternoon on one of those rare, green winter days among the islands, when the sky is clear and the sun shines at its brightest during all of the short day, when the Atlantic, weary of heaving and raging along the cliffs, decides to lie at peace, when blue smoke rises straight up from white cottages whence come cheerful noises—children's shouts, the barking of dogs, the cackle of cocks and hens.

There would be no doubt of the steamer being able to call at Stronn Island this afternoon, Mary Edzell reflected with satisfaction, as she looked from a window of the lodge across the pale calm waters. Indeed, there it was already, a black spot in the distance, a spot which would presently take life and shape with foam at its bows and smoke rolling back from its funnel. The men, she was pleased to see, were already down at the jetty, her friend Sandy among them, preparing to man the ferry boat that would go out to meet it.

Mary felt pleasantly excited now. Fetching her old cloth hat and her inverness cape, she went to see what her man Murdo Macdonald was doing, if he had got out the handcart and was ready to come. For there should be quite a load for the lodge. Will's baggage for one thing. That wouldn't be much. But, in addition to the usual boxes of provision, there would be presents for the islanders who were her special care, and also, she hoped, a small Christmas tree and toys and decorations to hang upon it.

Now, in half an hour more, the island's boat was lying off waiting to meet the incoming steamer as she slid in near to the land, her engines still for the moment, steam mixing white with the belching black above her. Now the little crowd on the jetty could hear the bell signalling the engines to go into reverse as she threatened to overshoot her halting place. Now the men were pulling at their oars to bring their boat alongside. Now the rope was thrown and the one or two who were coming ashore were stepping down.

Mary raised a hand to Will who, as he settled himself in the stern of the open boat, recognised the squat figure standing there on the jetty among the island children. Now the boat was being piled high with packages and luggage, Mary's Christmas tree and at last the mail bag. Now the rope was thrown off, the bell clanged again, and the island boat with its Christmas cargo was left bobbing in the foaming wake of the steamer.

"Is that a tree they're bringing?" a tiny boy beside Mary asked her timidly.

"Yes. I think it is, Colin. Who'll be wanting a tree, I wonder?"

An older child looked up at her with a knowing look of delight.

4

It was the letter with the French stamp, Mary decided, that was at the root of the trouble. It had come ashore with Will in the mailbag, and had been duly delivered along with other letters at the lodge later that evening.

Will had been his old self, excited and pleased to find himself back on the island, delighted to renew acquaintance with the lodge, the island and everything he found there. He had been about the house looking at this and that, going into the kitchen to greet Mrs Macdonald and the dogs, then, he had stood outside looking about him; across the green flat at the little white village; at the ragged, snow-blue shapes of the mountains, there, far away across a sea now turning slate colour as the afternoon breeze troubled its surface; up at the Hog's Snout, now beginning to turn to a dark outline as the early winter sun sank behind the island. He was behaving, Mary told herself happily, as though he had come home.

She had scarcely expected this behaviour from him. It was a little unusual, surely, in one so newly affianced, then forced to endure so quick a separation. She had expected to find him more serious, perhaps, more mature. At tea, responding to her request for news, he had talked of Rosamond and her family, entertaining her with his talk. Making it too much of a performance, it might be, but obviously enjoying the telling.

Then towards dinner the letter had arrived. She had given it to him, the clouds had gathered and there they remained during the next days. Will had been good and docile enough. She had taken him out with her to help with her Christmas charities. He had helped too, with the tree and even, at his own suggestion, impersonated Father Christmas in the island schoolroom. But it was now as though some trouble had descended, or perhaps some resentment he could not shake off. Other letters reached him from France, several at a time, as the steamer did not call each day. And on Christmas morning, Mary, having persuaded him to make a telephone call to Paris, was told that Rosamond was well and that her brother was now really improving. But these things did not serve to dispel the dispirited brooding that had, so unaccountably, fallen on that first evening.

If Will would only talk, only let her help him. Was he worrying over ways and means for his marriage? Had something happened to make the future difficult? Or had that first letter quite simply brought upon him a fit of sharp love sickness? For some days after Christmas Mary worried over these things. Will was not her son. And even if he had been, yet still she would have feared to force his confidence. But now as the days went by she told herself that she was tired of it; that she had brought him out here seeking to do her best for him. But what best could she do, when she did not know what it was that troubled him?

5

At last one evening she decided to go into the attack. They had been sitting in the light of a high-piled fire of peat and driftwood listening to a symphony on the gramophone; Will's Christmas present to herself; an attempt to convert her to classical music. Mary found she was not listening very much. And the young man there, staring abstractedly into the fire was not, she guessed, listening any more than she was. The movement of the symphony ran to its end and he got up to change the record.

"No, Will. Don't play any more just now. I want to talk to you."

He turned, came back and sat down.

"Will, you're quite different from what you were here in the autumn. There's something wrong with you. I wish I knew what it was. Something happened to you on the first evening you came here. If it was anything I did, I wish you would tell me."

"You did nothing whatever, Aunt Mary."

"Well, I can't ask you to tell me what it was if you don't want to. But surely you must see it isn't very fair to me to come over here and behave like a mourner at a funeral. I expected a very different young man. To tell you the truth, I've been wondering if I was foolish in letting myself get so fond of you." A little bewildered smile of thanks for these last words encouraged her to go on: "Is it that girl of yours? If you're missing her so badly, I might buy you a ticket for a quick trip to Paris."

"No!"

"I'm sorry. I was only wondering how I could help."

"Thanks. And I'm sorry if I've been queer."

She could only shake her head and smile at this then sit waiting, watching his troubled face lit by the flames. For now she saw that he had something to tell her and she was in hopes that she had succeeded in stirring him enough to tell it.

"The Priestlaw people want me to kowtow to that old man." He had turned upon her angrily.

"Old man, Will?"

"Old John Edzell. The one who was so damned uncivil to you!"

"I had forgotten all about that."

"Well, I hadn't."

It pleased her that he should insist so determinedly upon being her champion, but her only response was a gesture of brushing aside such nonsense. "All the same, hadn't you better go and see him? He's Rosamond's grandfather."

"I don't care."

"What does Rosamond say about it?"

"She wants me to go." He turned away from Mary and resumed his gazing at the fire.

"I would have thought," Mary hazarded in a moment, "that you would want to please her."

He turned round on her again. "I've no intention of being anybody's flunkey! I've been reared independent. And I'll go on being independent."

It was on the tip of Mary's tongue to say: "Well it seems to me, young man, that you're marrying into the wrong family for that!" But she merely said: "But what has that to do with paying your respects to the girl's grandfather?"

Now she was given the story of Will's meeting with Harold. And how old John Edzell was seeking to force Rosamond to drop Will, seeking to prise them apart, by an appeal, as it seemed to Will, to the girl's love of money.

Wondering what kind of girl Rosamond really was, Mary asked: "What did she say in her letter?"

He hung back as though shamefaced for a time. "Thinks at least I should try with him," he said presently. "Says she must agree with her father and Harold. And we haven't yet had time even to talk between ourselves about how we're going to live. But whatever we decide, I'm not truckling to that old man!"

Mary looked at Will sharply and chanced a question. "Suppose she were to drop you if you didn't?"

"She would never do that!"

"I hope not. But, Will, what would you feel if she did?"

He sprang up, thrust his hands deep into his pockets and stood looking down at her excitedly. "Aunt Mary, it would break my heart!"

His voice was trembling and his eyes were shining in the firelight. So he wanted this girl? There was no doubt about that. But Mary decided to appear to take his words lightly, laughing a little, consoling laugh. "Then we'd better see that doesn't happen, Will."

Murdo Macdonald appeared with a decanter and a siphon, set it down and went away again.

"There. Have your whisky. I'm glad you've told me. Now at least I know what's been worrying you."

6

The days that followed this conversation gave Mary Edzell much to think about. She had forced the confidence of this difficult young man and the result left her puzzled. But one satisfaction she had. Will seemed much happier for having told her his troubles and seemed too, now that the way was opened, quite ready to talk about them.

She felt touched, of course, by his strong bias towards herself. And remembering the affront she had suffered from the older Edzell family, she had no reason to be tender towards them. Indeed, she could not, in her heart, withhold her love and admiration from Will for the stand he was taking for her sake.

But was it sensible? Were not Frederick Edzell and his son Harold quite right in advising Rosamond to tell Will it was better to make his peace with that detestable old man?

As she thought about it, the behaviour of John Edzell outside the restaurant came back to Mary in all its grossness. And her memory, too, of how it had occurred to her that it was within her power to use her greater share in the family business as an instrument of revenge. She had dismissed the idea as crude. A thing born of a foolish resentment.

Yet now, as she went on thinking, other arguments came to her. Her fortune was, after all, her late husband Adam Edzell's fortune. Edzell money that would, had she been shown any affection by them, already have been willed back to the Edzells. Now here, under her roof, was an Edzell who *did* show her affection, who had never judged her except by his own standards, and who, in addition, was to be married into her husband's family. Why indeed should she not, and at once, arrange an income for Will? An income large enough to give him a triumphant independence over the others, so that his quick pride should be protected even from the very shadow of their condescension. And further, why not let it thereafter be known that she had willed to himself and to his future children all her remaining worldly possessions? She was a lonely woman, no longer young. What better could she do than attach this young man to her?

And now, as she turned the matter this way and that in her mind, yet another thought came to her. Would Will, with his almost maniacal independence, with the equalitarian ideas to which he had been raised, want to have an income and the prospect of a fortune thrust upon him? Now that she was beginning really to know him, she found herself wondering.

CHAPTER 16

1

AT the end of January it was at length decided that Oliver might, all due care being taken, be flown home. The body burns he had received had not, the French doctors judged, been deep enough permanently to affect his health, and the danger of other, more obscure injury, had receded as the weeks in Paris had gone by.

Everyone was delighted, of course, beginning with the sufferer himself who, now at the start of a somewhat prolonged convalescence, was anxious to spend the first part of it at least at Priestlaw.

"And I expect you're pining to get home to that strange young man of yours," he said to Rosamond who, standing by his bedside, had just been told the good news.

"Of course, Nol. Wouldn't you if you were me?"

"Thank God my hands and face are not marked, anyway," Oliver said irrelevantly. "Your handsome brother will look very much as usual."

"That *will* be nice for us all," she had replied in the language that was expected of her. "But why do you call Will strange?"

Oliver turned his head on the pillow to look at her. "Oh, I didn't mean anything, really. I like what I've seen of Will. But that's been very little, remember." He pondered for a moment, then went on: "What I do mean about him, I suppose, is that I don't quite understand his idiom. I can understand the big business world, because I was born to it. And I tell myself I can understand the world that wants to paint or write or make music, because I think I'm meant for it. But I'm not sure I understand Will's world, the world that only has knowledge for its stock-in-trade. A world where the frills don't, perhaps, count for very much. Oh, I don't know. Am I talking nonsense?"

"No. I see what you mean. But just because of that, people like Will need quite a lot of managing, I think. Oh, I'm all for good brains and his having his head in the intellectual clouds. But, as his wife, I want to be able to tell him where to put his feet, when he pulls his head out of these clouds for a moment and looks down at me."

"And if he doesn't want to be told?"

"Why does he want to marry me then?"

Oliver looked up at his beautiful sister objectively. He could think of quite a number of other reasons. "Well," he said presently, "good luck to you. You'll be glad to see him again anyway."

Yes. She would be glad to see the slim young man who had become so much her obsession; for whom she had longed so much that her first happiness had almost taken on an edge of pain.

2

Rosamond was not, however, much preoccupied with thoughts of Will's intellectual equipment as, some days later, the evening plane from London came down out of the winter starlight through the rain clouds that hung over Glasgow. She was in the grip of a high excitement as now the strung-out points of light swaying, moving and steadily rising nearer, told her they were coming in over a great city.

She found herself grateful for her brother's presence as at length they sat waiting in the standing plane until the other passengers filed out, one after the other, down the steps and into the drizzling night. For in the empty aeroplane, it had been decided, Oliver, who still moved with some difficulty, could most easily be supported out. It was a few minutes of respite before seeing Will, who must surely be there waiting to greet her along with her father and Harold. She was aware that she had longed to see him so much that now she was afraid to do so. It was a refuge that Oliver was taking the limelight.

"They've sent a chair across for you. That's good," her mother said as they slowly followed him down the steps. "There's your father beside it."

No. Nobody was looking at Rosamond.

"Hello, Nol," was all her father could trust himself to say as the trio at length reached the bottom of the steps.

"Oliver has stood the journey splendidly," Christine said, giving her husband a firm, businesslike peck. "How are you, Fred? Let's get in out of the rain." Her mother was being deliberately crisp with the easily emotional Skipper.

"Harold's waiting inside," Frederick said as they

moved off across the tarmac.

Rosamond could not for her life have asked if Will was with them, but almost at once her father obliged her.

"And Will too, Rosamond. He telephoned today to ask what plane you were coming by, so Harold picked him up. Harold's got his own car."

Rosamond was glad of the rain and the comparative darkness. Really, it was absurd to find oneself so intense about anybody. Yet, as they came into the air shed, there he was, looking much as usual beside her brother—this beloved stranger round whom, in the last weeks, her thoughts had made so many images—his hands thrust into the pocket of his old raincoat. So that was the flesh and blood Will again? The man who now, hat in hand, was disengaging himself from the crowd and coming towards them.

"Rosamond!"

"Will!"

They had met and he had given her a perfunctory kiss of greeting. For they were, neither of them, of those who allow themselves public demonstration. But since the young man's lean face was flushed and his eyes were shining: and since the girl had tears on her cheeks each was content with the other.

"Will, can't we go and have dinner somewhere together?" They stood isolated, while the others still occupied themselves with the invalid. "Harold can give us his car and go home with the others."

"Would that be wise, Rosamond? Haven't you had a long day? I've promised your father to come down tomorrow morning for the weekend. Aren't you dead beat with all you've had to do today?"

"Yes. I suppose I'm dead beat. But I don't care."

"But *I* care. You're going to look after yourself and go home now. I'll be with you in the morning."

3

It was on the Monday following that Mrs Adam Edzell arrived at what Sam Crabbe had once called his Aunt Jessie's twopence-ha'penny hotel. Since Christmas, the idea of making Will her heir had continued to grow in her mind. The affection between herself and this somewhat difficult young man had by no means diminished over the days he had been with her on Stronn. An affection that was, perhaps, hard quite to account for.

At all events, in the feelings, in the emotions of this elderly woman, Will Edzell was already—although she did not yet altogether admit this to herself—her adopted son. She had meant to ask him to come to see her. But on an impulse—because they would not be interrupted by Jessie's inconsequent talk, perhaps—she decided to take him by surprise.

"Good heavens, Aunt Mary! You!"

"Yes, me. I flew down today. It was like summer this morning. So I took the chance to come. Are you glad to see me? You're looking at me as if I were a ghost! Am I interrupting something?" She looked at his paper-strewn table and at the masculine untidiness of this cheerful, worn room.

"Nothing that matters. I don't think I've ever been so glad to see anybody, before."

She looked at him wondering, then let her face

relax into a smile. "Nonsense! What would the girl in that photograph say if she heard you talking like this?"

"I say, Aunt Mary. Do sit down." He took her coat from her. "Can I get you something?"

"Nothing." Mary settled herself comfortably. "Has Rosamond come home?" she asked.

"On Friday, as I wrote you. I spent the weekend at Priestlaw in the bosom of the family."

She knew Will fairly well by this time. But now, instead of finding the pleased young lover she had expected, she found herself at a loss to understand his nervous, almost exaggerated pleasure at seeing her—as though, somehow, she were a straw to be grasped at. And why had there been overtones more of contempt than of humour in his voice as he had spoken the words "bosom of the family?" She allowed herself a cheerful laugh. "It's a bosom you'll need to get used to, Will."

Her words were answered by a sombre, distracted "yes".

For a time she sat looking at him. "Come on, Will," she said at length, "out with it! There always seems to be something I've got to be told these days."

He took his time before he said: "Old John Edzell came down to Priestlaw to see Oliver yesterday."

"John Edzell!" So Will had been forced to see the old man whether he wanted to or not! "And so what, Will?"

"Well? From what I told you at Stronn, what would you expect?"

"I'm asking you to tell me what happened."

Will again took time to emerge from the gloom before he spoke. "He arrived yesterday afternoon. His man drove him down. He wasn't expected."

"And what did he do?"

"Everyone was in the room when he came in. Frederick Edzell did what he could. He told the old man who I was and reminded him he had seen me before. I wasn't going to make any trouble. I held out my hand. He looked past me without taking it and sat down and began to ask Oliver Edzell about himself. Then Rosamond said something like: 'Grandfather, you know I'm engaged to Will?' He looked straight at me and said: 'You think you're engaged to my grand-daughter, do you?'" Will stopped.

And again Mary had to prod him: "What happened then?"

"I walked straight out of the room and out of the house and refused to come back until the old man had driven away. If I had had my motor bike, I would have come back here."

"What did Rosamond do?"

"Came out after me."

"Poor girl!"

Will looked at Mary unhappily. "It wasn't *my* fault. What could I be expected to do?"

"Weren't you sorry for her?"

He nodded gloomily.

"I should hope you were! And after that?"

Will considered for a moment. "After that nothing much. They all did their best, I suppose. Tried to say he was old and this and that."

"In fact, after that you had a nice dreary evening together?"

"That's about it."

4

For a time Mary sat considering. Will had, she realised, given her the outline of what must have been a very unpleasant happening, for himself, for Rosamond and—if they had any feelings whatever—for Rosamond's family. She wished she had had time to get to know this girl who must have been so badly hurt on Will's account. But now it seemed to her that the young man was in immediate need of all the support she could give him. "Will," she began at length, "I've come here to Glasgow to talk to you."

"To me?"

Suddenly and unaccountably in the face of what she had to tell him, Mary Edzell felt shy. "Yes. I had meant to think about this a little longer, but after what you've just told me, I feel you must hear what I intend to do." Here she stopped but presently went on again. "Will, I'm lonely and I'm rich and I'm getting on in life. And I happen to be very fond of you."

The colour had risen in Mary's face as she spoke. Now, as the young man began to guess what was coming, a flush spread over his own.

"Will, I want to give you an income and make you the heir to all I have."

"No! No! Aunt Mary!"

She looked at him astonished. "Now why?"

"Because I'm like that! Because what you want to do will take away my freedom! I'm used to working for what I spend! It's the way my father brought me up!"

She understood his sense of shock. She had even foreseen it. "Not a bad way, Will. I was a working woman too, once. But don't be too hard on yourself—or me. If it's only for that girl's sake, you'll have to change your ideas. Whether you like it or not, you've decided to marry into a family where the value of money counts. If it's only to protect yourself and her you must think over what I've been saying."

"I sometimes feel it would have been better if I had never met Rosamond Edzell," he said glumly.

"Don't go into a pose, Will! Don't talk that bitter, theatrical nonsense to me! You would think I was trying to ruin you instead of handing you and your girl a fortune!" Mary got up. And now, standing on her feet looking down at the brooding figure in the opposite chair, her voice softened. "I respect your independence, Will. But you had better take time to think over what I want to do for you."

He looked up at her uncertainly. "You've taken me by surprise, Aunt Mary," he said.

She went to him and laid a hand on his shoulder. In this emotional moment she was taken by a strong impulse to kiss him as though he were a beloved, sulky child. But at once she decided this was altogether too sentimental. "I know I have, Will. But by the time you've slept a night on it, I think you'll be glad to accept. I must say I think you're a strange boy. Now I'm going back to your Aunt Jessie."

"I'll take you."

The rain had come on. Will held her umbrella over her as they walked the short distance together almost in silence.

5

Glad to be back and out of the rain which, on his way home, had become heavier, Will climbed upstairs, took out his latchkey and let himself in. In the dim hallway he took off his hat and raincoat, shook the drops from them and hung them on a peg. Now he crossed to the fire and took from its place of honour on the centre of the mantelpiece the large photograph that Rosamond had given him. For a long time he held it in his hand, staring at it until at last he realised he was not really looking at it at all, that he was entirely preoccupied by the turmoil of his own thoughts.

And turmoil it was. He put the photograph back, flung himself into a chair and felt in his pocket for his cigarettes. Mary Edzell's offer. The happening of this weekend at Priestlaw.

Will felt trapped. It may seem strange that any young man who had been accepted by a beautiful girl with whom he was much in love, and who had, in addition, just been offered a fortune, should feel trapped. But that, at this moment, was what Will felt. He had been brought up to a life of freedom, of improvising. He had up to now—and with a good confidence in himself and in his own bright mind—hitch-hiked through life. He had been conditioned to this, and now he realised he had enjoyed it. The knowledge that he could have a shining limousine waiting to convey himself and his girl for the rest of the journey did not, for tonight at least, appeal to him.

And then the incident at Priestlaw. Rosamond had found him angrily walking about outside in the dark of the late winter afternoon and had flung herself into his arms. "Will, I'm so ashamed of what happened just now."

"Are you sure that anyone wants me down here very much?" he had answered. Why in heaven's name had he wanted to hurt her?

"Will! You know you didn't mean that!"

"I'm not going back in there."

"Yes you are. When grandfather has gone. He'll only stay for a short time. And I'm staying out here with you."

It was Frederick who had found them later. He had taken Will by both hands, asked him to accept the apologies of all of them and begged him to say no more about it. Thereafter it had been an awkward, unhappy evening with everyone trying to seem normal, with nothing said further and nothing resolved. He had been glad to escape this morning.

And what, after all, had been the cause of this unhappiness? The behaviour of a detestable old man and, he supposed, the Priestlaw family's respect for his money! And it was now within his power to snap his fingers at the lot of them. And yet—

He got up, thrust his hands deep into his pockets and leant, back to the fire, against the mantelpiece. "That rich and distinguished young couple Mr and Mrs William Edzell!" he said half aloud in a voice which his Priestlaw cousins would most certainly have called "red brick".

He swung round, hands still in pockets and stared again at Rosamond's photograph. But presently he found that the image had become blurred by the water that hung unshed in his eyes. No. He didn't know. He just didn't know.

CHAPTER 17

1

THE repercussions of John Edzell's unexpected, yet quite understandable visit to his grandson had been, of course, immense. The old man had not bothered himself over Will's angry escape from the house, nor yet over Rosamond's disappearing in his pursuit immediately afterwards. He had come to Priestlaw to see the condition of Oliver for himself. This might be called grandfatherly anxiety and affection. As no doubt it was.

They had all humoured him as best they could, given him tea and finally got him back into his old, black car with feelings of intense relief.

Then presently Frederick had gone off to look for his wife whom he found restlessly fussing about her bedroom, tidying up what did not need to be tidied. He knew the symptoms. In moments of stress, such as this, these fussings helped her to think things out.

"It's quite dark now," she said turning to her husband. "Rosamond must have followed Will outside, Fred. Harold had better go and look for them."

"I've brought them in. She's giving Will tea."

"Good." Christine sat down at her dressing table needlessly rearranging such things as she found there, while her husband, bringing round a chair,

sat down beside her and waited. Presently she let
the articles in front of her be, turned on her dressing
stool and looked at him. "All this has been extremely
awkward, hasn't it?"

"My father's behaviour to Will?"

"Yes."

"Will seemed very angry, Christine, I don't blame
him. I have apologised to him."

She thought of this for a moment, then she nodded
slowly. "I'm glad. But it doesn't make the situation
easier, does it?"

"You mean the question of the old man's money?
The question of reconciling him to the idea of
Rosamond's marrying Will?"

Again she did not answer at once. "Yes. I suppose
I just do mean these things. Oh, you know how I've
always hated thinking about money. But really—
well, your father has rather forced us to think about
it, hasn't he?"

For an instant Frederick reflected that his wife's
claim to hate the thought of money arose from the
fact that she had never known the want of it. But all
he said was: "There are other considerations too,
of course."

"Yes. Lots of them. That's what's been so unfortunate about what happened this afternoon. You
see, we've had no time, since I came home, to talk
anything out with Will and Rosamond."

At this moment the bedroom door was opened
and Harold looked in. "Hello," he said. "Sorry to
put my head into the love nest. Or is it an em-
ergency meeting? I was wondering where everybody
was."

"You all saw your grandfather's behaviour to Will," Frederick said. "Your mother and I have been talking about it."

"What's Oliver doing? He should have gone back to bed." Christine rose.

"That's where he is now. He's very angry at the old man. We had better go into a committee of four. Damned awkward, wasn't it."

The move took place and presently all three stood round Oliver's bed.

"Well?" he asked, sitting up in bed and looking at them fiercely. " What do we do now?"

Frederick thrust his hands into his pockets. "What is there to do, Nol? I've already told your mother I've apologised to Will."

"It's grandfather who ought to be doing the apologising! Do you know what I should do if I were Rose and that young man? I should go and get married at once, before the registrar."

Harold shook his head. "It wouldn't help, Nol. It would only make the situation with grandfather much worse."

"What do you mean? This infernal money business? Is everything always to come down to L.S.D.?" Oliver took a pillow, punched it as though it were a moneybag, put it behind his head and lay back looking up at them indignantly.

"Now look here, Nol. Don't get worked up and start talking through your—your artistic temperament! You know what grandfather has proposed to do. In fact you went to Paris on the promise of it. Didn't you? Whether we like it or not, it's important to you—to them—yes, and to me too!"

"I don't think we need go into that again, Harold," Christine said, taking command of the meeting. "I think we all know just how things stand. We don't like it, of course."

"I should think not!" Her younger son looked glum. "It's abominable!"

"We're agreed about that too," his mother continued. "It upset Rose very much, poor child, when she got Harold's letter in Paris. Still, you know, having talked to her I feel she is quite able to manage Will."

"What do you mean, Mother?" Oliver asked. "Bring Will round? Bring *grandfather* round? Persuade them both to love each other dearly and let us all pocket the swag?"

"I'm not quite sure what swag means, darling," Christine smiled at her younger son soothingly. "She wrote to Will about it. But I'm not sure quite what has happened. She may already have had him persuaded. That's what makes this afternoon's happening so unfortunate."

"I don't like the idea of Rose doing anything so calculating."

"She wants to get married, doesn't she, Nol? And you say you want to go back to Paris?" Harold burst out.

Christine turned. "Come along. It's time we were going downstairs, or those poor things will wonder where we've got to. No. I think the thing to do is to leave it to Rosamond. She's been very sensible, really."

2

This Sunday evening was to be one of the most unhappy of Rosamond's life. In her shame and vexation she was glad, at the end of it, to find herself alone in the privacy of her own room. Was glad too, to see Will go off with Harold and her father early on Monday morning.

"Better run up and see that Oliver is having his breakfast, darling," her mother said to her as they turned from the door.

Rosamond understood Christine's matter-of-fact tones very well. As usual, she was trying to keep things normal.

Sitting up in bed, Oliver answered his sister's enquiry for his well-being, poured himself out another cup of tea and looked up at her. "Big business gone off to the office?" he asked. "Taken Will with them, I suppose?" Then, as she merely nodded assent: "You're looking a bit woebegone this morning, Rose. I don't blame you."

"I don't blame myself." Rosamond's voice was gloomy. She turned away, crossing to the window. In the poor morning light the fields looked wet and wintry. A ceiling of grey cloud cut off the distant mountain tops.

"There was a family confab up here after grandfather went away yesterday." And as she did not answer: "The Skipper and mother, Harold and myself."

"Oh, was there?" Still turned away, her voice sounded indifferent.

"Rose, do you know what I should do, if I were you?"

"Do? Do about what?"

"About what do you think? About yourself and Will and this ridiculous money question."

"Well, then? What would you do? I'll be only too glad if you can tell me!"

As she came back he saw there had been tears.

"Go to Will and say you'll marry him right off. And let grandfather with all his squalid money threats go to blazes!"

"They're threats that affect you and Harold too."

"Rose! Look at us! Are we living in poverty?"

She stood for a time deliberating. Then she shook her head slowly. "No. We're not. But as things are—well, I'm only the daughter of a rich man. I haven't much of my own."

"Will is paid for his job, isn't he? You can live with him on what he's got? That's to say if you really think he's your man."

Yes. Rosamond was in no doubt that he was her man. She went back to look out of the window at the wet fields and the low hanging clouds. Oliver's suggestion attracted her. To marry Will at once and take the consequences, whatever they might be. To cut the abominable knot that was of her grandfather's tying. She had, she assured herself, love enough for Will and quite enough fight in her. But then? Had she not told Oliver just now that the old man's threat affected her brothers too? Suppose he were vindictive enough—and she thought him quite capable of it—to leave this promised money right away from the family? Harold, she knew, could fend very well for himself. But what about the young man in the bed behind her?

She spun round on her heel. "Nol, I can't do that. You haven't any more money of your own than I have. I can't do anything that may cut you off too. You want to go back to Paris, don't you? Isn't painting the thing you really want to do with yourself?"

"I'll be all right. Don't consider me."

"But I have to! However noble *you* want to be, the Skipper and mother would never forgive Will and me if anything we did spoilt your chances. Besides, I hate to say it, and you seem to be getting better, but you don't quite know how this Paris smash is going to leave you."

Her brother was looking serious now. She saw that he understood very well what she meant. But all he said was: "Need we take all this so heavily?"

"Yes, Nol. I *do* think we need! After all the worry you gave us in Paris! There were days at the beginning when mother and I didn't think you were going to pull through." For a moment Rosamond stood remembering. "No. I couldn't face mother— ever again—if Will and I just selfishly considered ourselves."

"I seem to have given you a deal of trouble."

This time, Rosamond's words came through tears. "No! No! It's not you, Nol! It's all—all grandfather's fault!"

"And Will's too, a little, Rosie?"

"Can you blame him?"

"Not much. No. Not at all, really. Considering yesterday. But look here. When are you next seeing him?"

"I'm having lunch with him tomorrow."

"Very well then. Why not say everything to him that we have been saying to each other now? Isn't he a reasonable being? He seems to like Mrs Adam Edzell very much. And hates the old boy for his treatment of her. But surely he likes you more. Surely you'll be able to make him see?"

"And what if, even with all our trying, we don't convert grandfather?"

"Sufficient unto the day—"

3

This talk with Oliver did much to comfort Rosamond. Indeed, as the day went on, her spirits had begun to rise. When she left him, she had called her spaniel and gone for a long damp tramp in the green February morning in order to think things out. Now, as she saw it, here was her first real chance to guide the difficult young man who was to be her husband in the paths of wisdom and practical sense. To protect Will, indeed, from his own quick defensiveness. She had, she felt, been quite honest with herself. Had there been no Oliver, she would have been quite ready to marry Will at once and take whatever consequences came. But now her conscience would not let her be satisfied until she and he had, at least, gone to the old man and done everything they could to melt him into going on with the division of his money. For Oliver's sake first. But for the sake of Harold too, and, of course, for herself and Will.

Rosamond was well aware that, Will being Will, her task might be delicate. But now, as, on the following morning, she drove her car towards Glasgow, she felt elated by that task: and the challenge it had thrown down to her.

Yes. Mr Edzell had come in.

But already Will had heard her voice and had come out to greet her. "Rosamond! I had just got in before you." He led her into the sitting-room and closed the door behind them. "You're looking a bit hot," he said brushing each of her cheeks with his lips. "Look. I put out the sherry bottle. Then, if it's all right for you, Mary Edzell, who is here from Stronn, wants us to have lunch with her. She wants to get to know you. And now I've got something to tell you!"

But Rosamond was too full of her mission. "No! First I've got something to say to you, Will. It's about grandfather, it's about all of us, and it's very important."

"What? Are you going to take me by the nose and lead me up to old John Edzell and tell him I'm going to be a good boy?" He turned to pour out.

"No, darling! It's not a joke." Rosamond sat down at the table and clasped her hands in front of her. "Will, I really want you to hear what I have to say."

"Fire away, old lady." He pushed the full glass towards her, then sat down with his own on the other side of the table from her.

"Will. We've said nothing about money yet. But

I simply must now." Here she found herself wondering at the flicker of amusement that crossed his face, but she must get on. "I'm going to ask you to do something. Something that's not quite for ourselves. No! Please be patient with me! I know you think grandfather is an old monster—well he is, really—but if you're going to belong to our family like the rest of us you'll have to learn not quite to ignore him."

"I can have a good try."

"Listen to me. Five years ago he gave one half of everything he had to my father. Now he wants to take the other half and divide it into three. For Harold, for Oliver and for myself. It will be quite a good sum. It will certainly make life easier for you and me."

"I see."

"Darling—" she stopped for a moment, troubled, and stretched a hand across the table towards him. "This is difficult, and you've got to help me. You see, the old man, as we know only too well, doesn't like our engagement. We needn't go into that. But as I—as, I think, all of us in Priestlaw—see it, you and I have got to do our best to bring him round. Will! Don't smile and shake your head like that! I don't know what you mean by it. No. Let me finish. Will; I'm doing this not just for ourselves. You see, Oliver may never be right after his crash. And if he is, he wants to go back to Paris. Actually he had gone on the strength of this money coming to him."

"Don't tell me your father couldn't send him,

whether he got money from your grandfather or not!"

"How do you know? You may not think it, Will, but Oliver is as sensitive—yes, and as independent— as any of us. And, believe me, he's a responsible creature, however lighthearted he may sound! He would never ask the Skipper to pay for something that may, as you and I know, very well come to nothing."

"We seem to be talking a great deal about your brother Oliver." Will seemed amused and puzzled.

These words struck Rosamond in the face like cold water. "But Will darling! Can't you see that just at this point we have to? If it were only ourselves—"

"Would you like *me* to send Oliver to Paris?"

There was anger in Rosamond's reply. "I don't know what you mean!" Then, as he got up to come to her: "No! You *must* sit down again, Will, and tell me what you mean!"

"Rosamond. I wanted to tell you at once. But you wouldn't let me. Mary Edzell was here last night. She has offered me an income and wants to leave everything she has to me when she dies. That's why I talked, just now, about sending Oliver to Paris. A poor joke, maybe."

"Oh, yes!" Rosamond merely felt bewildered and vexed. "That doesn't solve Oliver's problem though, does it?" she found herself saying.

"But really, why should your brother Oliver be such a problem to *us*?"

Rosamond did not answer. Somehow her new

world seemed to be crumbling about her. She was asking herself if Will really needed her now. Her pride, her self-confidence, the mental picture she had made of her future self as the wife who would bring him everything was falling to pieces. She did not know quite why. Was it that he seemed insensitive about others? Were the planes upon which they lived too different? Would she be of any use to him if Mrs Adam's money came to him? Was it that she actually did not like him to have money on his side?

Yet very little would have turned the scale just then. Had Will not seemed so inconsequently cheerful. Had he succeeded at this moment in coming near to her, in bringing home to her how much he loved her, Rosamond might have acted differently.

But now he was merely saying: "Well. Drink up your sherry and we'll get down to see Aunt Mary."

"Will. I'm sorry. I'm not coming."

"But Rosamond—"

"No. I'm not coming now."

"But Rosamond, what has happened? What have I done?"

"I'm going home, I tell you!" Her self esteem was sorely wounded and she was weeping bitterly as she stood up. "No! Don't come near me! I've had enough of you for one morning! You haven't tried to understand anything!" She turned at the door and this time she spoke more quietly. "Will, it's no good. Please let me go home."

He did nothing more to stop her. He was standing in bewilderment and in deep distress as she turned and went out.

4

Once again, late that night, Frederick Edzell and his wife found themselves discussing their daughter.

"She had gone to Will who was taking her out to lunch, Fred. But something happened. They quarrelled over—I don't know what. She has been very calm and closed up about it. She merely said she didn't want to see Will any more."

Frederick watched Christine as she sat once again in front of her mirror. "Didn't you ask why?"

"No. And I'm not sure that I'm going to. Wouldn't it be a good thing if we just said nothing and let her get over it?"

He considered this for a time. He saw, of course, what Christine meant. Rosamond's and Will's attachment had brought complications of which all the family down here at Priestlaw would be glad to be rid. And yet Frederick could not quite accept this ruthless, easier way. Not at once at least. "I wonder if she would tell me anything?"

"Well, as I say, is it wise to ask?"

"I don't want to know just out of curiosity, my dear." His voice was a little impatient. "Rosamond is a detached little person, but all the same, I should like to help, if I could."

"We should all like to help her, Fred."

"I know." He got up, laid a hand upon his wife's arm affectionately and turned. "Has she come up to bed? I'll go and see what I can do." He left Christine's room, crossed the landing and knocked upon his daughter's door. "Can I come in, Rosamond?"

He heard a noise which he took for assent. He found her sitting on her bed, still fully clothed. In the privacy of her bedroom she had allowed herself the luxury of tears. "Rosamond, what has happened? I hear you've broken off with Will. Is there anything we can do?"

She wiped her eyes, smoothed her fair hair and looked up at her father. "I don't suppose so."

"We all thought you were very much in love with him."

"Were, I think, is the word."

"But what did he say to you today? Or you to him? What did either of you do?"

"I really wish I knew exactly."

"Rose, you're unhappy. I happen to be your father and I want to help you, as I told your mother just now."

"Skipper, it's wonderful of you. But what am I to say?"

"Is it all a part of the unfortunate business with your grandfather on Sunday?"

Softened by his sympathy, she laid a hand over his and went on: "Skipper, I'll try to tell you what happened. Of course I was dreadfully upset about his treatment of Will. And I had been talking to Nol about it. Nol told me to go and marry Will at once, before the registrar; or however you do it— and let grandfather do what he liked about the division of his money. But for Nol's sake and for Harold's too, I felt I couldn't do that. I felt Will and I had no right to do something that my brothers, yes, and you and mother, might blame us bitterly for later. It was difficult. I was all on Will's side, of course. But it was only sense to try to go more carefully, to be a bit diplomatic. Detestable but necessary. Skipper, tonight I hate the very smell of money!"

Frederick nodded. He could understand. "And?"

"Well, I decided to tell Will everything today. I decided that, much as he hated grandfather, he would be certain to like me enough to try to understand; to do what I wanted and at least attempt to make his peace with the old man."

"What did he say?"

"Sat and smiled at me. For being so crude as to want to grub money out of my grandfather, I suppose. I pled Nol's illness, our anxiety in Paris, everything. Will simply refused to understand. Or couldn't."

"But that can't have been all."

"No. It wasn't all. He then told me Mrs Adam wanted to give him an income and make him her heir."

"My dear child!"

"That didn't solve my obligation to my brothers."

"But Rose, do you believe Will was in earnest?"

"We were supposed to be having lunch with Mrs Edzell."

For a time Frederick sat silent. "Did you see Mrs Edzell?" he asked presently.

"Certainly not."

"Rosamond, I don't yet quite see why this should have led to such a bad quarrel."

"It's not only a quarrel. Tonight I feel that the best thing I can do is to put Will right out of my mind."

"I wonder."

She did not reply to this.

"Don't you want Will? Don't you want to be his wife now he's likely to be a rich man?"

"I don't want to be Will's wife at all."

He got up. "Rosamond, I can't understand you." He stood for a moment looking down upon her. "Or I wonder if I do? I wonder if you've been making all kinds of unreal plans and schemes for that boy and yourself? Think about that. And I'll do some thinking too. And we'll both see where we get to. Good night. And don't be too unhappy." He bent down, kissed her brow and went, closing the door behind him.

His wife, still sitting at her dressing table, was waiting for him. "Well, Fred?"

"Christine, I've got news for you," he said. "It's something that, in spite of everybody's talk, I never really thought would happen!"

16

CHAPTER 18

1

"I'M sorry I can't bring Rosamond to lunch with you today, Aunt Mary."

"Why?"

"She's been here and gone away again."

"Didn't she want to see me, Will?"

"It wasn't that."

"Will, you're sounding as if something was wrong. Or is it only your telephone voice?"

"There *is* something wrong."

"Well, then. You had better come now to lunch and tell me about it."

"I don't want any lunch."

Having come to his rooms late that evening, Mary sat drinking the tea that his landlady had forced upon her and tried to understand what had happened. Of one thing she was in no doubt whatever. The young man before her was very unhappy. "Will! Please stop walking about and sit down and tell me what you said to each other."

"Rosamond came up here and wouldn't give me time to tell her anything. She started talking about her brother Oliver."

"Why Oliver?"

"It was about a money division. Old John Edzell is dividing his money into three and giving it to his grandchildren. But on one condition. That she drops me. Doesn't think I'm good enough for her, I suppose. Oh, he's a dear old man!"

For a moment Mary sat saying nothing. She was caught up in a surge of rage against John Edzell. But almost at once she remembered her own power in the family. She smiled. "We don't need to worry about that, do we, Will? Not if you accept my last night's proposal. Didn't you tell her about that?"

"Of course. But it only seemed to make her angry."

"Angry?"

"She seemed to think she must stick by her brothers—or something, to make sure that this division takes place. As if they weren't all wading in money down there at Priestlaw!"

"But what did she want you to do about it?"

"Go with her and crawl to John Edzell, I suppose. So as to get him to make the division." Will leant forward in his chair and looked at his guest fiercely. "Aunt Mary, I am doing nothing of the kind!"

"You can go so far as I'm concerned. It won't harm me."

"I tell you I'm not going!"

Mary did not reply. All this needed thinking out. She could not quite grasp the situation. But now she found herself wishing that she already had met Rosamond. Will's gaucheness, she feared, had in some way seriously wounded the girl. But now, looking at the young man, his hang-dog aspect touched her. What was she to say to him? "You've never really known what it was to live in a family and to recognise family ties, have you, Will?" she said presently.

He shook his head drearily.

"Nor yet have you lived among people with certain—I don't know how to put it—well, resources. People like the Priestlaw Edzells just look very rich to you, I suppose, and that's the end of it."

"What are you trying to say to me, Aunt Mary?"

"I don't know. Just thinking." Once more she became silent. Then: "But Will, what are we going to do?"

He shrugged.

"You don't want to finish with Rosamond, do you?"

"The question is: does she want to finish with me?"

"There's only one thing to do then. Go down early tomorrow morning and apologise."

"Apologise for what?"

"Never mind about what, Will. Apologise first and find out what it's all been about afterwards."

"She may refuse to see me."

"Will you please go when I tell you! She's probably waiting for your apology now. You know, I would advise you to accept what I suggested last night. Especially being—if you will allow me to say so—the touchy sort of young man that you are. It will put you on a level with—shield you, if you like—from the family you want to marry into. And what's more, you must tell them down there that you mean to accept my offer."

"I hadn't made up my mind about that," he said moodily.

Mary got up. "I think you are the silliest young man I have ever had anything to do with! Some-

times I wonder why I like you. While you're seeing
Rosamond tomorrow I'll see my lawyer and tell him
to get something drafted out. You and Rosamond
can consider it when you've both come back to your
senses."

"You're good to me, Aunt Mary."

"Yes. Of course. I'm far too good. And let me
know at once what happens. No. Don't bother to
come with me. I can get myself back to the hotel."

2

Having seen her husband, her elder son and then,
surprisingly, her daughter go off after breakfast,
Christine took herself upstairs to see the convalescent
who was not yet out of bed.

"Hello, mother! Good morning." Oliver put down
the morning newspaper. "You don't look too cheerful. What's the trouble?"

"Rosamond has gone away. The idea suddenly
seemed to take her. Nothing would stop her."

"Gone!"

"Yes. She said she wanted peace to think. I don't
know what to make of her."

"But where *has* she gone?"

"I don't know. And she didn't. She said she would
telephone. Not far, I expect."

"But why go away at all, mother? Was she afraid
Will would come out here?"

"Yes. Perhaps it was just that."

"Seems as if she were really determined to finish
with him."

"Yes." Christine looked about her worriedly. "I don't know what to think." She took a chair, set it by Oliver's bedside and sat down.

He looked at her. "You know you never really wanted Rose's engagement to Will," he said.

Christine took up the newspaper from Oliver's bed and occupied herself for a time putting the pages straight, quite unconscious that her restless hands were doing so. "Yes. I suppose I didn't. But— I don't know. There are complications."

"Complications? What *did* actually happen between Rose and Will yesterday?"

"Nobody quite seems to know. Your father went to her last night and she told him they had quarrelled. But he didn't quite understand about what. One thing Rose did tell him, however, and that was that Will had said Mrs Adam Edzell wanted to give him an income and make him heir to everything she has."

"I don't believe it!" Oliver lay back on his pillow laughing.

His mother looked down upon him unmoved. "I don't see what's funny about that."

"Look here, mother, for all our sakes, I think we should send someone after Rose as quickly as we can and bring her back in chains to marry Will before the situation gets any further out of hand! What if Will and Mrs Stronn Island suddenly decide to take a wicked revenge and turn the Skipper and Harold—and grandfather—out of Edzell's?"

Christine got up. "Darling, you've talked quite enough nonsense for one morning," she said. "I think you're getting much too well to stay in bed for breakfast. Was that someone knocking?"

A servant appeared. "It's Mr Will Edzell downstairs. I told him I didn't think Miss Rosamond was at home, so he asked to see you."

"Thank you. Tell him I'll come in a moment."

"He hasn't wasted much time, has he?"

Christine's colour had risen. Her son could see she was taking control of herself. "So Rosamond was quite right in thinking he might come here today." Her voice sounded more casual than she felt.

"What are you going to say to him?"

She turned, her fingers on the handle of the door. "My dear boy, I haven't any idea."

3

But it was not difficult for Christine to fall back upon a show of good manners. "Good morning, Will. This is an early visit. Do sit down and I'll ask them to get you a cup of coffee."

He sat down, but declined her offer. "I came down early to see Rosamond," he said. "Has she gone away?"

"Yes."

"Cousin Christine, I must see her. Tell me where she has gone. I didn't sleep at all last night."

She could believe him. His lean face had a tired, nervous look and his aspect was unkempt and careless. "I'm sorry," she said.

"Did she go away to avoid seeing me?"

"Yes. I think so."

"Where?"

"I simply don't know. She went off in her car about half an hour ago."

"You're saying that because you don't want me to see her."

Christine stood up and turned towards the door. "I'm not used to having my word doubted, Will," she said.

He rose too. "No! I apologise. Please! Cousin Christine, I'm very unhappy." His voice was hoarse.

She made a little gesture of forgiveness, sat down again and signed to him to do the same.

"I seem to have hurt Rosamond very much yesterday. Far more than I meant to hurt her."

"It seems to me strange that you should want to hurt her at all."

He dropped his voice to say: "Yes. I have a poor sense of humour, it would seem."

There was nothing to reply to this. She merely sat watching his distress. He was very penitent and, she guessed, very miserable.

"I suppose she told you what happened?"

"Not much, Will. But enough to allow us to know that she wanted to break her engagement to you."

"And I daresay all of you are glad that it has happened. You never wanted me, did you?"

She frowned and turned her face away, leaving Will to wonder what effect his quick, angry words had had upon her. She was passing through a crisis of conscience. No. Looking into her heart she must admit she had not wanted this uncomfortable young man for a son-in-law. She had looked to her daughter marrying someone quite different. Had she not suggested to Frederick, only last night, that the best thing to do would be to give this unequal engagement a chance to die, by merely doing nothing to bring the two together again.

But now, surprisingly, her feelings had changed. She felt within herself a strong desire to put things right between them. Why? Because she was sorry for him? Because she liked him better than she thought? Or was it because he might now inherit more than half of the firm of John and Adam Edzell Limited? Would become rich and could have power and influence among them, if he chose to use it, and whether they liked it or not? Some minutes ago Oliver had made a joke of it. He had said they had better bring back Rosamond in chains and make her marry Will. And she, Rosamond's mother had scolded him for talking nonsense. But Christine saw the pros and cons clearly enough.

She turned to look at him. It seemed absurd, somehow, that this unhappy creature might be having so much given to him. But she felt she must disregard all that. It was only what Rosamond and he felt for each other that must matter.

Again she stood up. "I'm sorry, Will, to keep you waiting for the answer to what you said just now. I had to think about it." She paused to look at him, then went on: "Very well then, the answer is this. Frederick and I quite naturally want Rosamond to be happy with whichever young man she marries. And you seemed to us, rather unexpectedly, if you

will let me say it, the one who would make her so.
But really, you know, both of you must expect to
resolve your difficulties with each other for your-
selves. Why should Frederick and I interfere? When
I know where she has gone I'll try to let you know.
But more than that I won't do. It's not for us to
influence either of you in one way or another."

Will had stood up too. "Did Rosamond tell you
what Mrs Adam Edzell was proposing to do for me?"

But Christine was determined to sound detached.
"She said something about that to her father last
night, I understand."

"Mrs Edzell wants you to know that she would
like to make me her heir and that I have accepted
her proposal."

Christine smiled a little remotely. "I'm so glad
for your sake. My congratulations." Will did not in
the least look, now at this moment, a subject for
congratulation. "But that has nothing to do with
your feeling for Rosamond, has it? Or Rosamond's
feeling for you?"

He looked bewildered, as though he did not know
what to say. "No. I suppose it hasn't."

She smiled. "Look, Will. Time is getting on.
Oliver usually comes down about now and we have
some kind of elevenses. I really wish you would stay
and have it with us. You're looking very tired."

But his mood this morning would not consent to
mere friendliness. So, once again obtaining her assur-
ance that he should be told Rosamond's whereabouts
at the soonest moment, Will thanked Christine and
went.

4

Once more, old Jessie Edzell became the channel through which news reached the rest of the family. Mary, coming back from Will's room in a state of trouble and preoccupation, had found an emotional vent in telling Jessie, who was nothing if not in sympathy, of Will's unhappiness at the break with Rosamond and of her own, Mary's, plans to make him her heir. All of which confounded and astonished Jessie. "Of course you don't want me to mention anything about this!" she said to Mary as they bade each other good night.

"If it's your family you're thinking about, Jessie, you can tell them what you like," Mary replied with more than a touch of impatience. "I daresay they'll all hear about it soon enough!"

And thus Jessie was given permission to spread the news.

On the following evening the Crabbes held a family conference. Alice had, of course, heard from Jessie that morning and had, forthwith, telephoned her sons at their office. This had led Sam to inviting Joseph and his mother to come across to Doune Terrace and to his telling young Patrick to come across too, bringing, if possible, his Aunt Jessie with him.

Despite some anxiety, the mere fact of their all coming together could not fail to generate among these hearty people an inescapable atmosphere of cheerfulness. Alice, who was nothing if not sociable, felt this as she entered Babs' drawing room with its blazing fire and with the inevitable sandwiches, cakes and tea things on a side table. "Just like a Christmas party! What's that you're asking me to eat, darling?" Minnie had been making fudge for the occasion.

For once Jessie was the subject of much consideration and found herself being listened to with respect.

"No later news since this morning, Jessie, dear?" Alice settled down beside her sister.

"I've heard none."

"You haven't heard if the girl has turned up, I suppose? Have a cigar Joe?" Sam took one for himself and held it between his fat fingers, smelling it.

"Very good-looking girl." Paddy helped himself to one of his father's cigars unasked. "Strong look of Grace Kelly."

"Princess Grace," Babs amended.

"How are Ruth and the baby, Patrick dear?" his grandmother asked.

"Could have flown very high, a girl like that. Now that we're all here, plug in the kettle, Min." Babs was fussing among the plates on the side table. "Fancy ever wanting a boy like Will Edzell!"

Jessie sprang at once to Will's defence. "Nobody can say that Will isn't handsome too."

"No. But all the same—"

"All the same what, mother? What with all Mrs Adam says she's doing for him! Look here, Aunt Jessie, now just what *did* Mrs Adam say about that?"

"Oh, I don't think anything is really settled yet, Patrick. You see— I don't know—or perhaps it is that I didn't quite understand. But Mary seemed not to be quite sure that Will would consent to accept anything from her."

"If she thinks that, Aunt Jessie, she needs an operation in her head! Or *he* does!" Patrick took a pull at his cigar and blew out the smoke slowly and luxuriously. "You can tell Mrs Adam to try *me* and see what happens."

Alice heaved a sigh. "I wish we knew, exactly; for all your dear sakes. You see this young man would own so much in Edzell's. And that means—"

"Oh, I know that Mary *wants* him to agree," Jessie assured them.

"Well. That's that then. We can call it settled." Now Sam was looking serious. "He'll accept all right. Was that the telephone? Paddy, go and see who it is."

"I don't think poor Will is thinking about money at all. He's terribly distressed about Rosamond disappearing. Mary says he's looking awful."

"Money, like time, Aunt Jessie, can be a great healer," Patrick said solemnly as he went out of the room.

"Joey, dear," Alice turned to her elder son and patted his hand. "There you are sitting saying nothing. What do *you* think?"

"I think that girl had better come home and marry the young man. That would keep everything in the family. Then we wouldn't need to bother. We don't see much of Fred and his boy Harold, but they remember who we are when it comes to business and treat us very well."

There was an impressed silence until Alice again spoke: "There you are, I knew Joey would say something sensible."

"But none of us here can do anything about her coming back, granny, can we?" Minnie disliked the idea of any romance coming to nothing.

"No, darling. Still, I wonder what Freddie and his wife are doing?"

"Or your old Uncle John," Babs said patting down a plateful of bloater paste sandwiches to make them look neater.

"Yes, indeed, Euphemia. Your Uncle John. Do you think I would do any good if I—?"

"Leave him alone, mother. Don't go out to Bearsden and bother Uncle John just now. It won't help. He'll be in touch with Fred."

"Still, I don't know, Joey. Or perhaps a telephone call?"

But there was to be no more discussion on this point for Paddy burst into the room. "Friends, Romans, countrymen! Do you know who that was? It was Mr Harold Edzell of Priestlaw House, Stirlingshire, asking if I knew if Mrs Adam Edzell of Stronn Island was still in Glasgow and did I know her address!"

Here was news to confound and delight them. Now the party was really worthwhile! Minnie began to hand round the fudge again.

"And did you give her address to him, dear? Alice inquired, imposing a gentle control upon their excitement.

"Of course, granny."

"But what does this mean, do you think?" Jessie asked. "Does it mean that Frederick—"

"It means that Fred's on the warpath. That's what it means." Sam shook a fat, knowing finger. "Good

for Fred! Don't you leave that hotel of yours to
morrow, Aunt Jessie, till you see what's going on."

"But Sam, wouldn't that be spying?"

"Oh, never mind about that, Aunt Jessie." Babs'
large face was flushed. "Oh, there's the kettle boil-
ing, Min. Don't let it spout hot water on the carpet.
Here's the teapot to fill."

CHAPTER 19

1

ROSAMOND put down the receiver and came back into the lounge of the wayside hotel on the Scottish Borders where hurt and anger had brought her. Reaction had set in. Already she had begun to feel lonely and rather foolish. And the sound of her father's voice over the telephone had not diminished these feelings.

She was relieved to find that she was, at least, to have this log blaze in its commercial-rustic fireplace, these polished horse brasses, these chintz cushioned, oak benches to herself. The two business men with Yorkshire voices who had, from their own table at dinner, tried to open a conversation with her, were, she was relieved to find, gone to spend the rest of the evening in the hotel bar; whence, now and then, she could hear distant talk and bursts of laughter.

"I've brought your coffee here to the fire, Miss. Did you get your telephone call all right?" The landlady was standing over her.

"Yes. Thank you."

"I told the boy just to leave your golf clubs in the car. You'll not be wanting them tonight?"

"No. Thank you."

"You'll play a lot of golf?"

"Some."

The woman hovered for a moment longer, then went back to report in the kitchen that the elegant guest, who had dropped in so unexpectedly this afternoon, was no great hand at a conversation.

"My dear girl! Whatever are you doing there?" Her father's voice had exclaimed, when she told him where she was.

"I had to come somewhere. It's all right, really. Quite comfortable."

"Rosamond, your mother and I think you are behaving absurdly."

"I'll be back soon."

"Were you afraid of Will appearing?"

"Yes."

"As a matter of fact, Will did come. Half an hour after you left this morning."

There had been a moment before she replied: "Which all goes to show that I was right to disappear."

"I don't know about that. Your mother says Will is looking wretched."

She made no reply to this.

"Rosamond. Are you there?"

"Yes. I'm here."

"Your mother promised to tell him where you were."

"What! Mother did? She had no right to! Then I shall move on tomorrow morning!"

"My dear child! Look here! This is quite ridiculous! Much better to come home to your own house and to the people who can help you."

"Skipper! Please leave me to have a day or two

17

to myself. Listen. There's one thing you can do for me. You can put a notice in the papers cancelling my engagement."

"No, Rosamond. Not just yet. Leave it for a little."

"So the family now want me to hold on to Will and his money do they?"

"Rosamond! That makes me very angry! What kind of people do you think we are? All right. I'll leave you to it. And I hope to get some sense out of you the next time we hear from you. Good night!"

Her father had hung up and she had come back in here to think, cast down, diminished and made stubborn by the anger in his voice, while the horse brasses twinkled in the firelight and shouts of a darts competition came from the bar.

Why had she been so furious with Will yesterday? What hurt had he inflicted to rouse her to such a pitch that now she could tell herself she hated him?

"Your mother says Will is looking wretched."

Well, let him be! And yet these words, now that they came back to her, hung in her mind, rendering her yet more unhappy, leaving a picture of Will. The picture of a wretched Will.

She had meant to do so much! She had felt so certain that once he belonged to her she would be able to plan his life for him. Their marriage was going to be different from the every-day marriages of others. She had had, she felt, so much to give this brilliant, homespun creature. Her own bright person. Her knowledge of the world. Her sophistication. And of course in the end, although they would have

to wait for that, her own share of the family resources. Which couldn't be nothing, even if that
detestable old man carried out his threat. And why
hadn't Will consented to help her with her grandfather? It was here that Rosamond—not quite
honestly—fixed the hurt he had inflicted. Even
though it didn't matter to him now, why had he
been unable to see how much it mattered to her
brothers? No one grasped better than herself how
difficult a meeting with her grandfather would be
for Will. But why hadn't he even tried to understand that it must be?

"Thank you. Yes. I've finished coffee."

The woman again returned to the hotel kitchen.
This time to report that the solitary young woman
in the lounge looked as if she had been having a bit
of a cry to herself, poor thing.

And now Will was to be rich. Richer, for all she
knew, than her father, even! Why did the thought
of this please her so little?

Now, Rosamond took out from her memory the
older, more familiar pictures of Will. Will limping
and difficult on that first autumn afternoon in the
Priestlaw gardens. Will dishevelled and rapturous
when, up there in his rooms for the first time,
she had broken from him and held him at arms-
length to look at him. Will on that tense afternoon
while they waited for news from Paris. Will at the
air station, when they had stood together oblivious
of everyone and everything but themselves. In these
last months, that strange, disturbing young man had
become the mainspring of her being. And now the
spring seemed broken!

Rosamond got up, walked to the window and thrust back the curtains. She could see nothing in the black darkness. Rain was striking the window-panes. Bewildered and unhappy, she turned back to the fire.

2

Frederick had gone to take Rosamond's telephone call alone in his study. Now, returning to his wife and sons, his face was troubled and glum.

Christine looked up at him. "Well?"

"Yes, it was Rosamond."

"Where had she got to?" Harold asked.

Frederick told them, adding: "But she said she was moving on first thing tomorrow when she heard you had promised to tell Will where she was."

"But Frederick—!" his wife was beginning, but for once he snapped back at her.

"Oh, she may as well stay away until she comes to her senses!"

"And I promised Will to tell him at once!" Christine said somewhat lamely, realising her husband's displeasure.

"She asked me to put an announcement into the papers that her engagement was off."

Harold emitted a low whistle.

But it was Oliver who asked: "And are you going to do it, Skipper?"

"No. Not in the meantime."

"Did you tell her so?"

"Yes. I did."

There was silence for a time, then Oliver asked:

"Look here. Do we really want Rose and Will to patch things up?"

Nobody replied to this. For a time all of them sat turning over the question in their minds. But all of them—each for different reasons—knew that the answer was yes.

Christine's conscience refused to see her daughter and the young man who had come here in search of her this morning as anything but two people who had, with great foolishness, made each other needlessly unhappy. Will's changed circumstances and its bearing on family interests, she felt obliged to shut from her mind.

Harold, on his side was frankly thinking of Mrs Adam's fortune and had decided, just as Joseph Crabbe was deciding on this same evening, that the sooner Rosamond held out her hand to Will and led him safely back into the family fold the better. From there it was easy for Harold to persuade himself that Will wasn't at all a bad chap and could be shaped into a very likeable brother-in-law indeed.

Oliver's ideas were romantic—to a point. Rose, he told himself, although perhaps she didn't think so at the moment, was hopelessly gone on Will, anyway. And so too, from all the signs, was he on her. Very well then. 'In delay there lay no—' and so on. The sooner for their well-being, mental and physical, they stopped this nonsense and got on with it the better. But beyond this point, even Oliver could not avoid a certain self interest. He could not but be worried about the money that might or might not come to him from his grandfather; the money that would send him back to Paris.

"Yes, Nol. I think we all want Rosamond and Will to patch things up." The irritation was leaving Frederick's voice. "They like each other too much." He stopped to reflect for a moment. "Besides," he went on "and this is on quite a different plane, it would simplify worldly relationships too, wouldn't it? Now that Mrs Adam Edzell—"

The three others found themselves ready to agree. Frederick appeared to have tied together their different points of view into one benign knot.

"Can't we do something to help?" Christine asked.

"We shall have to wait meantime, I am afraid. Until that silly girl—"

"Listen, Skipper. I've got an idea."

They turned to Oliver.

"Wouldn't it be a good thing if you went to see Mrs Adam Edzell? She's in Glasgow somewhere, isn't she?"

Oliver's father looked surprised. "I don't see how I can. You see—"

But Oliver was pleased with the idea. "Look. If she's doing all this for Will, isn't it time you and she got together?"

"I feel it would be an impertinence, Nol. After all these years of—"

"Oh, *you* can manage her beautifully, if you want to. It's the obvious thing to do."

Frederick looked towards his elder son.

Harold smiled encouragingly. "If you *would*, Skipper. We can find out where she is from the Crabbes. I'll ring and ask them if you like."

"I really think you should consider it, Fred," Christine said.

"What about seeing her yourself, Christine?"

"You know I'm no use at that kind of thing."

"Give me time to think about it. Perhaps I ought to," Frederick the ever dutiful said uneasily.

3

It was still early next day when Frederick was driven away from his father's house in Bearsden towards the city. As on so many occasions before he was leaving Lockview with feelings of disgust. Now, still more heartily did he wish that he need not go to see Mrs Adam Edzell this morning, a meeting which the family's insistence and Harold's practicality had forced upon his reluctant sense of duty.

And yet, strangely, old John had put no further difficulties in the way of reconciliation between Rosamond and Will. Quite the reverse. But to Frederick, his father's tone had been altogether nauseating.

"I brought you here, Fred, because your Aunt Alice telephoned me late last night. She tells me that young man is to get all your Uncle Adam's money."

"We don't know quite for certain, father."

"Well, you'd better make sure. Alice seemed sure enough. She says Adam's widow is leaving him everything. What are you going to do? And what was Harold wanting her address from the Crabbes for?"

For once resistance had risen up in Frederick. He could not quite have said why. He could not, he found, bring himself to tell his father, just then, that he was on his way to see Mrs Adam Edzell. "What *is* there to do, father? Haven't we thought that Mrs Adam might do this for a long time now?"

"And your Aunt Alice said that now that girl of yours doesn't want any more to do with him."

"Aunt Alice has no right to be mixing into this."

As usual, any annoyance shown by Frederick made no impression upon his father. "That's all very well, Fred. But is it true?"

"Yes. For the moment it's true."

"Just when there might be some sense in holding on to him!"

"You were doing everything to keep them apart, the last time I saw you, father."

"Well, I'm not doing it now! You can tell her that. And you can tell her at the same time that if she marries the young man, your family will get the money I meant to settle on them."

There had been more of this. Used as he should have been to old John's coarseness by now, yet Frederick was once again revolted by his habit of reducing every kind of relationship to pounds, shillings and pence. He felt, somehow, that he had no right to go to Mrs Edzell with this sordid talk in his ears. His family had pushed him into this meeting, strongly against his inclination. Harold had arranged everything; and now disinclination was redoubled.

"Whatever your father says, Fred, you will see Mrs Edzell, won't you?" Christine had said as she found his hat and coat for him.

"I feel it's a great impertinence. Considering how we've treated her in the past."

"You'll do it for Rosamond's sake, won't you? And

a little for Will's too, perhaps. It's the young people we must try to help."

As his man drove him on, Frederick thought how the motives of all of them had now become so strangely mixed. Even Christine's. For would she not have been glad to see Will drop out of sight only two days ago?

But here he was before the door of what must be the small hotel to which he had been directed. And there was his old Aunt Jessie Edzell coming out of it.

"Fred! Here already! Mary told me you were coming at eleven. And it's only quarter to! How are you? And all the Priestlaw cousins? Of course— poor Rosamond! But that will be all right, won't it? Mary is just inside. She'll see you at once. I'm sure she will. I'll run in and tell her. No. No trouble in the world!"

4

Mary Edzell had relished the thought of Frederick's visit just as little as he had relished the thought of paying it. From Will she had heard little but good of Frederick. But for so many years now she had, very naturally, been used to thinking of him merely as John Edzell's son. When Harold Edzell had telephoned her last night, she had consented to this meeting only because she had felt that, for Will's sake, it was her duty to allow it. And now here was the hated John Edzell's son standing before her holding out his hand.

"It's kind of you to allow me to come here this morning, Mrs Edzell."

Even at this agitated moment Mary felt surprised. This large, handsome man of obvious consequence, yet with an oddly sensitive face, was not what she had expected. "They said we would be left in peace if we went in here." She indicated the way into a little empty smokeroom. Her reception of him was austere. She had fallen back instinctively on her old hospital matron's manner, unsmiling and correct. A manner she had developed to mask her feelings when she had been forced to assert authority, or at such times as she had been forced to defend some happening for which she was responsible. She motioned him to take a seat, took one herself and sat upright on the edge of it, her hands clasped in front of her, firm lipped, attentive and waiting.

It was for Frederick to break the ice. "My family thought it would be a good thing if I came to see you, Mrs Edzell. They thought we might together do something to clear matters up between my daughter Rosamond and Will. Will has told us that you have become—how shall I put it?—more or less his guardian."

"I'm very fond of Will, if that's what you mean, Mr Edzell."

"Yes. So we gathered." He waited for a moment, but as again she did not speak he added: "Will may have told you that my daughter Rosamond has gone away. But she telephoned last night. She wants to break her engagement with him. She wanted me to have a notice put into the paper at once."

Mary felt the colour rising in her face. She had

spent a distressing hour with Will in his rooms last night. An hour of misery and self-blame. Despite his foolishness, Will was desperately in love with this girl. A formal breaking of his engagement would hit him very hard. "What did you say to her, Mr Edzell?"

"I was very angry. I told her I would do nothing of the kind. I told her she had better come home and talk things over sensibly."

Mary's expression softened. She was pleased with this reprieve for Will. The hospital matron began to withdraw into the background. "What kind of girl is your daughter, Mr Edzell?"

Frederick was surprised by this blunt question, but he did not dislike it. "The main thing about her at the moment, so far as you and I are concerned, is that in spite of herself—or so I firmly believe—she is still very much in love with your young man." He stopped for a moment to consider, then went on: "What kind of girl? That's a hard question for any fond father to answer, isn't it . . . Headstrong, with fixed ideas that she'll have to learn to unfix as she grows older, like any other young person. She's certain she knows the world and its ways much better that her father and her mother do. Perhaps she's right. But it can be highly annoying."

Mary found herself laughing a little at Frederick's look of displeasure. The ice could not but begin to melt between these two people of goodwill. "When I saw her once for a moment, I thought she was a raving beauty," she said.

"She looks all right, I suppose. Quite a number

of young men seem to have thought so too, it would seem." He smiled at her a little wistfully. "Oh, Rosamond's a good girl and we want her to be happy. That's why I've come here to see you. And what about the young man?"

"He's not my son, Mr Edzell."

Frederick merely nodded, waiting.

"But I'm getting old, and I'm lonely. And this, maybe, has made me stupidly fond of him. You see, I've got no one else. Perhaps it is that I want to feel I've someone to belong to. Can you understand that?"

To this question Frederick could only manage an encouraging nod of sympathy. There had been many times in his responsible and harassed family and business life—and this morning was one of them—when the idea of belonging to no one whatsoever had seemed to him the ultimate, unattainable happiness.

"When I asked just now, what kind of girl your daughter Rosamond was, I really wanted to know, Mr Edzell. From all I hear she's not quite the right kind of girl for an independent, difficult young man like Will who doesn't much care whether he travels through life hard or soft, so long as he can enjoy the use of his brains and his scholarship."

"Then you don't want Will to marry her?"

Mary looked at him earnestly. "Yes. Now I want him to marry her. Because I don't want to lose him."

"I don't understand."

"I saw him last night. He's quite broken down. He has made up his mind to leave this country if Rosamond won't have him. You know, of course, that I mean to make him the heir to everything I have. He said last night he wouldn't think of accepting a penny of it except for Rosamond's sake. Whether that's his final word or not, I can't tell you."

Frederick Edzell made no immediate comment upon this. He merely sat with a bewildered, quizzical expression on his face, looking about the scruffy little smokeroom in which he found himself. Really, the situation was becoming more and more fantastic! Everybody, every circumstance seemed to be pushing these two young people into each other's arms! What was the use of Christine and himself indulging in highflown feelings when everybody else saw nothing but expediency, some personal advantage in this union? A smile broke. It was absurd, and somehow comic, to think that Mrs Adam Edzell and his father, old John, should now, of all people, be anxious to bring about the same happening. "All this is quite extraordinary, Mrs Edzell," he said. "Her mother and I did not much want Rosamond to fall in love with Will. For very much the same reasons as you have given me. Only from the reverse point of view, of course. Now we all seem to have the same ideas." Frederick laughed apologetically and went on: "Still, the kernel of the problem remains: would these two young people be happy if they *did* marry?"

"As happy as most people, Mr Edzell. Will is intelligent. So, I hope, is your daughter. They'll shake down as other young people do, I daresay. Will can be very forceful, you know. He'll make her do what he wants."

"I wouldn't be too sure of that, Mrs Edzell. Rosamond is a wilful little minx with some very highfalutin ideas!"

"He'll knock them out of her."

"She'll fight back."

Mary laughed aloud. "We're, each of us, backing our own side!" she said.

Frederick stood up. "I'm afraid I must go," he said genially, looking at his wrist. "And we've come to no kind of decision, Mrs Edzell. Is there anything to be done?"

"Bring them together and see what happens."

"Then we had better keep in touch, hadn't we?"

"Yes. I think we should."

"Your daughter must come home soon. She can't stay away for ever, can she?"

"But that may not mean that she'll consent to see Will."

"Perhaps I might help there. Perhaps she'll allow me, if not him, to see her."

Frederick held out a hand. "Perhaps. Who knows?"

She was smiling benignly as she led him to the entrance and said goodbye. As she stood watching his man hold the door for him and saw them drive away, Mary was surprised to find herself liking Frederick Edzell.

CHAPTER 20

1

ALICE CRABBE's importance found the news—immediately reported by Jessie—of Frederick's meeting with Mary hard to bear. That it was of tremendous import to the family, goes without saying. But apart from the fact that Mary and Frederick had been in amicable talk, nothing was known. And Jessie dared not ask. This vacuum was torture to Alice. As the self-appointed centre of her family, she must, she felt, know more. And this was difficult.

"I went out to see your Uncle John, just after your Aunt Jessie told me," she said to her younger son, Sam, who had called up on his way home from town. "He was a little crotchety, Sammy, and rather implied it was not my business what was happening. You know the way he talks, dear. We have to keep making allowances. But I pointed out, as gently as I could, what a pity it would be if these two, really very delightful young people missed each other through—well, just some foolish misunderstanding, and that in so far as we all were relatives of both of them, it couldn't but *help* being our business."

Sam allowed himself a smile at this. "And what did Uncle John call you for that, mother?"

Alice coloured a little. "Whatever he called me, dear, doesn't matter. You know he doesn't always mean what he says. I did find out, though, that Rosamond had not come home yet. But Freddie told your uncle that he and his wife think she will come to her senses and reappear very soon."

This at least was something. "And what's the young man doing?"

"Nothing new, so far as your Aunt Jessie can hear. She's really being very good, Sammy. She's telling us everything now. She realises how worried we all are."

Sam looked sly. "Worried about these two very delightful young people?" Then, as she made no comment on this: "Fred was quite right to go and make his peace with Mrs Adam. Surely if these two put their heads together—"

His mother was looking wistful. "Yes, dear. It's always nice to think of old quarrels being brought to an end." Alice gazed into her sitting room fire for a time. But presently her son saw the spark come into her eye. "Do you know, dear, I've just been thinking. Wouldn't it be a good thing, perhaps, if I went to see Mrs Adam Edzell and tried to make friends with her too?"

Again Sam allowed himself a fat smile at this.

"No. Really, dear. I mean it. It's never too late to try to heal old wounds, is it? And I've been thinking of this too: wouldn't it be a good thing for me to suggest to her that being poor Will's— well—benefactress, she might try to see Rosamond whenever she comes home and do her best to make peace between the young people?"

"If you do that mother, we'll give you a medal!"

"But if Freddie has seen her, Sammy, and found

her reasonable, why shouldn't I? No, dear. The more I think of it, the more I feel I ought to make the effort for all your nice sakes."

Same looked at his mother. Now she was pink and excited. The old warhorse was pawing the ground.

2

On the following morning, as she was finishing breakfast, Mary was told there was someone to see her. This someone, she found, was the driver of Frederick Edzell's car with a letter which he had been asked to put directly into her hands. Having left a talkative Jessie still at breakfast, Mary decided she had better take the letter to the peace of her own room. It was from Frederick.

"Dear Mrs Edzell,

"I'm writing this very late tonight as it is impossible for me to see you to-morrow. I am flying to London early. But I shall leave this with my man to be given to you after he has taken me to the plane.

"Tonight, about nine o'clock, Rosamond came home. Neither her mother nor I can get at her frame of mind. She was tired, poor child, and anything but communicative. And therefore we felt that the only thing to do with her was to try to make her eat something and go to bed. We have not, I need hardly say, dared to ask her intentions towards Will. A word she dropped to her brother Oliver, however, rather pointed to the fact that she does not want to stay at home for any length of time.

"Finding myself alone with her for a moment, I felt I might chance telling her I had been to visit you; just to see what she would say. She looked surprised. But merely said: Oh, had I? And there it ended. No questions about Will, or when had I seen you, or anything. I should guess, however, knowing my own daughter a little, and going by her not quite successfully casual voice, that she is still very upset and that her running off, as she did so foolishly, has decided nothing for her.

"Having got her to bed, we, her mother and I—and, indeed, her two brothers with us—have just had a long talk and have come to the conclusion that it might be a good thing if you, who are so close to Will, came out here, saw her and told her about him. To see Will, himself, at once might, we feel, be altogether too abrupt. I think you will understand what I mean. I am writing this now because we do not think any time should be wasted.

"I shall be in London, but do telephone Christine, my wife, here at Priestlaw. She will, as Rosamond's distracted mother, be only too glad to send the car for you.

"She is hoping to have a telephone call from you very soon after you get this letter.

> Very sincerely,
>
> Frederick Edzell."

Having read this twice, Mary did not take long to make up her mind. Last night, Will's state of mind had been worse than ever. She had not known what to do. And she was tired of it. To go out to Priestlaw and see this girl would at least be doing something. And the sooner the better, it seemed. She went to her room telephone, but it was not to telephone Christine. It was to ask the hotel to find a car that would take her into the country. The hotel had a car, she was told, and it would be at her disposal immediately.

Mary's toilet took not much longer than it would have taken her, were she merely going out into her garden at Stronn Lodge. In a few minutes she was on her way downstairs.

In the entrance hall she found Jessie talking with another woman.

"Mary! Going out already! Mary, this is my sister Alice. I don't know if you—she felt it was a pity she had never—you *did* meet a long time ago, didn't you?"

So this was Alice Crabbe, with the sweet, ingratiating smile and the outstretched hand? But now Mary's thoughts were upon her meeting with Rosamond and what might come of it. She returned Alice's greeting distractedly. "Yes. I have to go out," she said turning to Jessie.

"Oh, I'm sorry, Mrs Edzell. Jessie thought you wouldn't be going out quite so early." Alice's cheek showed a tinge of pink.

"Well, yes I am, Mrs Crabbe. I must go at once." Mary looked towards the door. "I'm getting the hotel's car."

At which Jessie, glad to escape, perhaps, ran outside leaving Mary face to face with her sister.

"We're all so sorry about this—this difficulty between that dear girl of Freddie's and that poor boy Will, that we all like so much, Mrs Edzell."

"Yes. It's a pity."

"We're all so hoping that you'll be able to put things right for them. We've all heard how fond you are of Will."

"I'm very fond of him."

Alice's cheeks became pinker. "Wouldn't it be a good thing for you to see Rosamond whenever she comes home? And talk to her? I don't know—poor Will has no mother to speak for him, has he?"

Mary stiffened. From the old days she had no reason to like Alice Crabbe. And she had always heard she was a busybody. Yet this presumption, as she told herself afterwards when she had time to think about it, passed everything!

But Jessie saved the situation. "George, that's the hotel chauffeur, is waiting for you, Mary. He's not quite in front of the door. There's a silly grocer's van that has—"

Mary gave Alice her hand once more. "Thank you, I'll come at once. No. Don't trouble to come out with me, please."

And she had gone before they could follow her.

3

When Rosamond came down in the middle of the morning, she found a grey haired woman in rough tweeds drinking coffee with her mother. For a moment she hesitated, wondering who this person could be. But a smile of recognition from the visitor told Rosamond her name. This was Mrs Adam Edzell to whom she had apologised on that unhappy occasion in the restaurant.

There was nothing to do but give the visitor her hand. But really it wasn't fair! Why hadn't her mother come to tell her that Mrs Adam Edzell was here? Surely she must have guessed that this was the last person, with the exception of Will himself, that she, Rosamond, could possibly want to meet. What was she doing here?

"We've seen each other once before," Mrs Edzell was saying. "Do you remember?"

"Yes, I do." Rosamond helped herself from the coffee tray and was poised for flight. "Was I interrupting something? I'll take this somewhere else." She was making towards the door when her mother's voice halted her.

"Darling, please! Mrs Edzell has come here to talk to you." Again there was nothing to do, short of giving a display of childish rudeness, but to turn back. She stood now, saying nothing, her eyes watching two cock finches as they fought and fluttered on the rain sodden turf of the lawn just outside the window. Presently she became aware that her mother was standing up too.

"I'm going to leave you for a little," Christine said.

Rosamond watched her mother go with an emotion very like panic. In these last days she had passed through all kinds of moods. She had, perhaps, done better than she knew by going off on her own. She had done so in the first place because she was angry. But as her anger had smouldered down, uncertainties, questions, had arisen in her mind. The girl who now faced Mary was, as Mary could see, emotional and on edge.

"How did you know I was here, Mrs Edzell?"

"Because your father sent me word. He came to see me, you know."

"Why?"

"Because he and your mother were distressed about what had happened and very rightly thought I would be distressed too. My dear girl, sit down and let me talk to you."

There was a warm firmness about this stocky, weather beaten woman that Rosamond, even in her unhappiness could not dislike. She laid aside her coffee and sat down near to Mary, facing her.

"Of course you know very well why I've come, Rosamond—if you'll let me use your name. I've come to tell you that Will is a very unhappy young man. And that it's about you he's unhappy. And also that, whatever he may have done to offend you so much, he's bitterly sorry and wants to come to you and apologise."

"Why hasn't he come then?"

"Because nobody has told him you're home. I don't know if you know it, but he was out here the next morning to ask you to forgive whatever he had said."

"Yes. I knew." The girl was looking very near to tears. "But why should *you* come, Mrs Edzell?"

"Because I happen to love Will as much as it's

decent for an old woman to love any young man. And I don't like to see him miserable. Nor you either, Rosamond, now that I'm having a look at you." Mary stopped for a moment, watching, perhaps, the effect of her words, then went on: "Surely the only thing for you and Will to do is to make up your quarrel."

"It's no good, Mrs Edzell!" Rosamond had risen to her feet and was turned again to look out of the window. She had done this, as Mary rightly guessed, to hide tears.

Mary spoke gently. "Rosamond, my dear, come back and tell me about it."

"About what, Mrs Edzell?" Rosamond pulled herself together, dabbed her eyes and turned to Mary.

"About why you've made this break with a young man you're quite obviously in love with. What did Will do to hurt you so badly? He spoke to me about a division of your grandfather's money and something about your brother Oliver. That you wanted him to see your grandfather. But I didn't understand."

"It was how he took all that, Mrs Edzell."

"I told him it didn't matter two straws to me whether he made his peace with your grandfather or not. Please try to explain to me."

"He was—I don't know. Smiling. Cynical. He didn't get near to seeing—and certainly didn't try— that I could be anxious and worried about Oliver and that I was trying to make him realise that a visit to grandfather might be the only way out. Oh, it's difficult to explain. But it shocked me and made me afraid. I had gone to him so full of confidence that, of course, he would do anything for my sake. And instead of that—" Rosamond shrugged.

"I see."

"I suppose he felt that now he's going to be your heir he could laugh at other people's money problems."

"Rosamond. Sit down again and listen to this." Mary watched her earnestly as she did so. "Will has made up his mind to leave Glasgow and go abroad without taking a penny from me if you break with him finally. Your father knows that. But perhaps he hasn't had a chance to tell you. It would be a great blow to me. But he's determined. You don't know him very well, if you don't realise that Will is an odd, independent young man, who—as I said to your father yesterday—doesn't mind whether he travels hard or soft through life so long as he can use his brains. I sometimes think he hardly knows the value of money. I didn't ask him to fall in love with you. Nor ask you to fall in love with him. But here you both are! And he seems to be the man you want. Will is the kind of person who is going to take a great deal of knowing by the wife he marries. It all depends if that wife will love him enough to find the patience and understanding to mellow his ideas for him. It won't be easy. But, for myself, I think Will is worth it. You see, he has never had any money and he has never had any family life. The girl he marries will have to teach him about these things and a great many other things too. And at the same time not allow him to see that she is teaching him anything." The handle of the door turned. Mary stood up. "Think about that, Rosamond. And I'll go back to Will now and tell him you're going to see him, shall I? It's for him to go on with the argument now."

For a moment she laid a friendly hand on the girl's arm, then she turned with a smile to Rosamond's mother.

4

He had turned at the door saying he would go and find her. Christine had told him she had gone out directly after lunch. She had no idea where. And he had gone straight to where she was, to the glasshouse inside the walled garden. He did not know why. Never had he pictured Rosamond as a fine lady pottering among her hothouse flowers. But now, as he came through the door in the wall and caught sight of the sleek, fair head appearing for a moment behind the sky-reflecting glass and the green of growing plants, everything seemed to fall into its place. Rosamond had come home and he had found her. There was only that fair head and the certainty it belonged to him.

And yet, when later he came to look back, he was to remember odd details of things and happenings. He had left his motor bicycle in the negligence of excitement and it had fallen over. He stopped to set it up again. He had noted a mist of snowdrops in the grass beneath a great tree beyond the drive. There was the shine of recent rain on the flagstones of the front terrace. And with the certainty coming to him that he must find her just here, he had hurried his going and had bounded recklessly down the terrace steps, forgetting the habit he had fallen into of saving his wounded leg. At the bottom it had struck him that he need not save it any more. That his leg was sound. He had to struggle with the stiff, old-fashioned handle of the door into the garden.

Mary Edzell had found him just before lunch. "Will, Rosamond is home. You had better get down to her as quickly as ever you can."

"How do you know?" He had been dumbfounded.

"I've just come back from Priestlaw. That's how I know. She'll see you."

"Grant me an interview?"

"Will you ever stop being a fool? And if you've work to do this afternoon get your landlady to say you're dead and buried. But go! Do you hear me?"

"Who told you to go to Priestlaw?"

"Never mind now. Come to me when you get back and I'll tell you."

The sleek head behind the glass did not move. By now she must have seen him; must be waiting. And she was still waiting down there, as he turned the handle and went in at the other end of this corridor, damp, warm and aromatic, of hothouse flowers and forced winter greenery. Waiting to grant an interview?

But now that he was standing before her, confidence began to evaporate, and all that he could find to say was: "Why did you run away?"

"So even yet you don't realise?"

"I've come to say I'm sorry for everything. That you've put me through hell. That I want you to forgive me." He held out both hands to her, but she stepped back out of his way.

"Very well. I'll forgive you. But we must finish it at that."

" What do you mean, finish! We can't finish, you and I! We belong to each other! We *are* each other now!" It was a cry. Whatever he had expected her to say he had not expected words like these; and, all self possession ebbing before their hardness, he now was amazed to find himself standing there before her, his body shaken by distress. In all his adult life, Will had never before felt tears run down his cheeks.

His unhappiness had some effect, although it did not yet appear to melt her.

"Will, you and I would make a mess of it. I've been thinking of what Mrs Adam Edzell said about you this morning. She seems to think your wife will need a world of patience and love for you. No! Let me say this! Will, I'm frightened. We're too different. Temperament—point of view—everything."

"Rosamond! Frightened of *me*!"

She nodded. "Yes, Will."

"Rosamund, I'll be good! I promise you I'll be good! Even if at first I don't always understand what you want of me! But you must have patience until you do understand. And not ever run away from me again! And then everything will be all right."

"How do you know?"

"Because I love you."

They stood now saying nothing, eyes searching eyes, each feeling increasingly the force of the other's nearness, yet still unable to cross the gulf.

At length he spoke in a whisper of desperation. "Rosamond, what else can I say to you?"

She did not answer but merely continued to search his eyes with her own.

Again he tried and now his voice sounded hoarse and weary. "On the night you brought Oliver home from Paris, you knew then that we belonged to each other. Have you forgotten?" And then, in an explosion of schoolboy weeping: "We just stood together in the crowd and didn't say anything at all!" Strange words with which to break down his girl's defence. But he had done it.

She went to him, put her arms about his neck and drew his head down to comfort him.

5

And of course everybody else expressed delight. As Oliver put it to his father when he got back two days later: "Well, that's that, Skipper. It's all been rather a storm in a teacup, really. It means business as usual now, doesn't it?"

"Hardly for Rosamond and Will, Nol. They're going to find business very unusual indeed. But at any rate they can't escape it. Oh, they'll shake down."

"Which will win, would you say?"

"It's not a case of winning or losing. It's a case of fitting in. And they'll do that, I think. People tend to, you know, when they begin marriage very much in love with each other. You'll come back from Paris for the wedding?"

"Yes. By train. I don't suppose you've heard yet that grandfather says he's coming to the wedding too? To see Will and Mrs Stronn Island's money safely into the family, I suppose. You know, Skipper, he's an old rascal! No more trouble about the money for his dear grandchildren or anything! But then I expect he can't help belonging to the to-every-one-that-hath-shall-be-given brigade, can he? Victorians were like that, weren't they?"

"My dear Nol! Very much younger people than Victorians!"

"Anyway, he assured Rose and Will everything would be all right when they went to see him yesterday."

"Have they been to see him already? I've been worrying about that. Did Will go quietly?"

But Frederick need not have worried. Will and Rosamond had been received with all the dignity that Loch View could muster. Old John had even gone the length of calling upon Alice, much to her delight, to act as hostess.

And if Will had behaved rather like a menagerie panther that had been made safe with drugs before his performance, only Rosamond could be aware of this.

"And do you know anything about money?" Old John had asked with a gnarled geniality as they settled round the tea table.

"I've never spent any more than I had, sir."

"Good. And did you ever save any?"

"A little. I've never set out to make very much,

you know. I've never had much interest—"

"Johnnie, dear. *Must* we have this kind of conversation?"

"Hold your tongue, Alice! Well, you'll need to have an interest now. I'll speak to Fred. You'd better come into Edzells and learn to look after what's coming to you."

"I'm staying at the University, sir. It's the only useful thing I can do with myself."

"How do you know? You don't seem to me to be a fool. You'd better join the board anyway, and come to the meetings and learn what you can."

Here Alice tried again. "You see, Will dear, how good Rosamond's grandfather is! He insists on taking all the family anxieties on his own shoulders. Now he's beginning to take yours too. Aren't you, Johnnie dear?"

For which she was again told to hold her tongue.

But Alice, as usual, had not been daunted in the very least. What could have been greater good luck for her than to meet the affianced pair, and to be able to tell the family she had seen them and heard such plans as they already had made?

"Will told your Uncle John he was staying on at the University," she told the assembled Crabbes that evening.

"Fancy! And with all that money coming to him too!" Babs' substantial hands fumbled with the pink pearls at her neck. "And what's he going to get out of that?"

"A professorship," Patrick said grandly.

His mother considered this. "Not my idea of fun," she said. "That girl's got too much style to be a professor's wife. You'll see. She'll get him away from all that."

"Nice harmless job, a professor," Sam said ruminatively. "Other folks can look after your money for you."

"I haven't had time to mention it, dears." Here Alice stopped to look a little important and a little coy. "But I'm going to tell you about a little thing I did." She stopped once more to pat the hand of her eldest son who happened to be sitting beside her. "Joey knows, don't you?"

Joseph looked fiercely before him and said: "Come on, mother. Let's hear what you've got to say."

"Well, dears. I've met Mrs. Adam Edzell!"

"Mrs Adam, granny!" Minnie exclaimed. "And what did you think of her?"

"No. Let me finish, darling. She was just going out. But I had time to advise her to see Rosamond the moment she came home. I don't believe it had occurred to her. But I put the idea into her head."

Knowing the old lady, Alice's family took this with varying degrees of belief. And it was, perhaps, Minnie's good nature that made her say: "Well done for you, granny!"

"I suppose we'll all be meeting Mrs Adam now," Babs said.

"I don't know about that. I wouldn't count on it." Joseph looked at his sister-in-law.

And, for the time being at least, Joseph was right. For just at that moment Mary was sitting in the West Highland train as it puffed its fiery way across the Moor of Rannoch in the winter darkness. She had done what she had meant to do. And now she was answering the call of her island. Tomorrow early, Murdo McDonald would be coming in with the white launch to take her home.

(at Craiting Bhan Mc Sedburgh)

x How extraordinary — !
Am I answering the call of my Island — ? By going to Mull —

Sept 19th 1968.

Betty H Shields.

" My heart was always Highland "